THE BLANKET CATS

Kiyoshi Shigematsu

THE BLANKET CATS

Translated from the Japanese by
Jesse Kirkwood

MACLEHOSE PRESS
QUERCUS · LONDON

First published in Japan as ブランケット・キャッツ
by Asahi Shimbun Publications Inc. in 2008
First published in Great Britain in 2024 by

MacLehose Press
An imprint of Quercus Editions Ltd
Carmelite House
50 Victoria Embankment
London EC4Y 0DZ

An Hachette UK company

The authorised representative in the EEA is Hachette Ireland, 8 Castlecourt Centre, Dublin 15, D15 XTP3, Ireland (email: info@hbgi.ie)

A CIP catalogue record for this book is available from the British Library.

ISBN (HB) 978 1 52943 523 8
ISBN (TPB) 978 1 52943 528 3
ISBN (MMP) 978 1 52943 524 5

10 9 8 7 6 5 4 3

Typeset by CC Book Production
Printed and bound in Great Britain by Clays Ltd, Elcograf S.p.A.

Papers used by Quercus are from well-managed forests and other responsible sources.

THE BLANKET CATS

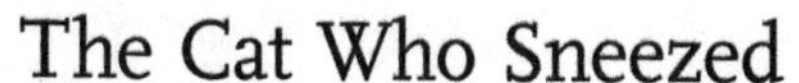

The Cat Who Sneezed

I

Two nights, three days. That was how long you could keep them.

"You're probably thinking that isn't very long," the pet shop owner would say to his customers once they'd signed the contract. He would deliver these words in an identical tone, and with an identical expression, every single time.

"Any longer and you start to get attached. Meanwhile the cat starts worrying it might never be coming back here. Doesn't work out well for anyone, believe me."

Buying them wasn't an option. Nor, as a general rule, was hosting the same animal more than once in the span of a month.

"Three days. That's it," the owner said, driving the point home in the same quiet but firm voice as always.

They didn't come cheap either. For the same upfront cost – the fee plus a deposit several times that amount – you could easily buy one of the purebred kittens the owner sold through the more conventional "pet shop" side of his business.

And yet the customers kept coming. Each of the seven cats would return from its latest assignment and, after just a night or two at the shop, move on to another new home for the next three days.

They came with their own toilet, and you weren't allowed to feed them anything except the special cat food supplied by the owner. In particular, he insisted that, like any cat, they should never be fed onion, abalone, or chicken bones.

"Onion is poison to a cat's bloodstream. It breaks down their red blood cells and turns them anaemic. Abalone makes their ears swell up and turn bright red. In bad cases they develop dermatitis, and if you don't do anything about *that*, their ears fall right off. As for chicken bones, they splinter when a cat bites them. Don't want them piercing their throats or an organ, do we?"

The customers would react to his warnings in all sorts of ways – some took notes, while others gasped in surprise; some simply nodded in silence, while others barely even listened because, in their opinion, they'd heard it all before. When it came to looking after cats, people's level of experience varied.

The owner welcomed customers who'd never had a cat before. But he was always sure to give them a particularly stern warning:

"The cat sleeps on its own. When it's bedtime, you put it in this carrier, and you make sure the blanket is laid out just like it is now. And never, ever, wash the blanket – no matter how dirty you might think it is."

Cats are not known to relish a change of environment. For any normal cat, this lifestyle would undoubtedly be stressful.

"Which is why . . ." said the owner, still using the same words as always, the same expression and tone of voice. It was quite possible that the precise duration of the explanation up to this point was identical every time too. "They have the blanket."

From an early age, each of the seven cats had always slept with their own rotating collection of blankets. As long as they were equipped with one of their familiar favourites, they could sleep soundly wherever they found themselves.

"It's like that scene you see in old manga comics. You know, the kid who leaves home and stuffs his pillow into his bag for comfort."

At this point, he liked to give a chuckle. The same chuckle every time.

Today too, he chuckled right on cue.

"Well, here you go. She's yours," he said, picking the carrier up from the counter and holding it towards the customer. "Take good care of her, okay?"

The customer – who, like the owner, looked to be in his mid-forties – clutched the carrier close to his chest, a nervous look on his face.

"You don't have to hold it like that, you know."

"Ah . . . sorry."

"You don't have to apologise either." For the first time, the owner offered what seemed to be an unscripted smile.

The customer smiled back awkwardly, then shifted the carrier to his side.

"Sorry. It's just I've never had a cat before . . ."

"Don't worry – she's well-behaved. Takes to people quickly. Go on, have a quick peek. She's a cute little thing. Big round eyes."

The customer did as the owner suggested. Still holding the carrier, he peered in through the small window in its side.

There she was, gazing right at him.

She was curled up on a beige blanket. The owner hadn't lied: she had enormous, staring eyes.

A calico, just as he'd requested.

". . . She's adorable."

"Isn't she?" the owner said with a satisfied nod. "Still only a year old, so she has that kitteny look about her – but she's all grown up and well behaved. A real charmer."

The customer nodded, then stole another glance inside the carrier. The cat was still looking at him.

It mewed softly.

"Oh . . ." The customer looked up. "I forgot to ask her name."

The owner nodded, as if he'd seen the question coming. "Well, what would you like to call her?"

"What? You mean I get to . . .?"

Another nod. "You get to name her whatever you like. Call out to her a few times and you'll be surprised how quickly she picks it up."

"Really?"

"Yep. I told you, she's a clever one. And it makes sense for you to name her, don't you think? She *is* going to be your cat – even if it's just for three days."

The owner chuckled, then cast his eyes over the form his customer had filled out, which he was about to type into the computer.

"Mr . . . Ishida, is it? Well, for the next three days, this cat is a member of the Ishida family. So make sure you give her a nice name, okay?"

"Erm . . . what do you call her when she's here, at the shop?"

"Cali, as in 'calico'. Doesn't seem much point in *us* giving them fancy names, see . . . In any case, talk it over with your wife or kids, and find a name that feels right for your family, okay?"

Just then the telephone rang. As the owner made to take the call, Norio Ishida bowed politely and left the shop.

On his way back to the car park, he turned around and took another look at the shop.

Alongside the ordinary-looking sign for the pet shop was another that read: BLANKET CATS. Above the Japanese characters, the English words for the same thing had been squeezed in like an afterthought.

Blanket Cats. The phrase had meant nothing to him when he'd found the shop online, and still less when he'd walked in there. Now I get it, he thought. Cats that come with their own blanket. Blanket Cats.

The carrier felt surprisingly heavy in his hand. Doing his best to keep it steady, Norio made his way to his car.

The sky towered above him, expansive and blue. In the distance, the mountain ridges shaded off imperceptibly into the haze.

It was spring. The day before, the clouds of fine yellow sand that often blew in from China at this time of year had, once again, made landfall in western Japan.

For now, though, Tokyo remained out of the sand's reach. Instead, the morning news had forecast high levels of cedar pollen in the city's air.

The forests that covered the mountains, on the outskirts

of Tokyo, were almost all cultivated cedar plantations. Norio himself wasn't allergic to their pollen, but a colleague of his who had a surgical mask practically glued to his face at this time of year swore that sometimes he could actually see it swirling through the air.

"Seriously," he had said, "you know those old yokai manga, where the smoke spewed out by factories turns into a monster that chases after people? That's what it feels like."

Norio grinned to himself, imagining the face his colleague might pull if he brought him out here to the suburbs, where the pollen was particularly fierce.

Just then, a tiny sneeze came from inside the carrier.

Hang on. Did cats really sneeze?

. . . What if *she* had a pollen allergy?

Surely not, he thought as he opened the rear door of his car.

"We'll be there in a minute, okay?" he said, setting the carrier down on the floor behind the front seat.

In response, the cat sneezed again. It wasn't as vocal as an "*achoo*" – more of a breathy *shoo*, like fabric rustling.

"Don't tell me you actually have a pollen allergy," he said, astonished.

But the cat simply carried on sneezing. *Shoo! Sha-shoo!* . . .

Norio took the expressway across central Tokyo back to the satellite town in Chiba where he lived. For early on a Saturday afternoon, the Metropolitan Expressway was surprisingly empty. On the way to the shop, the journey had taken him almost two hours due to a traffic accident. But now, even with a break along the way, it took him less than half that to get home.

When he was almost there, he pulled the car up outside the nearby station and called Yukie on the phone. He'd expected his wife to still be in, but apparently that wasn't the case.

"It's so nice outside, and I was bored, so I went for a little wander."

She added that she'd just walked into a café near the station, where she'd been planning to pass the time until he got back.

"Right. I'll come to you, then."

"What, and leave the cat in the car?"

"Of course not. I'll bring her with me."

"Is that okay? Bringing a pet into a café, I mean."

"Should be alright if she's still in the carrier, don't you think?"

"I don't know. Hang on, I'll ask one of the staff."

The phone switched to the hold melody. Norio leaned back in his seat and gave an exasperated sigh.

It would only be three days. But Norio had never had a cat before – or any pet, for that matter.

Just as he was becoming convinced the café would be a no-go, the melody cut out.

"They say it's fine as long as we don't let her out."

"Right. I'll head over there now, then."

Once he'd hung up, he twisted around in his seat to look at the carrier. It was a pretty cramped little container, and yet the cat was just sitting inside it patiently. The sneezing that had continued for a while after they'd joined the expressway had stopped now.

Was this stillness due to her training, or was it just her personality? Or was she asleep? Or . . . maybe . . .

Feeling a tremor of panic, he jumped out of the car, opened the rear door and lifted the carrier up to look inside. He heard a vague snarl, presumably in protest at this rough treatment, and the container shook violently.

"You're alive, then. All okay in there?"

Relieved, he placed the carrier on the rear seat, then gave another sigh. Three days was starting to sound like quite a long time.

"Just hang on a bit longer, alright?" he said, then opened up the hatch on the carrier. The least he could do was give her a bit of fresh air. You better not run off, he thought, preparing himself for the worst. But the cat remained curled up meekly on her blanket.

He remembered the pet shop owner's words: "Only the top kittens get to be Blanket Cats."

Norio wasn't sure the cats themselves considered it much of an honour, but she did seem fairly well-behaved.

There was one other thing the owner had said.

Talk it over with your wife or kids. The cat's name, that is.

He closed the hatch of the carrier.

"Mummy's waiting," he said to the now-hidden cat. On second thoughts, maybe "Mum" was better for Yukie.

I'd prefer "Dad" to "Daddy" myself, he thought. Though it would be up to the kid to choose.

The cat sneezed again.

Shoo-shoo-shoo! Three in a row this time.

"You sure you don't have a pollen allergy?"

Shoo! Sha-shoo!

"Yeah, you definitely do."

Shoo-shoo! Shoo!

"Well, at least you're like Mum in one respect," he murmured before swallowing a sigh.

Yukie was sitting by the window of the café. When she saw him approach, she removed her face mask and took a series of cautious breaths. After inhaling, exhaling, and twitching her nostrils for a few moments, she allowed her expression to finally relax into a smile.

"How are you doing?" asked Norio, pulling out the chair opposite her.

"My nose was ticklish earlier, but I think I'm alright for now."

"Loads of pollen about today, apparently."

"Yeah, they said on TV. Glad I didn't go with you to pick her up."

Norio held the carrier out, and Yukie carefully took it in both hands, then placed it on the seat next to her. She gently stroked the hatch.

"Hello," she said, in a rounded, mellow voice. "Nice to meet you."

At some point, the cat had stopped sneezing.

"I want to see her, but I feel like, weirdly nervous . . ."

"She's a cute little thing."

"A calico, right?"

"Yeah. One year old."

"And she's a girl?" she asked – before adding, almost apologetically: "Didn't you want a boy?"

"I don't mind. Anyway, calicos are always female."

"What? Really?"

"Yeah. Apparently, with male chromosomes, it's impossible to have the genes for both ginger and black hair. Occasionally a male will be born through some kind of genetic abnormality, but the odds are like one in a thousand. And the ones that are born aren't exactly very . . . manly."

"What do you mean?"

"They're infertile." Norio glanced out of the window, where a mother and child happened to be passing. "You know, like someone else in your life."

He'd meant it lightly, but he felt his voice tremble, and Yukie offered no reply.

2

The cat would sleep in the small Japanese-style room that adjoined the living room, they decided. It got plenty of sunlight, and the lack of furniture meant there was plenty of space. Even if the cat scratched the tatami mats, or the fusuma or the shoji—

"We can deal with that, right?"

"Yeah."

It was settled. If anything, they were more worried about what the cat would make of the distinctive grassy smell of the tatami.

"If she doesn't like the tatami room, she can sleep in mine, right?" Yukie had asked.

"I reckon she'd prefer mine," Norio replied. "Yours stinks of cosmetics."

"Well," Yukie pouted, "while we're on the subject of smell, yours absolutely reeks of cigarettes."

"Yeah, but I bought one of those air freshener sprays."

"That's cheating! Well, we'll just have to spray my room too."

Norio nodded and smiled softly. If the cat was going to sleep in one of their rooms, of course it would be Yukie's. He'd just wanted to tease her a bit.

"Well, it's only three days," he said, deliberately keeping his expression calm, his voice distant. He was hoping she'd tell him to lighten up. But she was play-acting too – and had decided to go for full-on childish excitement.

"Hey, do you think I can hug the cat straight away?"

"Yeah, I guess. She's super comfortable around people, apparently."

"I bought a cat teaser. Reckon she'll play with it?"

"Oh, definitely. I mean, she's a cat, right?"

"Can she sleep with me?"

That, unfortunately, was a no-go. It said so clearly on the website. Separating the cats from their blankets was strictly forbidden.

When Norio had explained, Yukie had seemed pretty disappointed. But she'd soon gathered herself.

"In that case," she'd said, "I'll just have to sleep in the tatami room! I'm allowed to sleep *next* to her at least, right?" Her voice had been lively, her cheeks flushed, her eyes gleaming with excitement.

"Oh, sure," he replied, curtly. "I mean, do whatever you want." He turned away from her, as if he'd had enough of the conversation. Really, though, he was just trying not to let her enthusiasm infect him.

It wasn't the cat's arrival that he was happy about. It was seeing Yukie so thrilled to have her in the house. When had he last seen that smile on her lips, that carefree look on her face?

Even now, the following morning, as she played with the cat in the tatami room, she wore the same smile.

By this point, though, Yukie wasn't just calling her "the cat". She'd given her a name.

"You really don't mind me naming her?" she'd asked at first, doubtfully.

And yet the moment she let the cat out of the carrier she'd exclaimed, without a moment's hesitation, "Hello, Anne!"

As in Anne of Green Gables, Norio had assumed. But Yukie's reasoning turned out to be a little different.

"I mean, I guess that might have influenced me. But it's actually short for Anju," she said, picking the cat up and stroking it on her lap.

"Anju as in . . . *Anju and Zushio*?"

"No!" she laughed. "Why would I give her the name of the heroine from a tragedy?"

Good point.

Anju, she explained, was written with the characters for "apricot" and "tree".

"Thirty-three strokes in total, when you include our family name. The most auspicious number for a girls' name. It was tough to get the strokes to add up right when we have so few in our surname."

Anju Ishida.

Norio traced the characters in the air with his finger, counting the individual strokes. Sure enough, there were thirty-three of them.

"Would have been easier if I'd given her a three-character name, like mine." A name like Yukie's, which was written with three separate characters, would have meant more strokes. "But then you'd feel left out with your measly two characters, wouldn't you?" She turned to the cat and giggled. "Wouldn't he?"

The sliding shoji doors of the tatami room were open, the soft afternoon sun pouring in. There was Yukie, sitting in the amber-tinged light, hugging the cat. Hugging Anne.

"She really is well-behaved, isn't she?" she said.

"Yeah . . ."

"It's like she's always lived here, don't you think?"

"I guess . . ."

"Nori, what's wrong?"

Yukie turned to look at him, as did Anne on her lap. Even the look of surprise on their faces was the same.

"Are you angry?"

Norio looked away. "No, not at all."

"But you've gone all mopey."

"I told you, I'm fine."

"Ah, I know," she teased. "You're just wondering when it'll be your turn to hug her, aren't you?" She gave Anne another squeeze. "Sorry, she's all mine!"

Shoo! The cat sneezed again.

Shoo! Sha-shoo . . .

Achoo! This last one was Yukie. "Uh-oh, now I'm sneezing!" The sunlight made the skin on her face almost transparent.

Norio looked up at the clock, deliberately avoiding the smile that spread momentarily across her face.

"I might pop out," he said.

"Where to?"

"Thought I could buy her some toys and things. They had this climbing frame thing in the pet shop, plus a bunch of other stuff. Probably best to get her something like that, don't you think?"

He half expected Yukie to say, *Isn't that a bit excessive for a three-day stay?* But she didn't.

"Shall we both go, and take the cat?" he asked.

"Hmm . . ." She frowned and paused. "No, I think I'll stay here with Anne. I'd feel self-conscious taking her out."

She was probably expecting him to say, *What is there to feel self-conscious about?* But he didn't.

"I guess this must be how a new mum feels about taking their kid to the park for the first time," she said.

Norio cocked his head and gave a pained smile, but said nothing as he walked out of the tatami room and began briskly gathering his things.

"I won't be long," he called from the corridor.

"See you in a bit!" she replied in her airy voice.

Anne, for her part, offered a pleading, drawn-out miaow.

"Wow, you really are a clever cat!" he heard Yukie exclaim.

He wondered what sort of face she was pulling. But he left without looking, like a man on the run.

Driving to the local hardware shop, he smoked one cigarette after another. It wasn't the taste he was craving, but the feel of the filter, gripped tight between his lips.

It'll be alright, he thought. You worry too much, he gently chided himself.

There was nothing to be anxious about. The cat they'd spent the last few days looking forward to had finally arrived in their home. Yukie was over the moon. Seriously, he thought, when was the last time he'd seen her that happy?

As for me . . . You know what? I'm having fun today. I really am.

Their weekends were normally quiet affairs. It wasn't that either of them was particularly taciturn, but compared to homes with kids tearing around from morning until night, the atmosphere in their apartment was so hushed you'd barely know anyone lived there. In fact, on several occasions, the delivery man had slipped an "attempted delivery" note through their letterbox just because they'd taken a bit longer than usual to answer the door.

Their place had three bedrooms, as well as a combined living room, dining room and kitchen. It was certainly big enough for the two of them – too big, if anything. When they were each ensconced in their separate bedrooms, over half the seventy square metres of the apartment was nothing but dead space. They'd never had kids. More specifically, they hadn't been able to.

Norio was the problem. Sex itself went smoothly enough; the issue was his sperm, which were apparently weak and extremely low in number.

They'd found out in their early thirties, on the very first day they'd gone in for infertility treatment. The chances of conception weren't quite zero, they'd been told, but near enough.

They couldn't say it hadn't hit them hard.

At the same time, no matter how depressed the news made them, there was nothing they could do. All they could change was how they felt about it.

Maybe we're fine the way we are, they'd told themselves through their thirties. They weren't bluffing; that was really how it seemed.

But now, on the cusp of their forties, they felt the hushed quiet of their lives morphing slowly into sadness. The harmonious monotone interior of their living room began to feel strangely desolate.

A few months ago, reading a new year's card from a friend, Yukie had suddenly burst into tears.

The friend in question always enclosed a photo of their family in their cards. Underneath the standard printed greeting was a handwritten message.

Our eldest started middle school this April. We can't believe our little scamp has grown up so fast!

It was your average update from a friend, really, and yet something about it caught Yukie completely off-guard, like a sharp jab to the tenderest part of her heart.

"I wonder what that feels like," she'd said, her eyes reddening. "You know, looking at your kid and thinking wow, they've really grown up." Then, as the tears had really started to come: "I bet it means the world to them."

Once the sadness arrived, it never went away. But it wasn't sadness for their present situation that enveloped them, so much as a realisation that the quiet life they shared was simply going to roll onwards, indefinitely, into the future.

"Ah, kids are just a nuisance anyway," one of Norio's friends had said. "All the mess they make! Not to mention the noise."

A different friend had said: "The fewer mouths to feed the better, I say."

And another told him: "Kids are basically just half-formed adults. They can be *so* frustrating. And you're expected to do everything for them!"

Meanwhile, one of Yukie's friends had said: "As a couple, you get to choose your partner, but you don't get to choose your kids." Another had told her: "It just isn't worth quitting your job to raise them."

When they'd first heard these comments, they'd taken them at face value, but it was different now. Like playing cards – or the black-and-white disks in a game of *Othello* – being flipped over to reveal their true identities, their friends' complaints about their children had begun to sound more like attempts to console Norio and Yukie for not having any.

They'd probably say they were overthinking it. *Come on,* they'd say. *Don't take it that way.*

Over the past year or two, both Norio and Yukie had stopped inviting their friends over as much. Nor did they go out of their way to visit them.

They'd become unsociable people. And their quiet, sad weekends had slowly grown quieter and sadder.

It had been Norio who, about a month ago, had said, "Shall we get a pet?"

"Well, if we did," Yukie had replied immediately, "I'd want a cat."

They weren't allowed pets in their apartment block. If they were really going to get a cat, they'd have to move. They'd bought their current place back in the eighties, during the bubble era – and before finding out about Norio's infertility. It had been a bold purchase, made on the assumption that one day, there would be three or four of them living together.

These days, the market for pre-owned apartments was shaky to say the least. It wasn't clear they'd find a buyer, and even if the sale went through, the proceeds probably wouldn't cover the balance on their mortgage.

And yet Yukie had really taken to the idea. "Let's just go for it," she'd said. "We'll manage the money somehow." She'd seemed ready to rush out of the door that minute and start hopping between estate agents and pet shops.

In an attempt to humour her, Norio had suggested they try spending a few days with a cat before deciding what to do.

And now Anne had arrived at their house, and for the first time in a long time, Yukie was laughing that carefree laugh of hers.

Wasn't that a good thing?

I'll get the cat stuff, he thought, and then I'll pop by the estate agent's and see if they'll at least give me an estimate on that apartment.

At the hardware shop, he found himself hesitating. The truth was, he was a little taken aback.

Ranged in front of him were various models of cat tower. The pole on one of them was about two metres tall, with a hemp rope wound around it for the cat to scratch its claws on; a birdbox-like cabin was attached to the pole, together with various platforms and steps. They'd have no use for it once Anne's stay was over, he thought – and even if they did move to another apartment and get a cat, all that pink and blue was just so . . . garish.

At their place, a thing like this would stick out like a sore thumb.

With a look of astonishment still plastered across his face, he asked a nearby clerk if they had anything more muted.

"Nope," the clerk replied, without the slightest hint of an apology.

"Seriously? They all look this childish?"

"Cats love pretty colours," the clerk replied unconvincingly.

Glumly, Norio distanced himself from the man, then turned to face the cat towers once more.

The wood grain visible through the paint, the rounded edges, the over-the-top colours . . . eventually, he realised that what they brought to mind, more than anything else, were the children's toys he'd seen at the house of a friend who, a decade or so ago, he'd used to visit.

His friend had always prided himself on his collection

of over two hundred LPs, mainly old Japanese folk and rock records, but he had given up the shelves that once housed them to the robot figurines his son collected. Super Metal something or other, they were called. "That's the thing about kids," his friend had grumbled, "they take over your life completely." But the look on his face had been far from unhappy.

Alright then, Norio said to himself, before calling the clerk over again.

"That pink one, with the platforms and the little cabin," he said, pointing and smiling. "No need to pack it up. I'll take it home just as it is."

3

Their digital camera ran out of space in no time at all.

Norio chuckled weakly as he watched Yukie adopt yet another pose with Anne in her arms. "Hang on. I think I need to download these onto the computer first."

"It can't be full already," Yukie said, shocked. "You sure it's not just playing up?"

He shook his head, laughing louder this time, then pointed at the clock on the wall. "Wow. Look at the time."

"How is it eight o'clock already?"

"Yeah. I'm pretty hungry. And Anne," he said, playfully stroking the cat's belly, "you must be feeling peckish too, right?"

Brushing his hand out of the way, Yukie squeezed her into another hug. "Sorry, Anne! Are you hungry?"

Anne stuck her neck out, looking slightly disgruntled, but made no attempt to escape. She'd spent the last hour or so clasped to Yukie's lap, unable to move, but she seemed completely relaxed.

They ate the dinner he'd prepared earlier that evening, then fed Anne. "I wanted to give her something homemade," Yukie complained, but the pet shop owner had been clear: they were strictly forbidden from feeding her anything other than the cat food he provided. Any variation in the quantity or quality of her food could badly upset her health.

Norio stole a glance at his wife as she ate alongside him. That soft smile. That tender look in her eyes. The mellow, rounded timbre of every word that issued from her mouth. During all the weekends they'd spent alone, he couldn't remember her ever looking this happy.

"How about going for a walk after dinner?" she asked.

"What, with Anne?"

"Yeah. Give her a bit of fresh air."

"I thought it was just dogs you were supposed to take for walks . . . Anyway, what if someone from the building sees us? We'll get in trouble. Plus there's the pollen."

"Oh, I'll be alright."

". . . I meant Anne."

Whether from the pollen or some other allergic reaction, the cat was still sneezing. She'd be quiet for long stretches of time, but once she started it was like it would never stop.

"Maybe's she's just reacting to the house dust. In which case, wouldn't it actually be better to take her outside?" Yukie peered down at Anne, who was nibbling away at her food. "You'd *love* a little excursion, wouldn't you!"

When Anne glanced up at her, Yukie imitated a coy little *miaow*, to which Anne responded with a soft mewl of her own.

"See?" said Yukie, laughing delightedly.

That's cheating, thought Norio. "Alright, you win," he said, chuckling despite himself.

When, he thought, had *he* last laughed like that?

When they'd discovered they couldn't have children, they'd made each other a series of promises.

"If we'll never be parents," Yukie had explained, "that means we'll never be connected by blood, right? I mean, marriage is just a sort of social contract."

Norio had found this a rather dramatic way of putting things. But he could see where she was coming from.

"And without a bond like that, I think two people who are going to share a home for the rest of their lives need to agree on a few ground rules."

Firstly, they'd give each other as much space as they needed. So, separate bedrooms, each with their own locks.

Next, financial independence. They opened a new bank account that was solely for shared living expenses, to which they each contributed the same amount each month.

Then there was the need to respect each other as individuals, rather than confine each other to the roles of "husband" and "wife". That was why they still called each other by their first names instead of the usual generic terms of affection. Yukie carried on using her maiden name for her work, with both surnames featuring equally prominently on their apartment's letterbox.

"In other words," Yukie had explained, "we need to respect each other's freedom as much as possible. Otherwise, living alone like this, we'll end up sucking all the life out of each other."

This made sense to Norio too. She wasn't wrong, he told himself. Still, sometimes – just sometimes – he wanted to say, *I guess all these rules might suck the life out of us too*. But because he was never sure he'd be able to make it sound entirely like a joke, he always held his tongue.

In the almost seven years since the doctor had told them that conceiving a child was basically impossible, they'd never once argued. Whenever conflict seemed imminent, one of them always yielded to the other. They didn't want fights. If they fought, there would be no-one to come between them, no-one to rally around them, no-one to decide who was in the wrong; no-one, even, to complain to. Deep down, Norio found the idea frightening. So, he assumed, did Yukie.

Turning "two" back into "one" and "one" was easy enough. Two individuals, each their own person. Partners who respected each other's freedom.

But, as Norio had occasionally caught himself thinking of late, was that really what it meant to be a couple?

That evening, they let Anne out to play in the park.

Cats aren't like dogs, though; there was no running around after her owners or chasing frisbees. The moment they opened the hatch, Anne leaped out of the carrier, dashed into the bushes on the other side of the park, and showed no sign of emerging.

"Erm . . . are you sure she'll come back?" asked Yukie.

"Oh yeah. As long as we have her blanket, she'll always come back. That's what the man said."

"She could have at least stayed where we can see her." Yukie sank onto a bench, pouting slightly. "I mean, running off like that. It was like she couldn't wait to be rid of us."

"That's how cats are, I guess."

"I know, but . . . I was hoping she'd show us a little more gratitude or love or . . . something."

Yukie explained that it had been the same when they'd been taking photos at the apartment. Anne had patiently sat in her lap, but she hadn't seemed particularly happy to be there.

"She looked fine to me," said Norio.

"You probably couldn't tell just from watching. When I was holding her, I could *feel* it. You know, like she was just going along with it because that's what she was supposed to do.

"You're imagining things."

"Maybe *you're* just not being sensitive enough."

Shoo! came a sneeze from the bushes. Anne was closer than they'd thought.

Shoo . . . shoo . . . shoo . . .

The sneezes became increasingly distant, mingling with the sound of rustling leaves and twigs.

"Maybe she heard us," Norio joked.

Yukie hunched her shoulders together and pulled a guilty face.

"So, what do you reckon?" Norio said.

"About what?"

"Getting a cat. Shall we give it up?"

"No. I still want one."

"A dog would be more, well, affectionate. And it might actually do what we told it to."

"No way. We have jobs, Nori. Who would take it for walks?"

She had a point.

The reason they'd opted for a cat in the first place was because they were more independent and less demanding than dogs. Or, to use Yukie's favourite word, cats were all about "freedom".

"Nori . . ."

"Hm?"

"Do you think I've become a bit . . . demanding recently?"

The question was so sudden that it took him a moment to answer. When he eventually replied, "No, I don't think so," his words sounded forced.

Yukie fell silent and looked up at the clouded night sky.

Shoo, sha-shoo, came the sneezes again. Anne was quite far away by now. All this space to play in, and she chooses the bushes, thought Norio – but maybe that was her own kind of "freedom".

"I think I have, you know," Yukie murmured, still looking up at the sky. "At work, and at home too. I keep getting upset over the tiniest things." She sighed.

She found herself bothered by the way her younger colleagues always bungled their polite Japanese, or the way their newly appointed account manager restlessly tapped his foot. She got angry at her computer, which kept freezing because of some new software she'd installed; she couldn't forgive her neighbour Mrs Midorikawa for the way she secretly mixed her recycling in with her regular rubbish; and she was well and truly sick of getting back from work to find the same Mrs Midorikawa standing in the entrance hall gossiping loudly with the other neighbours.

"That's not really the same as being demanding, is it?" said Norio.

"Well, I don't know what else to call it." She paused before continuing. "I guess what I'm trying to say is, things never seem to go the way I want them to anymore." Another pause. "Or I've become more sensitive . . . more vulnerable, maybe . . . Yes – it's like my immune system's gotten all weak."

She'd find herself upset by things that never used to bother her. Things she would have once happily shrugged off now seemed like unforgivable transgressions.

Norio knew what she meant, just about. In fact, he thought, he probably felt the same.

As two adults living together, almost everything went exactly the way they planned it. They stuck firmly to the rules they'd set. There was no-one to get in their way. If they wanted silence, they could have it for as long as they needed, and if they wanted to lose themselves in conversation, there was no-one to interrupt.

Our life is . . . immaculate, he thought.

Compared to their friends and colleagues, with their raucous kids, and the elderly parents who lived with them, all requiring constant attention, their nerves frayed from always having to play the good neighbour – it wasn't just their apartment or clothes that were cleaner, neater, tidier. It was life itself.

But, just as an overly sanitised body was vulnerable to the tiniest bacteria, wasn't it possible that this immaculate life of theirs was also a terribly fragile thing?

"So wanting to get a cat – that was . . ."

Yukie nodded slightly. "Well, partly they're just cute. But yeah, I do think part of me wanted something to look after – something I'd have to nurture, regardless of the hassle."

"And if it was something that would grow up over time, that would be even better?"

Yukie nodded again. "I guess."

Now it was Norio's turn to gaze up at the sky. The half-moon hung low, its outline blurred by clouds. Unlike in winter, when the air was crystal-clear, the night sky in spring always seemed slightly murky, as though seen through a veil.

He could feel the words jabbing at his chest.

Instead of a kid, you mean?

He knew the answer. He knew it, and that was why he said nothing. And so they sat side by side on the park bench in silence, sharing another immaculate moment.

Half an hour later, Anne still hadn't returned. Occasionally they heard her sneeze, almost dutifully, so at least they knew she was somewhere in the undergrowth. But she showed no intention of coming back.

"Should we whistle for her?" Yukie said. "Oh, wait. That's dogs, isn't it . . .?"

She chuckled as she turned her jacket collar up. It had been a warm and humid day, but the night air carried a chill.

"You can head back if you like," Norio said.

"No, I'm fine," Yukie replied. "I mean, why should she want to go home just because *we* want to."

". . . You know what, Yuki?"

"Hm?"

"Maybe we should give up on the cat idea. Just think how tough it'd be. I really don't think it's how we imagined it."

Yukie cleared her throat quietly and moved her head in a way that made it unclear if she was nodding or shaking it.

"There's something else too," Norio continued.

But as he said these words, they heard a loud rustling from the bushes, followed by a short squeal. It sounded like some other animal. Something smaller than a cat.

"Is that . . . Anne?"

"I don't know . . ."

They got up from the bench and turned to look at the bushes just in time to see Anne slowly emerging. In her mouth was a mouse.

With a gasp, Yukie sank back onto the bench.

4

Yukie couldn't bring herself to hold Anne anymore.

"It's not like she ate the thing," Norio said, smiling ruefully. "And catching mice is in her nature." He turned to the cat, now back in her carrier, and stroked her head. "Isn't that right?"

"I know, but . . . I still can't believe it," Yukie said, turning away in distress. "I feel like I might be sick."

Norio stroked Anne again. "Cats aren't dolls, or toys, Yuki. They go to the toilet. They get ill."

"I know *that.*"

"And . . ." He paused. "Eventually, they die."

"I know that too," murmured Yukie, pouting like a sulking child. She still hadn't managed to look at the cat.

Norio silently closed the hatch on the carrier.

There was one other thing he'd wanted to say. *They even have babies.* But he knew those words were best left unspoken.

"Let's go home."

He picked up the carrier. There was no reply from Yukie. Instead, Anne, curled up in her blanket inside the carrier, mewed softly.

"Come on, Yuki."

He began walking, a briskness in his step. Yukie followed him wordlessly.

Their apartment was barely a five-minute walk from the park. It being a weekend evening, the streets were practically deserted. On the other hand, lights glowed in almost every window of the housing complex that loomed ahead of them.

They passed a bulletin board with a poster recruiting players for a boys' baseball team. Alongside it was a poster from an environmental group that declared: PRESERVE THE EARTH'S BEAUTY FOR THE NEXT GENERATION!

"So, what should we do after we give Anne back?" Norio asked Yukie as they walked.

"What do you mean?"

"I mean, are we going to get a cat?"

Norio didn't mind either way. He'd go along with whatever Yukie decided.

There was a pause before she replied, "I don't know."

"I guess cats can be pretty demanding," Norio said with a smile, unsure how Yukie would take this comment. He'd leave that up to her too.

She fell silent, then sniffed.

Tomorrow's pollen forecast looked even worse than today's. And what about Anne? Just as he was wondering whether cats really could have pollen allergies, another sneeze issued from the carrier.

Shoo, shoo, shoo . . .

"So, do you still want to sleep in the same room as Anne tonight?"

"I don't know. Can we . . . wipe her mouth or something?"

"I don't think that'll work."

"Or wash her in the bath? . . . I guess she'd hate that, wouldn't she?"

"Yeah, I think she would."

"I guess I'm not going to get ill or something just by being in the same room. What about fleas, though? Yeah, I'm really not sure."

Shoo, shoo, shoo . . .

"Nori, did the pet shop owner say anything about her fur? Is she going to leave hairs all over the place?"

Norio gave a quiet but audible sigh.

Yukie didn't seem to notice. "Do you think she'll make the room smell too?" she continued.

"Hmm . . ." Norio said, tilting his head slightly. He sighed again.

Anne had finally stopped sneezing.

They were fast approaching the housing complex. The light from the other apartments was dazzling. Norio thought about the soft mood lighting they had at home, how it would never work if they had kids. A three-bedroom apartment like theirs – too big for just the two of them and probably too cramped if they had children – was never intended to be the rarefied space they had turned it into. It was supposed to be lively, noisy, crowded . . .

Norio repeated the question he'd murmured earlier, louder this time:

"So, shall we give up on having a cat?"

Without waiting for Yukie's reply, he lengthened his stride and, glaring at his own shadow, walked on ahead.

That night, Anne slept in Norio's room.

She curled up on her blanket inside the carrier with the hatch open, slumbering in complete silence.

When Norio woke abruptly in the middle of the night, the air in the room felt faintly damp. A distinctive smell tickled his nostrils, and he could sense a vague warmth in the room.

At first, still half asleep, he wondered if they'd left some food out.

Then he remembered, and felt the tension in his shoulders dissipate. Without turning the light on, he sat up in bed. The white carrier glowed faintly in the dark.

"Anne? You asleep?"

No response. He chuckled at himself. Had he been expecting a reply?

"Cheeky little thing. It's very different with you around, you know?"

He'd only carried on because it felt odd not to, and yet talking to the cat felt strangely satisfying. The words kept coming.

"Yuki went to bed in a right old huff, didn't she?" Then he corrected himself. "Mum, I mean. She was pretty angry, I think."

He felt a twinge in his chest, like when he'd gone swimming in the sea as a child and reached the part where his feet couldn't touch the bottom.

"Mum doesn't do proper tantrums, does she? Just goes off to her room like that, quiet as a mouse. That's when I know she's really angry. When she gets like that, I have to make sure I don't say anything that might tip her over the edge. All I can do is let her get on with it."

What the hell am I talking about?

"Your dad tries his best with her, you know."

His heart seemed to skip another beat.

"Not that it's a big deal, or anything."

Then he fell silent, and his heart felt heavy, as if he'd committed a terrible breach of the rules.

It had been ages since he'd spoken to anyone other than Yukie at home. Even if it was a cat he was talking to, with nothing to offer in reply, it was different from just talking to himself.

Yes, he had broken the rules.

*

On Sunday morning, the weather struggled to make its mind up. The sky was cloudy, but not enough for it to rain, and the strong wind that was blowing, damp and oddly warm, felt more like the kind that blew in the summer rainy season.

"If it's going to rain, I wish it would get on with it already . . ." grumbled Yukie, sniffling. She'd just applied eyedrops for her pollen allergy, and had been sucking special tian-cha lozenges all morning. None of these remedies seemed to be working. According to the forecast on the morning news, cedar pollen levels were set to reach a new high for the season.

"You probably shouldn't go outside today," Norio said.

Before, Yukie had been excited about the prospect of a Sunday out with Anne, but now she simply nodded and said, "Yeah, I guess." She was less sulky than the previous night, but still made no attempt to cuddle their guest.

The cat kept wandering around the tatami room aimlessly, occasionally planting herself down somewhere before moving on again. She had shown zero interest in the tower Norio had bought. Maybe she didn't like the colour. From time to time she sneezed. She should probably stay inside too, Norio thought.

Yukie only had soup for breakfast – partly because she felt all clogged up from her blocked nose, and partly because seeing Anne had reminded her of last night's mouse, triggering a fresh wave of queasiness.

"I know it's not Anne's fault, but . . . Sorry."

"I'll take her back to the shop. I'm sure the owner won't mind, as long as we still pay the full fee."

"No, I'd feel bad for her! Don't worry, I'll stay in my room.

I've got some work to get on with anyway. You play with her today, okay?"

"So, Yuki . . . shall we give up on getting a cat?"

She nodded wordlessly, without a moment's hesitation. She must have made her mind up last night.

"How about a dog instead?" he asked. "Or some tropical fish or something. Or we could try a reptile – apparently they're surprisingly easy to look after."

"I don't think the type of animal makes a difference, Nori. We've always done things at our own pace, and so that's all we know. If we add someone else into the mix now, I don't think we'll ever get used to them."

"But . . ."

But then the sadness will never go away.

He swallowed the words that were on the tip of his tongue. That would have been another breach of the rules.

"Thanks, Nori." The sparkle had come back into Yukie's voice. She sat up straight and, before he could ask what she was thanking him for, continued: "I really appreciate you bringing me and Anne together. I know I can be demanding, and I get really upset when things don't go my way. But having her here has made me see just how hard it's going to be for me to change at this point. There are so many things in life that you have to actually experience before you understand them."

". . . Is that really what you want?"

"It's not about what I want. I mean, just the idea that a cat would do exactly what I wanted it to – that's being demanding, isn't it? I guess I owe Anne a thank-you – or maybe an apology."

Yukie's nose had begun to run, and now she hastily dabbed at it with a tissue.

"Sorry, my head is so clogged up right now. I'm going to lie down for a bit."

Still holding the tissue to her nose, she got up and made for her room. Norio let her go. When he heard her door close, he rose weakly from his chair.

"Come on, Anne. Let's get you home."

Anne had finally decided to climb the cat tower. Sprawled on its upper platform, she was staring down at Norio.

Unsettled by her stony gaze, Norio glanced out of the window. Must still be loads of pollen flying around out there, he thought. He'd heard that, depending on the wind, pollen from the cedar forests in Okutama and Chichibu could make it all the way across Tokyo Bay to Chiba. Which was pretty crazy, when you thought about it.

Cedar trees of the world, are you that eager to reproduce? When you stand there on the mountainside spewing your pollen into the air, without a moment's thought for where it lands or how much it annoys people, is it because you're grappling with an unbearable sadness?

Just then, something flitted past his field of vision.

Before he could even turn around, Anna had dived down from the tower. She ran towards the shoji door, let out a feral hiss, and with a swipe of her claws, managed to tear right through not only the paper, but also the flimsy frame to which it was attached.

*

It took him a few moments to process what was happening. Anne had started tearing around the tatami room, hissing and yowling as she tore at the shoji panels, fusuma doors and matted floor. She scrabbled back up the tower, then jumped straight off it again, before turning her violent attention to the wooden chest of drawers instead.

Next, she darted past his feet and into the living room. She climbed onto the sideboard, where she proceeded to knock various photo frames, a vase and a clock onto the floor.

It was the sound of the glass vase shattering that finally jolted Norio into action.

"Anne! Stop!"

There was no way he was going to catch her. Still, he pursued her around the room, bending over to try and grab her, until he tripped over his own feet and barged into the floor lamp by the sofa. The lamp toppled over. He heard its lightbulb shatter.

"Hey! Anne! Stop it, okay? Stop it!"

His shin collided with the low table in the middle of the room, causing him to stagger forward and collapse. CDs rained down onto him from the rack above.

Now Anne was doing laps of the dining table, sending coffee cups, plates and a glass salad bowl flying onto the floor, before extending a front paw to a two-litre box of orange juice and, with a well-judged tap, knocking it over like a bowling pin. Norio, sprawled on his hands and knees, stared dumbfounded as an orange stain spread slowly across their immaculate, snow-white rug.

"Are you okay? What's going on in—?"

Yukie fell silent as she reached the doorway to the living room.

Anne leaped energetically off the dining table, then, with a hop, skip and jump, mounted it again, before diving straight into the kitchen sink.

"What on earth got into her?" said Yukie, her voice cracking slightly as she scrubbed away at the floor with a cloth.

"Don't ask me!"

"I thought she was supposed to be all clever and well-behaved?"

"Like I said, don't ask me," sighed Norio. He was gathering the fragments of the Ginori coffee cup that had been one of their most extravagant purchases.

The contract he had signed with the pet shop specifically excluded liability for any damage caused by the cat. Eyeing Anne, Norio wondered resentfully if the shop's owner had secretly known she might do something like this. She was much calmer now, sitting there nonchalantly licking her front leg.

It took them a good hour or so to get the room back into shape. Afterwards, as if by some unspoken agreement, they sank onto the floor, their backs against the wall, and exchanged a glance.

"Well, that was an ordeal," said Yukie.

"Ridiculous," replied Norio.

So much for their "immaculate" life. Their quiet Sunday lay in tatters.

"Still . . ." Yukie said, gazing at the shredded remains of the shoji. "I think that cleared the air."

"Yep," nodded Norio.

"We've learned our lesson, thank you very much," she said, in an exaggerated voice. "Having a cat is hard work – we get it!"

Still sprawled against the wall, she called out to the cat. "Hey, Anne, come join us."

Mewing softly, Anne walked over to her – and into her waiting arms.

"You were soaking wet a moment ago, and you're all dry now," she said, sounding impressed as she stroked the cat's back. But Anne's fur was far from clean. The sink she'd jumped into had been full of dirty dishes.

"Maybe we should give her a bath," said Norio.

"You reckon that'll work?"

"She might wriggle about a bit, but . . . if we do it together, we should manage."

Together. He'd tried to emphasise the word slightly, though he wasn't sure if Yukie noticed. She was busy giving Anne a mock-stern look and saying, "You'd better behave yourself, okay?"

Anne stretched lazily, then sneezed three times.

"See, you've caught a cold from getting wet!"

No sooner were the words out of her mouth than Yukie herself sneezed loudly. Norio, smiling and shaking his head, got to his feet, then made his way to the bathroom.

He began running the water hot, then wondered if Anne wouldn't prefer it lukewarm. Cats were sensitive creatures, after all. Adjusting the temperature, he felt a laugh welling up from somewhere deep inside him.

Maybe this is what we need sometimes.

Without removing his clothes, he stepped under the jet of water and let it run down his face.

Not always. But sometimes.

“Hey, come on!” he called to Yukie. “I’ve got the shower running.”

As if in reply, two sneezes came from the living room. One loud, the other soft.

The Cat in the Passenger Seat

I

It was always the black cat she wanted.

For five years, she'd asked for Kuro, a Maine Coon whose name meant simply "black". And now that Kuro was too old to serve as a Blanket Cat, she always opted for her replacement, a mixed breed with a glossy black coat who went by the same name.

"I *do* like other cats, you know," Taeko told the shop's owner as she stood at the counter waiting for the younger Kuro.

She wasn't normally the talkative type, but whenever she rented Kuro she found herself chatting away. For the entire three days they were together, she'd be giddy with excitement.

"But black ones are just so beautiful, don't you think?" she went on. "Sort of like precious little . . . ornaments."

"Ornaments?" muttered the owner as he typed her details into his computer.

"Sorry. Maybe that's not the right turn of phrase."

"Oh, I don't mind. As long as it's just a turn of phrase." The owner smiled wryly and clicked his mouse.

The screen showed her rental history. As usual, it had been exactly three months since the last one. Taeko turned up here once a season.

"How's the old Kuro doing, then?" she asked.

"She's taking it nice and easy. She's past working age, so it's the quiet life for her from here on."

"What is it – two years since she retired? I imagine she's forgotten all about me. Being a cat and everything."

"Oh, I'm sure she remembers *you*, of all people. You took her on enough trips."

"I thought cats didn't get attached to people like that."

"They do. They're just don't show it the way dogs do."

"Isn't it three steps and they forget everything? Oh, wait," she chuckled, "that's chickens, isn't it?"

The owner smiled back at her. "Where are you taking her this time, then?"

"A couple of hot-spring resorts. One in the mountains, one by the sea."

"Sounds nice."

"Doesn't it?" she said proudly.

"The mountains and the sea, eh?" muttered the owner, glancing down at the floor. Then he looked up at her. "Listen. How about taking the old Kuro?"

"Really?"

"Like I said, she's getting on in years. Before long she won't be in a state to go anywhere. I was thinking it would be nice to take her off to the seaside or something while she's still in good health. She's been out of service for a while, but with you she'll be fine."

"You don't mind?"

"Not at all. If it's alright with you, that is."

"You're sure?" she asked, tilting her head down while

looking up at him hopefully, like a little girl who scarcely dared to believe she'd been given a present. "Really?" she added, wiggling her hips excitedly.

She was in her fifties. What was she playing at? The part of her brain that was still operating normally told her to calm down. And yet that giddy feeling was becoming even harder to contain than usual.

The younger Kuro was good company. But she was no match for the original, the cat Taeko had come to know so well over the years.

The large Maine Coon would always sit there so proudly, and with such beautiful poise and posture, that it seemed inadequate to say that Taeko had merely taken her somewhere. Kuro was her companion, and any other description failed to do her justice. It was just like those dog-lovers you saw driving about with their golden retriever sitting happily at their side.

‘This will probably be her last trip," said the owner as he cancelled the reservation for the younger Kuro. "Make it one to remember, okay?"

Taeko smiled, nodded, then watched as the owner disappeared into the back room to fetch the cat. It was only once she was sure she was alone that she allowed the smile to fade from her face.

Kuro had aged visibly in the two years they'd been apart. Her black fur had lost some of its glossy shine and, on her chest, it had thinned out considerably.

"Kuro-chan, it's me, Taeko," she said, hugging the cat against her. "Remember?"

The cat didn't struggle or growl, though she gave no indication of being particularly happy either. There was a sort of sluggish reluctance about her movements.

"She's getting on a bit, that's for sure," said the owner. "But she's in good health, and she still cleans up after herself when she goes to the toilet." He paused. "Not sure we'll be able to say the same in six months' time."

He placed Kuro in the carrier, then wrapped the blanket around her.

This was a necessary procedure whenever a cat left the pet shop – even for a short journey like the one back to Taeko's vehicle in the car park. It was a signal to the animal that it was about to embark on one of its missions as a Blanket Cat.

What did Kuro think as she was placed into the carrier? Taeko had always been dying to know the answer to this question. As the blanket was wrapped around her, she would fix her gaze on a single point in space. Perhaps the penetrating gaze of the Maine Coone – so feral-looking it had inspired wild theories about them being the product of crossbreeding with raccoons – was capable of discerning things that the human eye could not. To Taeko, there were times when this seemed eminently possible.

"Give her a good time, okay?" said the owner as he saw them off. His smile, effortless and gentle, made her think of a soap bubble drifting into the air.

"New car," Taeko said to Kuro, after she'd set the cat down on the passenger seat. She started the engine. "Well," she shrugged, "technically it's second-hand." She sighed as she released the handbrake.

They had a long drive ahead. Their first stop was a secluded ryokan deep in the Nagano mountains, which they'd only reach after dark. It was the middle of April, but if the weather took a turn for a worse, there was even a chance it might snow.

Taeko turned onto the main road and accelerated. The engine began to whine, and the wind whipped loudly against the windows. The car was a subcompact, one of the high-bodied types that were so popular these days. Taeko imagined it lurching from side to side on the motorway or the sharp curves of the mountain road.

"Hey, Kuro. How about we rent ourselves a nicer car? You know, something a little more . . . spacious."

Kuro's pointed ears twitched slightly. Taeko decided this was her way of signalling assent.

"You *are* getting old, aren't you? I hope you're not going to tumble off that seat every time we go round a corner."

According to the pet shop owner, Kuro had lost almost all her teeth.

She was twelve now. By Taeko's calculations, she'd been five at the time of their first trip together. The first signs of aging in cats began at around eight years. In other words, when they'd first met, Kuro had still been in the prime of her youth.

"I was in my forties. Not sure you'd call that the prime of *my* youth. But I did feel young."

She ran a search for the nearest car rental on the car's navigation system.

"By the way, that owner of yours is a bit of an oddball,

isn't he? Friendly enough, but I'm never sure whether that smile of his is genuine. It's like he always knows what you're thinking. What do you make of him? I mean, you're basically part of the furniture at that place. He's not secretly abusing you or anything, is he?"

She giggled as they shot across a junction just after the lights turned red.

"Boring old name he gave you too. Bet you'd have preferred something a bit more . . . distinguished."

Though I suppose you could say the same about me, she thought.

Taeko's name was written with plain old hiragana characters. Her parents, now both dead, had initially opted for a more elaborate rendering using the kanji for "great wisdom". But then a fortune-teller specialising in names had warned them the total number of strokes would be inauspicious, and so they'd opted for the hiragana version. The fact that her surname would change when she got married, rendering all this fuss pointless, seemed to have slipped her parents' minds.

The first such change of surname had come thirty years ago. As far as the stroke count was concerned, it had been a disaster – the new total was, in divination terms, one of the most ill-omened numbers possible.

Three years after that, she'd regained her old name.

A year later came the next change of surname. Again, she'd ended up with an unlucky stroke count.

A decade had then gone by, during which she'd learned that these fortune-tellers weren't messing around: having the wrong number of strokes really did bring you terrible luck. Eventually, she switched back to her old surname and decided never to marry again. And yet along came surname number four. She was forty by this point. As before, she ended up with the worst stroke count possible. It was beginning to seem like a bad joke.

Still, you don't make it to forty without picking up at least a little bit of wisdom along the way. Life had offered plenty of lessons, even if she'd had to learn most of them the hard way.

The way her parents had eventually written it, Taeko had ten strokes.

But if you wrote it differently – with the kanji for "endurance", which no-one would normally think of using – you ended up with fifteen, one of the three luckiest numbers. With fifteen, everything in life would go your way.

If they could only have written it that way, maybe she'd have had better luck with at least one of her husbands.

The satnav had finished scanning the area. There were three car rental places within ten kilometres of her current position. Two of them were affiliated with specific manufacturers, while the other was a slightly shady-looking spot that claimed to specialise in luxury imported vehicles.

Please select destination, came the voice of a young woman from the satnav.

Please select destination. Please select destination.

"Oh, shut up!" grumbled Taeko, before turning to Kuro. "Hey, how about we spoil ourselves? We could rent a Volvo or a BMW. Maybe even a Benz."

She had the money, that much was certain. In fact, this

was probably the first – and last – time in her life she would have this much cash to burn.

"Hey, Kuro. What d'you reckon?"

The cat's long, bushy tail swished languidly.

This, Taeko decided, was her way of saying, *I'm all in.*

In the end, she settled on a Mercedes S-Class. You were supposed to book in advance rather than just turn up, which meant she had to provide an extra-large deposit. You'd think they'd be used to the sight of cash at a place like this, she thought, observing the startled reaction of the staff as she piled wad after wad of banknotes onto the counter.

Pets were against the rules too. She promised she wouldn't let Kuro out of the carrier, but had to pay a temporary advance to cover any cleaning costs. Again, the staff almost seemed to wince at the amount of cash she handed them.

At the first red light, she broke her promise and let Kuro out of the carrier.

"Pretty smooth ride, huh? It's a Benz. Probably set you back at least ten million yen. Maybe we can buy one on the way home if we decide it's a keeper."

If she wanted to, maybe she really could.

The staff at the car rental place hadn't batted an eyelid at the name on her driving license, meaning word hadn't got out yet about what she'd done.

It was a straight shot down the six-lane bypass to the motorway junction. When you were used to a subcompact, an S-Class felt like a bus or a truck. The interior was like a living room. With the steering wheel on the left, it almost felt like operating some entirely new type of vehicle.

"It's so quiet, isn't it? Now I know what they mean when they say it just glides along."

The sounds of the engine, the wind and the road were all so faint that you had to strain your ears to hear them. Meanwhile, the subcompact she'd left at the metered car park near the rental place was probably still sputtering away now.

"Guess what? The engine on that old thing always sounds like it's saying *poor-poor-poor-poor.* I'm not joking. And when you brake too hard, it goes *salaryyy–salaryyy–salaryyy*. What, don't you believe me?"

There was no reply from Kuro. She'd never been one to miaow, even in her youth, and she seemed to have only grown more tight-lipped in her old age.

Had she been like this with everyone? Or had she adapted her personality to match each of her temporary owners?

Despite Taeko's many years of custom, the man at the pet shop never really told her anything. All her questions about Kuro's other hosts – for example, whether they tended to be men or women – went unanswered. All he ever said was: "Only the smartest cats get to become Blanket Cats."

She wasn't sure the old Kuro qualified as "smart". If anything, her younger replacement seemed a lot sharper.

Still, it was the old Kuro she preferred. They had a sort of chemistry.

Going on drives with Kuro in the passenger seat – that was what Taeko loved best. Over the course of each of their three-day trips together, Taeko would feel the heaviness inside her – a sort of sediment of silence and sadness that accumulated during the three months between each trip – fall away. With the younger Kuro, some of that sediment always lingered – but with her predecessor, as she was now remembering, the liberation was complete.

"Oh, yeah – the wipers go *debt-debt-debt-debt,* and the indicators sound like they're saying *worn-out, worn-out, worn-out.*"

She could tell Kuro the most ridiculous things. This is such *fun,* she thought to herself with something approaching astonishment.

And now it had been a whole two years since they'd been together. The sediment was even denser than usual.

She was approaching the motorway junction. ROADS CLEAR TO NAGANO, said the electronic sign.

Scrabbling to find the indicator lever – it turned out to be on the other side to usual – she shifted into the leftmost lane. She still wasn't used to the left-hand drive, and they jerked abruptly across the road, but the driver behind noticed and slowed down accordingly.

"That's the power of a Benz for you. If this were my car, I guarantee they'd be honking us off the road."

Taeko couldn't remember the last time she'd felt this happy.

She wanted to go all out. To tell Kuro everything and anything. To laugh until her sides shook.

Which was why, she decided, it was the time to clear away the heaviest sediment of all.

"Hey, Kuro, guess what?" she said as they drove onto the on-ramp. "I pinched some money."

2

It wasn't quite accurate to say she'd pinched it. Technically, what Taeko had done was embezzlement.

Thirty million yen in operating funds, snatched from under the nose of the stationery wholesale company she'd worked at for thirty years.

It was a fairly small operation – exactly the kind of place the phrase "family-run business" brought to mind. Faced with the same problems as everyone else these days, the company had managed, against the odds, to keep growing. Rather than overreaching, its strategy had simply been to plug the gaps left by the bigger firms.

The company president trusted her. She was on first name terms with him – as well as the father he'd taken over from, and his son, now managing director. None of them had ever bothered checking the ledgers Taeko was responsible for.

"They're good people," she said to Kuro in the passenger seat. "Real honest-to-goodness types." The car was already doing close to a hundred and twenty kilometres an hour. Taeko nudged the pedal down a little further.

The other employees had been just as amiable as the president and his family. Of course, if you worked somewhere for three decades there was bound to be the occasional conflict. The office had seen its fair share of sulkers, shirkers and hotheads. But looking back now – now that everything was over – all she was left with was a bittersweet smile and the thought that they'd all been "good people".

She'd only been a few years away from an uneventful retirement. By the time her departure was approaching, the president's son ("Auntie Taeko", he'd always called her) had entered the company as managing director, and the president himself had even asked her to stay on after retirement in a part-time capacity.

She'd had no complaints. She had none now either.

Whatever happened from here on in, she couldn't imagine ever regretting her time at the company.

"Pretty rotten of me, wasn't it?" she murmured, flashing her lights at the car in front that was blocking the fast lane. There was a BABY ON BOARD sign in the rear window. The car made a panicked escape to the slow lane, like someone ducking hurriedly out of the way.

Once again, Taeko marvelled at the power, the authority, the dignity, the sheer *impact* of the S-Class.

She found herself thinking of the president's father, who in his days as head of the company had always talked about wanting a foreign-made car, yet never bought himself anything fancier than a Toyota Crown. And of the current president, how happy he'd looked when he'd splashed out on his own company car and got himself a Lexus.

Thirty million yen.

And it wasn't money that had come from cunning investments or property flipping, either. Every single yen had been earned through the unstinting labour of everyone at the company, from the president all the way down to the rank and file. All the endless bowing, the long days traipsing around after clients and bending over backwards to please them. Whenever business took a hit the operating funds went down, and when it recovered they went back up. They'd been the barometer of the company's health.

And she'd stolen the lot.

"Yep. Rotten's the only word for it."

Kuro, silent as ever, lazily stretched her large frame, then hopped onto the rear seats. If this was Taeko's car, the manoeuvre would have entailed an awkward squeeze between the front seats. But the capacious interior of the S-Class made it a breeze, even for an adult Maine Coon.

"Fancy stopping at the next service area?"

Kuro meowed back in a way that sounded, to Taeko, like another vote of agreement.

She pulled into the service area just past Kofu, where she decided to let Kuro stretch her legs in the small, wooded area adjoining the service station building.

But Kuro was no longer her youthful self. After a few plodding steps she eased herself down onto the ground.

Taeko sat on a nearby bench and, sipping on the paper cup of coffee she'd bought from a vending machine, gazed vacantly at the cat.

The black fur, so glossy in her youth, had grown dry and lacklustre. Her remaining teeth were so weak that the pet food she'd been provided with was a sort of paste specially designed for elderly cats. Even her breathing seemed laboured, her chest heaving up and down as though she were quietly urging herself on with each exhalation.

Taeko had first met Kuro seven years before, after separating from her third husband.

She hadn't borrowed her out of loneliness. In fact, when she'd first learned – in a magazine, was it? – that there was a company that rented out cats for three days, she'd been shocked more than anything else. Shocked that someone would make money out of a thing like that – and that anyone would actually take them up on the offer.

In the end, she'd tried it simply out of curiosity.

Ever since childhood, she'd heard people say that black cats were unlucky.

That was why she'd chosen Kuro. What could suit her more, she'd reasoned, than the unluckiest animal of all?

And then there was that fragment of a Shuji Terayama poem that had long occupied some remote nook of her brain. It went like this:

There is a cat named Sorrow,
It never leaves my side.

The poem didn't specify the colour, but to Taeko it was obvious: a cat that embodied unhappiness could only be black.

And so "Sorrow" had become her secret nickname for Kuro.

For five years – once every winter, spring, summer, autumn – she had gone on long drives with Sorrow at her side.

In the sixth and seventh years, she'd had the younger Kuro for company instead. The new cat had beautiful, glossy fur, but compared to her predecessor, Taeko always felt she lacked a certain depth. Now, reunited with the original Kuro, she realised that there had only ever been one cat named Sorrow, and this was her.

Sorrow lay there as a butterfly danced around her.

Sorrow closed her eyes.

Sorrow stretched. Sorrow yawned. Sorrow twitched her ears.

"Look, a cute kitty cat!" said a little girl as she walked past holding her parents' hands.

But her parents simply frowned and muttered something about how they'd have to be careful when they drove off.

Without getting up, Sorrow turned and looked at Taeko.

"Ready?" asked Taeko, opening the hatch of the carrier at her feet.

Sorrow paced slowly over and climbed in.

Taeko closed the lid and picked the carrier up by the handle.

And off she drove again, with Sorrow at her side.

Taeko pulled off the motorway at the first junction after Lake Suwa. From here, she would follow the winding road north into the forest. It would be another two hours or so – after sundown – before she reached the secluded ryokan where they were to spend the night.

She turned the radio on. Still nothing on the news. Maybe her happy-go-lucky boss and his family hadn't noticed yet, or maybe her crime had simply been too banal to be considered newsworthy.

"Not that it matters," she chuckled to herself as she drove.

She called the ryokan from a service station where she'd stopped to fill up. She'd already told them about the cat when making her reservation, but she wanted to be sure there wouldn't be any issues.

Some years ago, on a winter drive, she'd arrived at her hotel only to discover that some miscommunication with the travel agency meant they were unable to check her in. But she hadn't got angry. All par for the course when you're travelling with Sorrow at your side, she'd told herself.

In the end they'd spent the night at a shabby motel. Kuro had passed most of the time leaping up from the bed in an attempt to catch her own reflection in the mirrored ceiling. We were both still so young then, Taeko thought.

When she'd filled the car, she turned to Kuro. "Ready for the final stretch?"

Kuro had curled up on the passenger seat and begun nodding off.

"I'll take that as a yes."

She'd had no grudge against the company, no ill feelings towards her boss or his family. Nor had she been particularly desperate to get her hands on the thirty million yen. She knew all too well how much the money meant to the company.

"When they arrest me, they'll probably ask for my motive. What do you think I should tell them?"

She hadn't just been acting on impulse either. And as much as she could empathise with those who developed kleptomaniac tendencies in the wake of some psychological upset, that didn't seem to be the case with her.

"What would *you* tell them, Kuro-chan?"

No reply.

"Tough one, isn't it? I mean, I don't even know the answer myself."

All she could compare it to was a child suddenly tearing all the flowers from a flowerbed. Or demolishing a painstakingly assembled Jenga tower. Or dressing up a favourite doll in special clothes, lovingly brushing its hair and hugging it close – only to calmly rip its head off a moment later.

She smiled grimly as she realised that her imagined culprits all were children. What about someone who was edging towards sixty? What could her excuse possibly be?

The road narrowed as it entered the forest and the streetlamps disappeared. Steep slopes rose on either side, blocking the evening sun. It was suddenly very dark. Taeko turned on the headlights. With their pale cones of light bathing the road in front of her, the darkness inside the vehicle only seemed to intensify.

"What do you think it is, Kuro-chan? Why do things never work out for me?"

She'd already told the cat all about her three husbands, and her reasons for divorcing them.

Her first had run off with a lover.

Her second had turned out to be a violent alcoholic and gambler – and work-shy to boot.

Her third had been a widower with a daughter. A straightforward and largely unremarkable office worker whose first wife had died from cancer. Too straightforward, as it turned out: he'd walked out on Taeko once it became apparent that his daughter was never going to take to her. "I'm doing this for my kid," he'd told her before he left.

"Unbelievable, isn't it? You know, the other day my friend said I have such rotten luck with men I must have done something terrible in a past life. Told me to go see a medium. She even tried to recommend me one. I mean, really . . ."

There were almost no other cars on the road now.

As the temperature dropped, a layer of white mist began to form on the windscreen.

Taeko found the button for the air conditioning right away, but no matter how many times she pushed it, nothing came out of the vents.

"Why isn't it . . .?"

As she fiddled around, the rear and side windows began to mist up too.

"Never mind, we'll manage."

She carried on driving.

"How about you, Kuro?" she asked nonchalantly. "Was it fun being a Blanket Cat? Or did you secretly hate it?"

That was when she realised.

Kuro wasn't sitting on the passenger seat. She groped around with her right hand, but found only air.

"Hang on . . . Kuro, did you jump in the back? It's so dark in here I didn't even notice . . ."

She wanted to turn and check the rear seats, but she was approaching a series of sharp turns along a river and the windscreen was still fogged up. In this unfamiliar vehicle, with its steering wheel on the wrong side, even glancing in the rear-view mirror felt dangerous.

"Kuro? You asleep?"

No reply. No signs of movement in the back either.

"Guess you're asleep, then."

As she lowered her speed, telling herself that it might

have been a good idea to keep Kuro in the carrier after all, she spotted a sign for the ryokan on the side of the road. TWO KILOMETRES AHEAD.

"Right. Almost there. Let's just push on, okay?" Taeko said, accelerating again.

Her headlights seemed to grow weaker. A thick fog was rising up from the river.

When she pulled up at the ryokan, an elderly man came hurrying out in a traditional happi coat, as if he'd been waiting for them.

Taeko opened the window on her side and told him her name.

"I've got my cat with me too," she added. "Thanks for letting me bring her."

The man gave her a friendly smile. "Yes, I know all about her." Then his smile broadened, as if to signal that he had something more important to discuss. "Your friends have all checked in already."

"My . . . what?"

"If you could just park here . . ." the man said before disappearing back into the interior.

The dubious look on Taeko's face relaxed into a wry smile. She unfastened her seatbelt and turned to address Kuro in the back.

"Looks like they've mixed us up with some other guest. Can you believe it?"

She gulped.

Kuro wasn't there.

She turned the interior light on. Still no sign of her.

Taeko leaped out of the car in a panic. She opened the rear door and checked the footwells and the space under the passenger and driver's seats. But Kuro was nowhere to be seen.

She went around to the passenger seat and opened the door. Her hands were shaking; her jaw and lips quivered.

"Kuro? Kuro-chan? Where are you?"

She wasn't in the footwell of the passenger seat either. Taeko groped about in the darkness, her hands numb with cold, but found nothing. Could Kuro have jumped out of the car along the way? Impossible, thought Taeko. Or slipped out right after they'd arrived? No, that seemed even less probable.

Stay calm, she told herself as she got back to her feet.

Just then, she heard an eruption of merry laughter from within the ryokan. Must be some tour group, she thought.

But then she began recognising the voices.

3

There were at least four of them, each distinctly familiar. She began picturing their owners. They were all laughing. They all sounded happy.

But for them to be *here,* at this ryokan of all places – it was absurd.

For a moment, Taeko simply stood there, shaking her head over and over.

The fog around her was getting thicker by the minute, its pale dampness filling her lungs with each breath. It was stifling. She could feel its moisture clinging to the back of her throat.

Now she could make out a child's voice amid the din. A boy.

"Auntie Taeko!"

She wasn't hearing things. The boy really had called her name. She'd heard his voice clearly. Almost too clearly.

"I wish she'd hurry up!" came the voice again. "Where is she?"

"She'll be here any minute," she heard a man explain. "Probably just got held up."

Taeko furrowed her brow. The boy she had heard was the managing director's son, Taro. But Taro was in his twenties. The voice issuing from inside the ryokan sounded like he had when she'd known him as a small child.

The man who had replied was his father, the managing director. *His* voice sounded just as it should – like that of a man in his mid-forties.

"I wish she'd get a move on already."

Drawn by Taro's voice, Taeko made her way unsteadily towards the door.

She walked into the ryokan.

The elderly man who had welcomed her a moment ago was standing there, still smiling politely in his happi coat. "This way, please," he said, gesturing towards the end of the hallway.

"I can't find my cat."

"So I'm informed."

"I've lost her. My cat. She was in the car with me a moment ago, and now she's gone."

"Yes. We're aware of the situation."

"Listen. What's . . . going on? What *is* this place?"

"Everyone's waiting to see you."

"But—"

"They've been waiting for *such* a long time." Once again, the old man gestured towards the end of the hallway. "This way, please."

It was a very long hallway. Somehow, the fog had begun to make its way inside. It drifted over the lustrous black floorboards as Taeko walked along.

She wasn't wearing her shoes, though she had no memory of taking them off.

The fusuma door slid open, and out poked the head of the young Taro.

"Auntie Taeko!" Scrunching his face up into a grin, he beckoned for her to join them. "Come on!"

Behind him loomed the company president, who was in his early seventies.

"Taeko, where were you? We've been waiting for you." He was his usual age.

His wife appeared at his side. "We were starting to worry you'd had an accident or something!" Her face, meanwhile, looked as it had twenty years ago – at a time when she'd often confided in Taeko about her fractious relationship with her mother-in-law.

Taeko couldn't move her feet.

Somehow, though, her body kept gliding forward.

The fog was getting thicker and thicker.

Taeko felt as though she was floating.

*

The reception room was full of people from her company. Some of them were colleagues she'd sat alongside just the previous day; others had retired years ago. Their ages were a mix too. One, sipping on her drink, had reverted to her youthful self; another, reaching for a piece of sashimi with his chopsticks, looked exactly as he did in the present. Some sported old hairstyles Taeko had forgotten ever existed; others were dressed so familiarly that it would have been the most natural thing in the world to lean over and grumble, *Hurry up with that invoice, would you?*

They were all smiling.

Taeko had stolen the operating funds that were the firm's lifeblood, and they were all smiling merrily at her.

They still don't know what I've done, she thought.

Then: *That's not the issue here!*

She closed her eyes firmly, then opened them again.

It was all a dream. It had to be.

Yes, there could be no other explanation.

And yet, sitting there in the reception room, they all looked so *real.* She could smell miso wafting from the hotpot set on a portable stove on the table, and when a cup of hot sake was thrust in her direction and she absent-mindedly took a sip, the tang of the alcohol was unmistakable.

"Auntie Taeko," nagged Taro. "Why are you crying?"

"I'm not! Look. Do you see any tears on my face?"

"No. But you *are* crying, Auntie. I can just tell." He turned to the others. "She is, isn't she?" They all nodded in unison.

But she really wasn't.

Or was she?

"It's okay, Auntie!" Taro flung his arms around her from behind. "You can stop now."

She felt his voice through her back, shrill yet soft and gentle. Yes, she remembered, that's what little boy's voices sound like.

Next, Taro plumped himself down on her lap.

"Oh, get off her," called his mother, the managing director's wife, chuckling as she chided him. "It's bad manners."

Her husband gave Taeko a pained grin as he sipped from his sake cup. "Sorry about him. He can be a bit of a brat."

"Hey! I'm not a brat!"

"Shush, you. Stop spouting nonsense."

"But you called me a brat! Didn't he, Auntie Taeko?"

"I suppose he did," she said, stroking Taro's head.

Taro drew his shoulders in as if he found this ticklish, then looked up at her again. "Now, stop crying, okay?"

"So I'm really crying, am I?"

"Yep. You look *super* sad."

"I'm not sad. It's so nice to see everyone again. Brings back all sorts of memories."

She wasn't just being polite. The words had come naturally.

"Really?" asked Taro, delighted. The smiles on everyone else's faces seemed to widen too.

With Taro still squeezed on her lap, Taeko took another sip of the sake, feeling its faint warmth arrive in her chest.

"Come on, Auntie. Dry those tears!"

". . . I'm crying? You're serious?"

"Oh yeah, one hundred per cent," said Taro, twisting around

to look at her. "So, what's up? Did something sad happen?" He put a hand to her jaw. "It's okay."

He stroked her chin gently, as if to wipe away the tears that were supposedly trickling down her face. "You can stop now. When you cry, it makes me want to cry too." A note of sadness had entered his voice.

He went on, still caressing her chin. "We're not angry with you, Auntie. Not one bit."

Now the fog was seeping into the reception room.

She felt Taro's weight disappear from her lap. The smiling faces of her colleagues began to recede into the pale white fog.

"Don't cry, Auntie."

Taro's voice seemed to come from somewhere above her, far off in the distance.

She could feel something dry and rough in her lap.

The fog had eddied in around Taro. When it cleared, all that remained where he had been sitting was a small, weather-beaten skull.

Taeko gasped. Her voice seemed to crack in her throat.

"Taeko," came the managing director's voice.

"Taeko, dearest," came that of the president's wife.

The fog lifted, and where they had been sitting Taeko saw two skeletons, still clad in the padded kimonos given to guests at the ryokan. They were staring at her.

Everyone had turned to bones.

And everyone was looking at her.

"*Why*, Taeko?" someone asked.

"We were your friends," came another voice. "How could you do that to us?"

Taeko could scarcely breathe. She felt a scream rising within her.

"But we're not angry," said the skull in her lap. "No-one's mad about what you did, Auntie."

She wanted to push the skull away, but her hand wouldn't move.

She wanted to run, but she felt too weak to even get to her feet.

"Don't cry, Auntie Taeko," said the skull.

"Dry those tears, Taeko," said the managing director.

"That's right, dear," said the president's wife. "You've spent your whole life crying over this and that. You can stop now."

"Come on, Auntie. Smile!"

"Yes. Show us the Taeko we used to know."

"You're okay now. You're okay!"

The fog swelled. Now it swirled around Taeko too. As it began to obscure her vision, a white curtain falling over the world, she saw the skeletons start to crumble one by one. The skull in her lap disintegrated, shattering from the jaw outwards.

She clutched the bony remnants to her chest. In the instant before they dissolved completely, their texture felt strangely familiar, like that of someone she'd been waiting to meet.

Then the fog consumed everything.

In the distance, she heard the miaowing of a cat.

From somewhere on the other side of the fog, she felt Sorrow drawing closer, step by unhurried step.

When Taeko opened her eyes, she found herself soaking in an open-air stone bath.

Above her was Kuro, curled on top of the large boulder that acted as a screen.

Taeko patted her hand against the water and listened to it splash. It sounded just as it should. She let out a deep breath, then rubbed her hands together in the water and pinched herself.

Once she was sure she'd returned to reality, she felt a rush of sadness.

"Kuro-chan," she said, gazing up at the boulder. "That was a nasty trick to play."

Kuro, apparently pretending not to hear, didn't turn to look.

"So you're one of *those* cats these days, are you?"

According to folklore, cats could only transform into bakeneko – supernatural beings with mysterious powers, such as the ability to enchant whomever they pleased – when they were old, and close to death. It was the kind of thing you'd read in one of those "spooky stories" magazines for kids, but right now it all seemed quite plausible to Taeko.

"You must be angry with me. That's why you made me see all those awful things, isn't it?" Taeko frowned at her.

But maybe, she thought, there was another explanation. Maybe, by showing her these visions, Kuro was saying that she forgave her.

The cat gave no reply, but stirred, stretched and rearranged her ink-black body so that she lay belly-down on the boulder.

"That's the end of the show, is it?"

Looking back, it didn't seem like such a bad dream after all.

"Have your powers run out?"

She wanted to be holding Taro on her lap again. This time, she thought, she'd hug him tight and never let him go.

"Say something, Kuro. We're old friends, aren't we?"

She wanted to see her colleagues again. This time, she felt sure she'd find the words that had escaped her earlier – even if she had to speak them through a wall of tears.

And if she really *did* start crying? Would Taro tell her the opposite – that she was smiling? Would he be happy this time, she wondered.

Kuro hopped onto another nearby boulder. The forest behind her was a shade darker than the night sky, and she was darker still. Her eyes, lemon-yellow with the slightest hint of blue, glittered in the gloom.

Sorrow was staring her in the face. But Taeko didn't avert her gaze.

"They really were good people, you know. Every single one of them."

She could think of plenty of people she would have liked to get revenge on. But her colleagues weren't among them.

"Why *did* I do it, I wonder? What's wrong with me?"

She felt something gripping her deep in her chest, a feeling that words like "remorse" or "regret" could never capture.

"*You* understand, though, don't you, Kuro?"

Kuro stared at her in silence.

"I mean, we're friends, aren't we?"

No response.

Taeko slowly stood up, her naked body emerging from the bathwater. Just above her belly button ran a long, thin scar.

"Turns out I have cancer." She gave a little giggle. "Terminal.

They opened me up, had a look in my belly, but there isn't anything they can do."

It was then that Kuro finally let out a soft *miaow*.

4

Taeko woke with a shiver. She made her way across the tatami room to the wooden-floored area by the window with its rattan table and chairs. When she slid open the floor-to-ceiling window, the cold fog that had gathered in the garden came swirling in.

The nights here were longer than in Tokyo, and dawn was still some way off. The air smelled of moss. She'd never lived anywhere this deep in nature, and yet there was something intensely nostalgic about the smell.

Taeko sat on one of the chairs and reached for the glass of beer she'd only half-finished the night before. It had gone completely flat, but that just made it slide all the more smoothly down her throat.

There was a stir in the gloom. Kuro, who had been sleeping in her carrier in the tokonoma alcove, had awoken.

She padded soundlessly across the room and joined Taeko in the wooden-floored area. "Morning," said Taeko. But Kuro simply hopped silently into the chair opposite. Sorrow was back at her side.

"It's four in the morning. Don't tell me you've become an early riser in your old age?" There was a pause before she murmured, "Oh, but cats are nocturnal, aren't they?"

Ignoring her, Kuro jumped down from the chair and padded out into the garden. A few paces were all it took for her to disappear completely into the gloom. If it's in a cat's nature to go hunting at night, Taeko thought, then the black ones must be best suited to the job.

For a while she sat there, waiting by the open window, but Kuro showed no sign of returning. Taeko pulled the collar of her yukata tightly around her neck, then lifted her bare feet from the wooden floorboards where they'd been resting. It seemed too much effort to fetch her padded kimono and socks – and yet she'd probably catch a cold if she sat here with the wind blowing in any longer.

"Come on, Kuro, let's go back to bed. It's cold. I'm going to close the window. Okay?"

The garden was deathly silent. There was still no sign of Kuro.

Taeko turned back to the room, thinking she'd at least pull on the padded kimono.

But the room had vanished.

In front of her was a lake of fog.

Where Taeko's futon had been, a little girl now sat.

She had her hair in a bob and wore a pinafore skirt. She appeared to be around primary school age.

"Where did things go wrong, eh?" said the girl. "When did all this 'sorrow' turn up in your life?"

Taeko gave a pained smile, then gave her a look that said, *Did you really have to put it like that?* The girl giggled and shrugged.

"Is there someone you'd like to meet?" asked the girl. "I

can show you anyone you like," she added, looking at Taeko with a mischievous glint in her eyes.

Various faces appeared in Taeko's mind before vanishing again, like so many soap bubbles popping.

All that remained was the girl – the most familiar face of all, smiling at her from amid the fog.

"Are you mad at me?" asked Taeko. "For making such a mess of life, I mean. Do you hold it against me?"

"It was a shock, definitely," said the girl. "But no, I'm not angry."

"I gave it my best shot, I promise," said Taeko. "Nothing worked out the way I planned it, that's all. There were so many people who let me down. People who treated me terribly. I don't need to go into the details, do I? You already know."

The girl nodded silently.

"I'd . . . never done anything like that before," Taeko went on. "I wanted to see what it felt like to be the one to betray someone. To hurt them. To put them through hell . . ."

When she'd been diagnosed with terminal cancer, Taeko had felt strangely unafraid of dying. All it meant, she told herself, was that the lengthy drama that was her life would soon reach its conclusion. *Game over*, as kids were always saying these days.

A happy ending didn't seem to be on the cards. Nor was there much chance of an unexpected plot twist. The sadness only really hit her when she realised that, when she was gone, she'd leave nothing behind.

That was when she'd felt the urge to dig her claws into this life of hers, this endless slide into sorrow. To make her mark, even if it was nothing more than a cat scratch, before she went.

"Why them, though?" asked the girl. She looked baffled. "Why betray the people who were kindest to you?"

"Stop calling me *you*!" shrieked Taeko suddenly. But, absorbed by the fog, her voice became a vague and distant murmur, as if she had water trapped in her ears.

"There were so many others you could have hurt," the girl went on. "And with good reason too. So, why them?"

She spoke serenely, quietly, without a hint of blame or reproach. "Why the people you had least reason to harm?"

"'You'? Don't you mean 'we'?" shouted Taeko. She grabbed the glass from the table and made as if to hurl it at the girl. But again her voice was lost in the fog, and the hand she was so sure had seized the glass now met nothing but air, clenching into a powerless fist.

"What were you trying to prove?"

The girl wasn't asking the questions to get answers. She spoke like someone lecturing a small child, as if she wanted to stun Taeko into some sort of penitent silence.

Taeko gave her a long, hard stare.

The girl giggled, then repeated her question, this time correcting herself.

"Okay, okay. What were *we* trying to prove?"

As she was driving back through the forest to the main road, Taeko came out of a sharp curve and was greeted by a ray of late-spring sunshine, lancing into the car as if it had been waiting for them all this time.

"They did say it was going to be warm today."

Kuro, sitting on the passenger seat, gave an interested nod – or so Taeko imagined.

"We might get sunburnt at the beach!"

Did cats ever get sunburnt, with all that fur? Weather like this must be pretty hard going for a black cat, she thought.

Taeko pulled onto the main road and accelerated, heading north. She'd booked another ryokan for the night, this time at the end of a headland that jutted out into the Japan Sea. They had entered the second half of their three days together, and the moment was fast approaching when Taeko would have to make an important decision.

"So, got any more magic tricks planned for me?"

Kuro stretched slightly, then curled up again.

In the two visions she'd had so far, Taeko had been reunited with the people who meant the most to her. People she'd never expected to see again.

"I wonder what's going on at the office. Maybe they haven't noticed the money's missing yet. Or maybe they have, and they're running around looking for me."

They really had been good people. As Taeko's younger self had put it, she'd had no reason to hurt them.

"I really can't explain it. But . . . *you* get it, don't you?"

You get it because you're a cat. Cats aren't like dogs, are they? They don't care about obeying their owner. They do as they please. They take life at their own pace.

Kuro began purring loudly, as if to indicate her agreement. Or maybe as if she hadn't been paying attention in the first place.

They entered a long tunnel. In the middle of it Taeko

spotted a sign indicating that they'd reached the other side of the mountains. It was all downhill from here – about a hundred kilometres to the Japan Sea.

"Kuro, we've been all sorts of places together, haven't we? Too many to even remember."

On some of their drives, she'd checked in at their hotels only to collapse on the bed in tears. On others, back when mobile phones lost signal the moment you left the city, she'd spent longer standing in telephone boxes than behind the wheel. There'd been the turbulent nights of hard drinking. The evenings when she'd had the mischievous idea of bedding a man for the night, only to lose her nerve and end up sleeping alone. The time when she'd parked alongside a highland meadow, lowered all the windows, and simply dozed all afternoon. Or when she'd pulled up by a river and spent the whole day gazing at its swirling waters.

And through it all, Kuro had been sitting in the passenger seat. Sorrow – never particularly affectionate, but always content to sit there in the car – had always stayed by her side.

"This is our last full day together, you know," said Taeko.

As she approached the next curve, she straddled both lanes, jerking the steering wheel to the right.

Nothing came around the corner.

She took the following curve the same way. This time, too, there was nothing in the opposite lane.

Just before the third curve, she steered back into her own lane.

"Just messing around," she chuckled. "Don't want to ruin someone's day, do we?"

Kuro gave a low growl. She was glaring at Taeko, her fur standing on end.

"Are you angry?" said Taeko, turning her eyes back to the road. "Still, I mean . . . you've had a nice long life, haven't you? Sure you don't fancy coming along for the ride?"

Kuro only growled louder.

Finally, the sea came into view.

On the radio, they were talking about what Taeko had done. She was being described as a "female employee responsible for the company's accounts".

Police are currently searching for the woman in the belief that she may know something about the missing money.

It sounded like something from a cheesy TV drama.

Eventually, the clapped-out car she'd left at the metred car park would be reported. The number plate would give her away. They'd ask around the neighbourhood. At the car rental company, they'd learn about the S-Class.

Taeko found herself wishing they'd track her down via the pet shop instead, though she didn't quite know why.

They pulled up at the beach. In the summer this was a popular bathing spot, but there was no sign yet of the prefab buildings that sprang up every year to cater to beachgoers. In fact, the entire beach was deserted. The sea looked calm.

Taeko got out, then opened the passenger-side door. With a visible effort, Kuro got to her feet and hopped down.

The sunlight was dazzling on the water. Taeko found

herself wishing she'd stopped somewhere to buy a pair of sunglasses and a wide-brimmed hat.

"Hey, Kuro. Do cats like to swim?" She remembered reading somewhere that they hated getting their fur wet, but . . . "Maine Coons are supposed to be part raccoon, and *raccoons* can swim, right? Or have I got that wrong . . .?"

Chatting away to herself, Taeko drew closer to the shore.

For once, Kuro followed her obediently. Like a dog.

As she walked, Taeko took a long, slow breath of the salty air, then carefully exhaled. Then she stopped and took another series of deep breaths. She felt the air in her lungs being replenished.

While Taeko stood there breathing, Kuro overtook her, drawing even closer to the water's edge. Undeterred by the lapping waves, she plodded forward, her large body swaying from side to side.

"Kuro . . ."

Kuro ignored her and continued towards the sea.

"I've been meaning to tell you. I haven't decided where exactly, but today, I'm planning to . . ."

She gulped, feeling the word at the back of her throat. *To die.* Then she let it sink back down into her stomach.

Kuro walked into the sea.

A wave washed over her.

At first the cat remained standing on the wet sand. But as the wave receded, it pulled her off her feet.

"Kuro, no!"

Taeko dashed into the sea, still wearing her shoes, not even bothering to lift up her skirt.

Kuro was a metre or so away from her, floundering in the waves.

Just as Taeko reached for her, another wave crashed in and Kuro was pulled even further out.

"Kuro!"

One metre became two, and then three. Weighed down by the sopping mass of her black fur, Kuro began disappearing between the waves.

Taeko, her legs now completely submerged, let out a silent scream as she pursued the cat.

The water came up to her waist, then her chest, her shoulders, her chin. Now she couldn't touch the bottom. Water flooded her mouth. She felt a stinging at the back of her nose, a salty pain in her eyes.

She swam. She thrust out a desperate hand, felt her fingers brush Kuro's fur.

Another wave crashed over them.

Kuro was getting further away again.

Taeko reached out again.

Another wave. And another.

She heard Kuro mewling loudly.

As the water beat against her eardrums it sounded for all the world like someone berating her.

Idiot! Idiot! Idiot!

It was a voice she seemed to recognise.

In fact, it was the voice of her long-dead mother. But this realisation only came to her much later.

*

Taeko was sprawled on the dry sand, her cheeks still stinging.

"What *were* you playing at, eh?"

She scowled briefly at Kuro, who was lying by her side, her wet fur coated with sand. She seemed to have forgotten about the near-drowning and was pawing at a piece of driftwood that had washed up on the beach.

"You look like a piece of tempura. You know, when it's covered in batter, before you fry it."

She was trying to make light of things, but as she gazed at Kuro, she felt a lump rising in her throat.

The word that had welled up inside her earlier seemed to have disappeared, though she wasn't sure where to. Maybe it was still in the pit of her stomach, or maybe it had been smashed to pieces in the waves.

"Was that your final magic trick? Or did you just . . .?"

No reply.

"Not that it matters," said Taeko, turning onto her back so she could look up at the blue sky.

"Kuro . . ."

The sound of the waves was receding. Her eyelids were growing heavy. Sleep was enveloping her.

"Let's go on another drive someday, okay? It might be a few years before I can come and find you again, but I'll be there as soon as I can. Just . . . stick around a bit longer, alright?"

She rubbed the scar on her stomach lightly and murmured, "And as for *you*, my tumorous friend . . ." A smile played briefly about her lips, then faded. "You can come too. We might as well try to get along, don't you think? I mean, you won't have anywhere else to go when I'm gone."

She heard a car approaching in the distance. Brakes squealing. Doors opening and slamming shut. Still lying down, she opened her eyes and looked over to see a police car parked in front of the Benz. A uniformed policeman was peering at the number plate and saying something into his radio.

Taeko slowly closed her eyes again.

"Me and you, Kuro. Back on the road . . ."

Kuro got up, padded over to Taeko's side, and curled up next to her.

Taeko reached out a trembling hand and stroked the cat named Sorrow. Then she opened her eyes just a crack, and watched the sunlight make rainbows on her eyelashes.

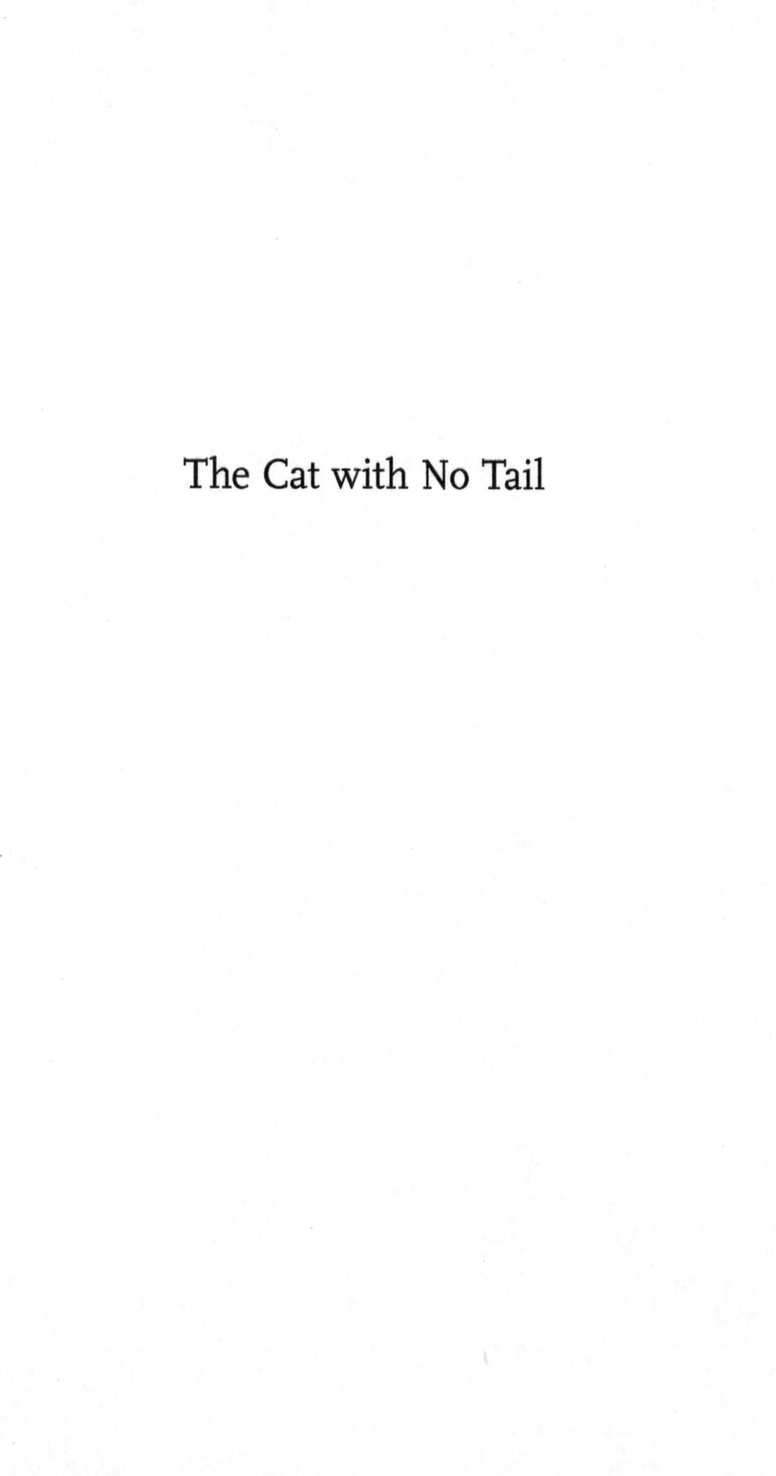

The Cat with No Tail

I

A boy was sitting on the sofa reserved for customers at the pet shop, flicking through the catalogue, when his hands suddenly froze.

"This one," he said, nudging his father, who was sitting next to him.

"Found one you like?"

"Yeah . . . I think . . ."

"Go on then, show me."

His father abruptly leaned over to look at the catalogue. Recoiling slightly, the boy pointed to a photograph at the bottom of the page. "It's a Manx."

"What's that, the breed? Never heard of it."

"Me neither."

"A . . . Manx, eh? Looks sort of . . . lopsided."

The father cocked his head, then addressed the man behind the counter.

"Are they always like this? These . . . Manx things."

"Yes," nodded the owner brusquely. "They're always 'like that'."

A short-haired breed originating on the Isle of Man in England. Also known as the "rabbit cat".

Having read the short text accompanying the photo, the boy looked up at the owner. "Why is it known as the rabbit cat?"

"Well," said the owner, suddenly breaking into a smile, "because it hops around like one."

"But . . . it's a cat, right?"

"Indeed it is. But if you look at that photo carefully, you'll see its hind legs are a lot longer than its front ones. So when they walk around, they sort of look like they're hopping. Just like a rabbit."

The boy's eyes widened. "Wow."

"Also," continued the owner with a grin. "See how it has no tail? That's another characteristic of the Manx."

"Oh yeah. It really doesn't!"

"There are different names for them depending on the length of the tail. If it has no tail at all, that's a 'rumpy'. Then, in order of length, it goes: 'riser', 'stumpy', 'longy'. The shorter the tail, the more valuable the cat." The owner smiled proudly. "And the Manx we have here is a rumpy."

The father broke in with a bemused chuckle. "So it's basically a deformity? And the more deformed the cat, the more valuable it is? Sheesh, humans really can be cruel. Depriving cats of their tails for their own amusement . . ."

"Not at all," retorted the owner flatly. "Manx cats are the result of a random genetic mutation."

"Well, whatever," said the father, wrinkling his nose and lighting a cigarette. "Come on, Koji, make up your mind. You want to go with this Manx thing?"

"Yeah. Just . . . give me a minute." The boy turned to the next page in the catalogue.

The father leaned over again to see what he was looking at, then chuckled once more. "They really do have all sorts, don't they . . . Personally, I'd have thought a cat's a cat." The smoke from his cigarette stung the boy's nostrils. Holding his breath, the boy flashed him a smile that wasn't really a smile, then turned back to the previous page.

"Yeah, I think I want the Manx."

"Alright. That's settled then." The father nodded, cigarette still in his mouth, then got up and went over to the counter.

"Can't say I see the appeal, but my son wants one of the ones without a tail, so that's what we'll get." He reached for the wallet in his pocket. "How much is it for the three days, again?"

"There's one thing I'd like to ask first," said the owner, his face impassive.

"What's that?"

"How old's your son?"

"Twelve. Just started middle school."

"And he's the one who'd be looking after the cat?"

"Well, I'm paying for it, obviously. And I can be the guarantor or whatever if you need one. I'm his father, and I'm a law-abiding citizen."

"Right," nodded the owner. "I see." Then he nodded again, this time with a slight sigh. He looked squarely at the father. "I'm very sorry, but we don't offer cats to minors."

"Now, hang on a minute," said the father, growing red in the face and leaning over the counter. "Why didn't you tell us that earlier?"

"I believe you found us via our website?" asked the owner,

his expression unchanged. "If you'd read the terms and conditions . . ."

"Who's going to read all that?" snapped the father furiously. "You should have told us when we walked in here!"

The owner shrugged, lowered his eyes, and waited for the father's anger to recede.

The boy, too, was simply sitting there, looking down at his lap with his shoulders hunched. The owner glanced over at him, then back at the man.

"When minors want to take a cat home, we normally ask them to do it in their guardian's name." He began extracting one of the rental forms from a filing cabinet.

"Which is why," fumed the father, "I told you to use mine! Go on, what do you need me to sign? I'll do it right now."

The owner sighed, paused, and returned the form to the cabinet.

"Sorry, but this isn't going to work. Please try somewhere else."

The father stared at him. "What do you mean? Why?"

He didn't exactly have an intimidating face, but the owner could tell he was the type who liked to boss the staff around whenever he was out shopping or eating. Like most such men, he looked somewhat ill at ease in his casual clothes, as though he'd much rather be wearing a suit.

"Manx cats are affectionate, delicate creatures. They're very good at knowing whether someone's likely to treat them kindly. And if you don't—"

"Oh, come on, it'll be fine."

"If there's a child involved, we need to know the parent will be able to take good care of it, too. Sometimes they can be too much for a kid to handle."

"And I'm telling you it'll be fine. What, you don't trust your customers?"

"It's not that . . ."

"You're running a business, aren't you? You've got a customer here asking you to rent him a cat. So why don't you?"

Short-tempered. Liable to flip out completely when he doesn't get his way.

"Tell me, have you ever had a cat before?"

"Course not. But I don't see what you're making such a fuss about. It's only three days."

Confident – and for no particular reason. In short, the guy simply isn't cut out for looking after a cat. Even – or especially – when it's "only three days".

Sighing inwardly, the owner turned away from the father and looked at the boy instead. Their eyes met.

The boy was still huddled in on himself, watching the scene unfold as if he were the one being scolded, wincing visibly at his father's arrogance.

"You like the Manx, do you?" the owner asked him.

The boy nodded silently.

"In that case, I'll make an exception and let you take it in your own name. Alright?"

"Really?" asked the boy.

"Really. Just make sure you take good care of him, even if it's only three days."

He pulled the form back out of the filing cabinet, then gestured for the boy to come over.

Left out of this exchange, the father wrinkled his nose, returned to the sofa and muttered, "Unbelievable." He looked around for an ashtray but, finding none, tutted and got to his feet.

"Koji, I'll be outside. Hurry up with that form, alright?"

When he walked out of the shop, his exasperation seemed to linger in the air.

"Sorry about that," the boy said in a thin voice as he wrote down his address. "Dad's always losing his temper."

The owner smiled wryly. "Well, that's not *your* fault, Koji."

"You were annoyed just now, weren't you?"

"Just now?"

"When he said that thing about Manxes being deformed."

"Oh, I didn't mind that," said the owner with another grin, before adding: "See, I'm not the friendliest person at the best of times."

This was enough to finally elicit a smile from the boy. His face was quite unlike his father's, with large round eyes. A little fragile-looking, but just the type to win the affection of his teachers – not to mention the girls in his class. Something about him suggested that his mother fawned over him so much that his father felt slightly left out.

"You like cats, then?"

"Yeah. I like all animals. Especially when they're all soft and, like, cuddly."

"And the Manx was your favourite?"

"Yeah. At first I just sort of chose it by instinct, but then I thought it was sort of cool how it hops about like a rabbit and doesn't have a tail and stuff."

"Want to know why they don't have tails?"

"There's a reason?"

The boy tilted his face up at him, his eyes widening. This seemed to be a habit of his whenever he was surprised.

"It's just a legend, really. People say they were the last ones onto Noah's Ark. Do you know what that is?"

"Yeah, I think so. The story with the flood?"

"That's the one. Well, the Manxes jumped on board just in time, but the hatch caught their tails as it closed. Chopped them right off."

The boy's eyes grew even wider. "Woah!" he exclaimed. "They must be really lucky animals."

"Really? The poor things lost their tails."

"But they made it onto the Ark just in time, instead of dying in the flood. If they'd got there a moment later it would have been game over. So they must be pretty lucky."

"I see what you mean," said the owner, nodding deeply. "You do like to look on the bright side, don't you?"

The boy grinned shyly in response.

"What a joke that place was, eh?" said the father, releasing the handbrake as the boy climbed into the back of the car, his voice still quivering with rage. "If he'd kept that up a minute longer, the gloves would've really come off, let me tell you."

The boy hugged the cat carrier on his lap in silence. Inside was the Manx, curled up in its blanket. He opened the hatch just wide enough to insert a finger and stroke its black back.

Ko–ji, he murmured.

"The way he talked to you! Acting all chummy, just because you're a kid. Guys like him really rub me the wrong way."

Feeling his father's gaze in the rear-view mirror, the boy forced a smile.

"You're a kind-hearted kid, so you might not mind, but he's got no right to talk to a customer like that."

Kind-hearted. The word made the smile on the boy's lips fade.

"Hey, Koji . . ."

"Yeah?"

"How's school these days?"

". . . It's alright, I guess."

"No-one's bullying you, are they? I mean, if they ever do – not that they will – but if they do, you come and tell us right away, okay?"

"I'm fine, Dad."

"Then what's all this about suddenly wanting to rent a cat? You had your mother worried too, you know. You *sure* you're alright?"

"Seriously, I'm fine."

"Alright, you're fine. It's just, you know, you hear about kids who get bullied and they keep it all bottled up and wind up doing themselves in or something. I'm not going to let that happen. If there's anything wrong – anything at all – you tell your father and we'll have a chat. I'll always fight your corner, son. Anyone bullies you, I'll beat the bastard up myself. And I won't let the school get away with it either." He took a breath before going forcefully on. "I'm serious. You don't want to mess with your father when he's mad. I'm not one of those wimps other kids have to put up with for a dad."

The boy smiled. "Okay, Dad, I get it."

He knew his father wasn't lying, or bragging, or bluffing. Past experience told him that much. In his fourth year of primary school, the boy had been involved in a minor scuffle – you couldn't even call it a fight – that had left him with a bleeding nose. His father had marched over to the other kid's house and bellowed at his mother until she got down on her knees for forgiveness. When, in his sixth year, the teacher had singled him out for punishment after he and his friends pulled a prank, his father had demanded an apology from the head teacher and his deputy, and even ended up writing a letter to the local board of education.

When it comes to Koji, I just can't seem to hold back.

He'd heard his father say this to his mother once. They'd been in the living room, unaware that he was listening from the corridor. In his father's voice he'd detected a peculiar blend of exasperation and pride.

They drove over the Tama River and into the area of outer Tokyo where they lived. A car pulled out abruptly from a side road. The father tutted as he slammed on the brakes.

"Bloody weekend drivers," he spat. "Not everyone has all day, you know!"

The boy opened the lid of the carrier and stroked the Manx.

Ko–ji, he murmured.

"What was that?"

"Nothing."

Koji. That was the name the boy had decided to give the

cat – the same as his own. It was the Noah's Ark story that had inspired him. If the Manx was lucky enough to avoid being swept away in the flood, the boy wanted in on some of that good fortune.

"Well, I suppose it's good that you want to look after an animal. You've always had a caring side." His father looked at him as if expecting a response. "Haven't you?"

Just then, the boy's phone chimed in his pocket. A new message.

"You shouldn't really have that thing," said his father, irritated at having his monologue cut short. "Middle school is too early for a phone, I reckon."

In fact, it was his father who'd insisted he get one the previous year, when he'd been attending an after-hours cram school, because "the streets are dangerous at night".

The boy got his phone out.

The message was from his classmate Hasegawa.

i heard yamashu snitched. told his parents last night. what do we do?

The boy felt a cold shiver race down his spine. At the same time, the pit of his stomach felt like it was on fire.

He flipped the phone shut and hugged Koji's carrier again.

"Seriously, though," said his father, "if you have any problems at school, you tell me, alright?"

A soft, plaintive mewl came from inside the carrier, as if the cat were replying on behalf of his namesake.

2

Back home, as he sat there playing with the Manx, the messages from his classmate kept coming.

update on yamashu. the guy's parents have gone into school

lights are on in the headmaster's office. think we're in big trouble

seriously, i'm gonna kill that guy

The boy didn't reply to any of the messages.

It was just like the man at the pet shop had said: the Manx really did hop around like a rabbit. The boy looked at its front and hind legs again, and saw just how unbalanced they were. He couldn't imagine how it could have ever survived in the wild. From a natural selection point of view, the species should have gone extinct long ago. Maybe that was where the story about just making it onto the Ark in time came from, he thought.

The messages that came after dinner had a slightly different tone.

apparently yamashu tried to commit suicide last night

i heard he put our names in his note. from a friend of his parents, so it's probably true

you're the ringleader koji. you better get us out of this (joking, but also like not)

you reckon they'll arrest us?

. . . and so on.

The boy snuck out and retrieved one of the house's cordless phones, then retreated back into his room.

If the school *did* call, he didn't want his parents answering the phone. His mother would be one thing, but if his father picked up things could get really nasty.

After all, the guy thought his son was a little angel. Good at his studies but, like a lot of only children, a little introverted – and so a natural target for bullies. That was how his father seemed to view him.

How little he knew. How little he'd noticed.

The boy's mother was as relaxed about parenting as she was about most things, but for his father it seemed to be a constant source of worry. He was always reading up on the subject, from self-help guides to investigations of real-life bullying cases complete with tips on how to spot "Signs of Bullying" and "Distress Signals". When the boy had found out about the cat rental place on the internet and said he wanted to get one, his father had agreed to it like it was no big deal, before – as the boy's mother told him afterwards – secretly flicking back through his books to find out what this might mean.

He really didn't have a clue.

He was a narrow-minded, self-obsessed man – which, paradoxically, seemed to be why he doted so idiotically on his son.

Whenever Koji found himself standing behind his father, the boy would watch him with cold indifference. Then, when his father turned around, he'd hurriedly look down at the floor before their gazes could meet.

The "Signs of Bullying" actually fell into two categories. Signs that your child was being bullied, and signs that your child was the bully. The books only ever discussed the first type. But his father hadn't noticed that.

*

He stroked the Manx and said its name. *Koji.* For some reason, the sound of his own name in his mouth seemed to ease, if only slightly, the weight he felt pressing down on him.

"Koji, can you believe Yamashu told his parents? I mean, what a loser. It's stuff like that that gets him bullied in the first place. Right?"

All the boys in the class disliked Yamashu, whose real name was Shugo Yamamoto. He'd never done anything to hurt anyone or incur a grudge. There was just something irritating about every little thing he did.

"Koji, you know what? Yamashu used to really like you. Yeah. Seriously."

He and Yamashu had begun hanging out together right after they started middle school together. The boy hadn't exactly thought of him as a "friend", but whenever Yamashu had a free moment he would wander over. *Ko-chan, Ko-chan,* he'd always called the boy. When the boy went to the toilet, Yamashu followed him without being asked, and when the boy sat down to eat his bento at lunch, Yamashu would unfailingly materialise at his side.

"The guy's so clingy. He must be, like, not getting enough love or something."

The cat seemed to have gotten bored of sitting still and hopped away from him.

"Or is it just because *you're* so charming, Koji?" The boy chuckled. Then he glanced at the cordless phone and suppressed a sigh.

Yamashu wasn't a *bad* kid. He was just so, well . . . annoying.

Always drivelling on in that reedy voice. Asking what the

boy's parents were called, what they did for a living, whether he had any brothers or sisters, why he was an only child, what his favourite food was, what his least favourite food was, his favourite sport, his least favourite sport . . . An endless slew of pointless questions, the kind where there was nothing you could actually do with the information afterwards. He just asked, and asked, and asked.

"The guy didn't know what else to talk about. But he was scared you'd go off him if he ever clammed up, so he just kept jabbering away. Talk about lame. Right, Koji?"

At first he'd put up with Yamashu's irritating presence. As long as the boy responded to the endless calls of *Ko-chan, Ko-chan,* Yamashu would do pretty much whatever he asked. Fetching things, letting him copy his homework, giving him the boiled egg from his bento . . . When, half joking, he'd asked him to buy him a McDonald's on the way home from school, Yamashu had actually gone and done it.

"Seriously, what an idiot."

The boy threw himself onto the bed, then lay there watching Koji. Seen from behind, the cat seemed incredibly vulnerable somehow. Maybe it was the fact that he had no tail.

No patting him on the behind – that's a rule, the man at the pet shop had said. Manx cats were missing the bone that would normally be at the base of the spine, meaning their rear ends were extremely sensitive. Another price they had to pay for making it onto the Ark at the last moment.

"You know what, Koji? I really can't work out whether you're lucky or unlucky."

Koji stretched lazily, then performed another rabbit-like hop.

The boy turned over on the bed so that he was staring up at the ceiling. No phone call yet. *You're alright,* he tried to console himself, *you've got this.* But the fear lingered. In fact, with each passing minute it only seemed to intensify.

He reached for his phone, opened up his inbox and reread the message.

you're the ringleader Koji. you better get us out of this (joking, but also like not)

Screw you, he thought, and deleted the message.

The fear continued to grow.

All of a sudden, Koji turned around and stared at him.

"What? You're not *scared*, are you?"

But Koji simply fixed his round, expressionless, marble-like eyes on the boy.

"It wasn't just you. They can't pin it all on you. That'd be . . ."

If his father found out about all this, would he say something along those lines? Would he stand up for him like he'd promised? Fight for him, even?

He carried on addressing the cat, imitating his father. "If anyone ever bullies you, I'll do whatever it takes to protect you. Even if it means laying my life on the line."

But his father had never mentioned what he'd do in the opposite situation.

Shortly before ten o'clock that evening, the cordless phone rang.

Quick, he thought as the display flashed green. Pick it up. But his body wouldn't react.

Then the caller number was replaced by the message MAIN HANDSET IN USE.

The boy held his breath. He closed his eyes.

Then he thought he heard his father's angry voice, though it seemed to come from far away. Perhaps he was just imagining it.

"*What are you talking about?!*"

In May, after a month or so at his new school, the boy had started making other friends. Before long, he was even getting on with the kids from different primary schools who had seemed so unapproachable at first.

Yamashu, meanwhile, was still following him around; he hadn't made any new friends of his own. The boy would be chatting with his classmates when he'd hear the familiar, pleading voice from behind. *Ko-chan, Ko-chan.* Annoyed by the interruption, the boy would turn and glare at him, but that only seemed to encourage him. *Ko-chan, what did you have for breakfast?* The reedy voice. The pointless questions.

Irritating. That was the only word for it.

One day in mid-May, when Yamashu, who was on monitor duty, had left the classroom to report to the staff room, Iijima had turned to the boy and said, "So are you and Yamashu, like, besties?"

"Yeah," laughed Yanase. "You two an item or something?"

Then Suzuki, with the nervous hesitation of someone

inserting the knife into the barrel in a game of Pop-Up Pirate, had said: "Don't you guys find him, like, sort of . . . annoying?"

At first, the others paused. But as soon as one of them said, "Yeah," the floodgates opened.

"Oh, definitely."

"Can't stand him."

"He's like, such a downer."

Only the boy remained silent.

"I guess he *is* Koji's friend, though," Tomiyama said, raising a palm in a gesture of mock apology before turning to the boy and saying: "You won't tell him what we said, will you?"

At this a shiver ran through him. *This is bad. If I don't do something right now, they're going to lump me and Yamashu together forever.*

The others carried on.

"I heard he got bullied a bit at primary school."

"Oh, I can totally imagine it."

"It's that voice of his. *So* irritating."

"And he always looks at you like he wants a cuddle. It's gross."

"Maybe *we* should pick on him too."

"What, you serious?"

"Nah, just kidding."

"He is, like, super annoying, though."

Tomiyama turned back towards the boy and said, "Seriously, Koji, you better not snitch on us." Grinning as he said it, like he was just messing around. But there was no telling where a comment like that might eventually lead.

Half panicking, he decided to take the plunge.

"I can't stand him either."

Then a pause. Maybe that wasn't enough, he thought. So he went further.

"Seriously. Let's pick on him."

A murmur of surprise rippled through his classmates.

"Well, if you want to . . ." said Tomiyama. "I guess I'm game." The others all nodded in agreement.

He felt another shiver roll down his spine. He'd somehow managed to turn himself into the ringleader. There was no turning back now.

Yamashu returned from his errand. He spotted the boy and came over as usual: "Ko-chan, Ko-chan!"

Tomiyama and the others watched the boy, smirking at one another. Like they were testing him.

"Ko-chan, guess what?" came the reedy voice. "When I was in the corridor just now—"

"Shut up," snapped the boy, before pushing the startled Yamashu in the shoulder. "Seriously. Clear off, jerk."

Yamashu, mouth agape, tripped and fell onto the desk behind him.

"Just get lost, okay?" the boy hissed, before marching off. Tomiyama and the others followed him.

"Woah, Koji, that was intense," someone said. He felt a wave of relief at these words – a reaction that, when he thought about it later on, made him feel utterly wretched.

He opened his eyes. The cordless phone still said MAIN HANDSET IN USE.

It was a long phone call. Maybe it was just one of his parents' friends calling.

The boy got up and reached for Koji, who was sitting by the bed.

His long, thick hind legs made him easy enough to grab. For a cat being embraced by a stranger in an unfamiliar house, Koji seemed remarkably calm. It had been the same when he'd eaten his food or gone to the toilet – as the boy's mother had commented, he basically looked after himself.

Only the cleverest, best-behaved cats get to be Blanket Cats, the man at the pet shop had proudly told him – and the Manx was clearly a member of that elite.

The boy was thirsty. He decided that when the phone call was over he'd go downstairs and get a drink.

"Koji," he said to the cat, speaking aloud in an attempt to dispel the fear still gripping his chest. "You thirsty too? A sip of juice or something won't hurt, will it . . .?"

As he sat there gently petting the cat, the light on the phone went off.

The call had ended.

"Right then. I'll go grab us a drink, okay?"

As he set the cat down on the bed, he heard his mother calling.

"Koji? Could we have a word?" Her voice was low, serious.

He hesitated. Then came his father's angry bark: "Right *now*, Koji!"

Flinching, the boy hugged Koji from behind. He told himself that he and the cat were one and the same. That he, too, had been lucky enough to make it onto the Ark.

Just in time too. If I hadn't turned on Yamashu that day, I could have ended up in his position. I had no choice. No choice at all . . .

But now the previously docile Koji let out a low growl and shook himself free of the boy's grip.

"What are you playing at?" shouted his father, his voice cracking into a falsetto. "Get down here right now!"

3

Attempted suicide. The moment his father's words burrowed into his ears, they seemed to lose all connection with reality.

It was just like on television, he thought.

Whenever a bully or their victim appeared in a drama or on the news, the boy always felt an odd twinge of embarrassment, one he would mask with an inane grin.

Which was why, right now—

"*Wipe that smirk off your face!*" bellowed his father, his voice cracking again. "This is serious, Koji. Do you realise what you've done?"

The previous evening, Yamashu had tried to slash his wrists with a razor in the bath. In the end he hadn't hurt himself too badly. At the first trickle of blood, he'd begun to panic; alerted by his cries, his parents had rushed in and found him.

On the pile of clothes outside the bathroom, they'd found a suicide note that contained a list of his tormentors' names.

That was just like on television too, the boy thought.

In fact, it all felt like the world of television had somehow merged with reality. Like he'd been suddenly handed the script for a drama or a news programme, assigned his role, and shoved in front of the camera. *And . . . action*!

"Your name was on that list," said his father. Then, as if to block his escape: "So don't give me your excuses."

His mother, who looked as if she was about to burst into tears, attempted to restrain his father. "Don't you think we should—?"

"Quiet," snapped his father. He began unbuttoning his pyjamas as he glared at the boy. "Looks like I misjudged you, son. What did I always say? Bullies are the lowest of the low."

The boy stared silently at his feet.

"You've let me down, Koji. Betrayed my trust. Well? What have you got to say for yourself?"

The boy's throat had clamped up so much he could barely breathe, never mind speak.

His father snatched a shirt from a hanger on the wall, pulled it on and began roughly doing up the buttons.

"Why did you do it? Go on. Look me in the eyes and tell me." His father's voice was growing hoarse.

The boy couldn't look up. His entire body had seized up by now. He felt his teeth chatter.

He was scared.

Not of his father hitting him. It was a deeper, more paralysing sort of fear than that.

"I'll ask again. Why did you pick on him?"

But the boy's brain, like his body, had frozen.

His father wouldn't take his silence for an answer. No

matter how remorsefully the boy gazed off to one side, there was no reprieve.

His father turned to his mother. "I can't go in my sports jacket. Get my suit out, would you?"

So his father was going into school. Their form teacher, Mr Toyama, would be waiting, as would the headmaster. On television, when all the parents were called into school, they always argued and tried to pin the blame on one another. The same thing seemed likely to happen in the real world.

"Who put you up to it? That's all I want to know, Koji. Who forced you into the gang? Tell me who it was, and I'll make sure their parents get what they deserve."

You've got it all wrong, the boy thought. No-one made me do anything. He felt the words catch in his throat, become a vague murmur, then shatter into a million jagged fragments.

His father clicked his tongue as he pulled on his jacket and straightened his tie. "Well, whatever happens, your father's still going to protect you. I'm sure there was a reason why this Shugo kid got bullied, and there must be a ringleader, even if you're covering for him. He can keep quiet all he likes, but you can bet it'll show on his parents' faces."

The boy frowned and carried on looking down at his feet.

"Don't worry. I'll protect you," repeated his father, though this reassurance seemed to be directed more at himself than his son.

Back in his room, the boy held Koji in his arms. Gently, he stroked the cat's rear end, the soft, tailless mound. The price the creature had paid for making it onto the Ark. It was as fluffy as a stuffed animal.

"Koji," he murmured. "Koji, Koji, Koji . . ."

He felt himself calming slightly.

"Hey, Koji." As he repeated his name, he felt himself becoming detached, somehow, from the boy he became in front of his father. "Your dad's serious, you know. He's really going to protect you."

Koji sat there meekly in the boy's arms as though he'd forgotten all about the growl he'd let out earlier.

"I can't believe the guy actually tried to commit suicide. But . . . Koji, you're the ringleader – what are you going to do? You're the one who drove him to it . . . If you hadn't rejected him like that . . . he'd never have been . . . bullied by everyone . . . would he? *Would he?*"

The boy's hand lay on Koji's spine.

"You're a coward, Koji. You know that? A spineless little wimp."

Now he slowly clenched his fingers, like the clawed hook of a crane.

"It's your fault," he said, mimicking his father. "You betrayed your father's trust. You're a total let-down."

He dug his fingers and thumb into the cat's fur.

"Your father trusted you . . . But you tricked him . . ."

The fur curled around his fingers. It was even softer than it looked. He could feel the supple skin underneath.

Koji gave an annoyed snarl and tried to wriggle away.

"Your father's never going to forgive you, you hear? Never . . ."

Pushing the cat down, so it couldn't escape, the boy dug his fingers deeper.

Just then, Koji tensed his powerful back muscles. The long hind legs sprang into action, and he hopped easily free of the boy's grasp.

Then, once he was clear of danger, he turned to face the boy – and came charging at him.

The boy saw the claws coming for his jaw. He watched them sink into the arm he raised in defence. For a brief moment, the cat's feral musk almost made him retch.

After dabbing at the blood on his cheek and arm with a tissue, the boy made his way downstairs.

The television was on in the living room, but his mother was slumped over the dining table, her head in her hands.

She remained in this position as he entered, though it was unclear if she hadn't heard him come in or if she was pretending. The boy sat down wordlessly on the sofa.

He glanced briefly at the family portrait on the sideboard in front of him, then let his head hang. In the photo he was still in his first year of primary school, looking shyly at the camera while his father, much younger than he was now, squeezed his shoulders from behind.

It was around the time of this photo that his father had started saying: *Koji, you're everything to me, you hear?*

The boy had been his hope. His constant worry too.

When he praised him, it had been: *That's my boy!*

When he scolded him, it was: *That's not how I raised you!*

He wasn't sure which of these he'd heard the most in the

twelve years he'd been alive. But he had a fairly good idea which he'd be hearing more often from now on.

His mother sighed, still resting her head on the table. "Koji, has the cat gone to sleep?"

". . . Not yet."

"What time is it?"

". . . After eleven."

They'd still had no word from his father.

"Go to bed," said his mother. "We can talk about Shugo tomorrow."

The boy nodded silently, but he didn't get up from the sofa.

He wanted to fall asleep, to dissolve entirely into a deep and dreamless slumber. He wanted to escape.

But even if he climbed into bed, sleep seemed unlikely to come. No matter how tightly he shut his eyes, he knew his mind would wander, frightened, towards the darkness inside him.

The scratch on his cheek still stung. As for the one on his arm, it had just begun to bleed again.

"Koji."

". . . What?"

"Why *did* you decide you wanted that cat all of a sudden?"

"I just saw it on the internet."

"Did you feel bad about the bullying?"

The boy glanced over at the dining table, saw that his mother was still slumped across it, then replied in a near-whisper: "Yeah."

"Were you worried Shugo might try and . . . hurt himself?"

"Well, I didn't think he'd go that far."

"Did you want to stop it?"

"I don't know," he murmured, his mouth barely moving.

"Was it a friend's idea to pick on him?"

No. You've got it all wrong. Once again, he felt the unspeakable words fracture in his mouth, their tiny shards scraping at his throat.

"Go to bed, okay?" said his mother again. "I'll talk to your father when he gets home."

He didn't reply. His mother's back began to tremble.

"Please, Koji," she said, the words catching in her voice. "Your mother needs to be alone right now."

The boy retreated from the living room where, he realised, he was no longer welcome.

Back in his room, he found Koji poking playfully at the pile of junk beneath his desk. The boy sat down on the edge of his bed and stared absently at the cat's fluffy rear.

A cat with no tail. A cat like a rabbit, with its oversized back legs. He remembered his father's little chuckle of astonishment at the pet shop that afternoon.

Sheesh, humans really can be cruel. Depriving cats of their tails for their own amusement . . . Of course, he'd been wrong: the Manx was simply the result of a genetic mutation.

The boy hugged his arms around his chest.

The Manx might owe its existence to a mutation, but he was different. His father had created him. He existed purely so that his father could keep happily proclaiming, *That's my boy!*

The boy had wanted his praise. He'd wanted to never let

him down. He'd been scared. Scared of the angry outbursts, but also the stern lectures from which there was no escape.

"Hey, Koji," said the boy to the cat. Feeling himself drift apart from his own body once again, he stared at the lopsided animal and gave a derisive chuckle. "What are you going to do? Stay in his shadow your whole life? Living in fear like that – it's pathetic."

Even as the mocking laughter issued from his lips, he felt his armpits growing hot and sticky with sweat.

"It's over now, though. He's never going to look at you the same way after this. He'll shun you for life. You'll never earn his forgiveness. You're too pathetic for that. If anything, it serves you right . . ."

He clutched himself tighter now, strengthening his grip in an attempt to squeeze every last bit of himself out of his own body.

". . . Why are you even still alive? Forget Yamashu – if anyone's going to do themselves in, it should be you."

The scratches on his cheek and arm throbbed painfully.

The cat came out from under the desk, keeping low to the floor.

"You shouldn't be alive," he murmured. "You don't deserve to . . ."

He pulled at the sides of his chest, his whole body quivering. The boy who killed cats – he'd seen that character on the news too. A child murderer who practised on animals before turning his knife on humans. It made for good television. The reporter giving a piece to camera from the scene of the crime, explaining how the perpetrator had been a model pupil, had always acted normally at home. Analysts and commentators in the studio making concerned faces and saying things like, *These are the times we're living in, when an ordinary kid can do a thing like this.* He felt the world of television come pouring into the room, enveloping him, smothering him, crushing him.

He heard their car pull up outside. Its door opening and slamming shut. The gate opening, and then the front door.

Footsteps coming up the stairs. Getting closer.

His mother's voice from the bottom of the stairs. "Can't it wait until tomorrow?" No response from his father.

The door flew abruptly open. The cat did a little jump of surprise, then dashed past his father's large frame and into the hallway beyond.

His father looked momentarily startled, but immediately reared up again in the doorway, paying no heed to the cat hopping frantically down the stairs behind him. Instead he glared at the boy.

"I heard the whole story."

He spoke in a low voice.

"I had to get down on my *knees*, Koji. In front of the kid's mother. She told me to, so I . . . had no choice." A thin, self-mocking smile appeared on his lips, only to be redirected at the boy instead. "This isn't how I raised you, Koji."

His voice was quiet, cold.

Finally, the boy unclenched his hands from around his chest and let them drop to his side.

Koji the cat had escaped. That version of himself, the boy

who would only ever be his father's creation, was no longer in the room.

"Now, Koji, you listen to me . . ."

That was when the boy jumped forward. Just like the Manx.

With a silent scream, he lurched towards his father, wildly swinging his arms.

His right fist slammed into his father's nose from the side.

As abruptly as a bubble bursting, his father crumpled wordlessly to the floor.

4

The next morning, a Sunday, as they were putting their shoes on by the front door, the boy's mother protested: "But all the other fathers will be there. I don't even know what I'm supposed to say . . ."

"You don't have to say anything," said his father tersely. He had a large, bluish swelling between his nose and eye, and he sounded like he had a blocked nose. "Just keep your head bowed. You're capable of that at least, aren't you?"

Glaring at the boy waiting at his mother's side with his shoes on, he opened his mouth as if to say something, then simply tutted and closed it again.

The boy looked down at his feet and waited for his mother. His eyes were bleary from lack of sleep, his stomach queasy. He hadn't eaten breakfast. He could still feel his father's face in his fist.

From the living room opposite the front door came the rustle of paper. Koji was playing with the newspaper.

"Well," said his father, "this is out of my hands now. You did it, Koji, so you better take responsibility for it."

The boy nodded silently.

"No running away, no excuses. You've embarrassed me enough already." With these words, he walked back into the living room. "Move it," the boy heard him growl. "Stupid cat."

Before the boy could see whether Koji had obeyed, his mother prodded him in the back. "We should get going," she said with a sad smile.

School was a fifteen-minute walk. The boy's feet seemed barely capable of moving – and yet in no time at all they had reached the post office that marked the halfway point.

As they passed the row of postboxes, his mother, silent until now, suddenly murmured, "Ko-chan . . . How could you do a thing like that?"

A thing like that. He didn't know which she was referring to – bullying Yamashu or punching his father. In both cases, though, the answer was the same.

He hesitated, then told her the truth.

"Because I was scared."

It felt good to get the words out. As a primary school student he'd always looked forward to the moment when, after lugging his bulky leather backpack all the way home, he could finally set it down and feel the breeze on his sweat-streaked back. That was how he felt now.

His mother paused, then asked: "Do you think you'll be able to apologise?"

This time the answer would be different depending on who she meant, and so the boy remained silent.

"You didn't get much time with the cat in the end, did you?"

"No."

"Is there a connection between you wanting it and . . . what happened to Shugo?"

". . . I dunno."

"Did you really get the cat because you wanted to be kind to it? Or did you want to . . .?"

What are you even suggesting, he began to think. Then he gulped, his feet lurching to a halt as the realisation hit him.

Of course, he could always deny it. It would be easy enough to dismiss her insinuation with a laugh, to say, *I don't know what you're on about,* to have a go at her for asking weird questions.

But the boy's face was turning paler by the second, his lips beginning to shake.

His mother said nothing further. She simply stood there with him for a moment, then slowly walked off again.

Eyes riveted to the ground, the boy followed her as if pulled by an invisible thread.

"By the way . . . What did you call the cat in the end?" she asked.

". . . Koji."

It had taken all his strength to get the word out, and yet he said it so quietly that his mother didn't seem to hear. Saying it brought him none of the relief he'd felt a moment ago either. Instead, he felt the helplessness that had often overcome him moments after that cooling breeze hit his back, as if he had deprived himself of something that might have protected him.

Hasegawa, Iijima and the others were already sitting in the headmaster's office. Eight kids in total. It was exactly the line-up he'd expected: no-one left out, and no-one dragged in unnecessarily. They were each accompanied by their mother or father. The parents looked even more sullen than the children.

Hasegawa's mother and the boy's mother knew each other well – after the parent-teacher meeting in May, they'd gone to the local Denny's restaurant together and chatted for hours. But now they both wore stark expressions, stealing glances at each other without so much as a nod when their eyes did happen to meet.

When the headmaster walked in, accompanied by their form teacher, Mr Toyama, the atmosphere in the room sharpened noticeably.

"Now, I spoke with the parents last night about what happened," the headmaster began. "But it seems that, erm, an apology is required from the individuals themselves . . ."

He went on to explain that Yamashu's father was waiting in the meeting room next door.

"In fact, Mr Yamamoto asked to see the children without their parents present, but we couldn't really, er, allow that, so . . . if you could accompany your child when your turn comes . . ."

The headmaster hadn't mentioned whether Yamashu himself was here. Not that this seemed to matter to the parents, who were busy exchanging wary glances to establish who would go first.

"So, er, who would like to . . .?"

By now, the parents' gazes had converged on a single target: the boy – the "ringleader" – and his mother.

His mother clenched her handbag tightly to her lap. The boy ran his fingers over the scratch on his cheek, then looked down at the claw marks on his right arm. He gently squeezed his right hand into a fist. He could still feel the blow he'd dealt his father. It occurred to him that even if the sensation faded over time it would probably never leave him completely.

Just as the headmaster was about to say something, the boy got to his feet, followed reluctantly by his mother.

"Erm," came a voice. "Sorry, if I could just . . .?"

The boy didn't recognise the portly man who had spoken, but Suzuki was sitting next to him, so this must be his father.

"I don't mind you going first, but . . . could you make sure you tell the truth in there? If you start making things up to try and get off the hook, you'll only make things harder for the rest of us. *My* son only got involved because the others talked him into it."

The air in the room seemed to thicken. The boy's mother and the other parents were all making faces as if to say, *Oh, sure, mister.* Still, no-one stepped forward to put Suzuki's father in his place.

If *he* was here, thought the boy.

If my father was here, he'd have really flipped. The guy wouldn't know what had hit him.

In fact, if it had been *him* there and not the boy's mother,

Suzuki's father would probably never have dared to open his mouth in the first place . . .

He looked at Suzuki. He'd turned crimson all the way to his earlobes and was staring down at his feet.

It was quite possible, the boy thought, that Suzuki felt just as suffocated by his own father. For some reason, this idea put him slightly at ease.

Yamashu wasn't in the meeting room. It was just Mr Yamamoto, sitting there with his arms crossed.

He was a small man, but there was something intimidating about his crew cut and sun-tanned face. The boy seemed to remember that he worked in construction. He fixed them with a glare as they walked in.

His mother introduced herself in a shaking voice, then launched into a long, rambling speech. She spoke so quickly that the boy could barely catch what she was saying. All he grasped was that she was apologising.

The boy was the ringleader, the villain of the piece. If this was television, the part would have been played by a child actor with narrow, menacing eyes.

But . . . said the voice inside him, the voice that no-one else could hear. *But* . . .

After that one word there was nothing. Or at least nothing that could or should be put into words.

But, but, but . . .

"Enough with the excuses, okay?" said Yamashu's father, as if brushing some minor nuisance out of the way. The boy's mother broke off mid-sentence, her shoulders shaking.

"You can apologise all you like, but I need to hear it from the kid's mouth. Are we clear?"

But . . . The boy heard the voice again in his chest.

But Yamashu's not here.

The person who really deserves my apology isn't here.

The boy looked up and, in a faltering voice, asked: "Is Shugo . . . not . . . coming?"

"Course not," snapped the father. "He's only just calmed down. If he sees your faces again, he'll probably . . . Well, surely you can imagine."

He's protecting his son, thought the boy. Just like Suzuki's father. Just like the man at home with the black eye thought he was.

"I'm really sorry," said the boy, bowing as deep as he could go. If Yamashu's father told him to get down on his knees, he would. If he wanted to punch him, the boy would let him. This was the world of television. He wasn't going to give his real apology here. All he wanted was to be released from the room as soon as possible. But if it was a television script the father wanted, he was happy to supply all the contrition in the world.

"I'm really, really sorry. I regret what I did so much. Thinking it was fun to hurt Shugo like that . . . I'll never do it again . . . So please, please, forgive me . . ."

As he reeled off the words, he felt tears running down his cheeks.

Even though his heart wasn't in it. Even though it was all just television.

It was only as he listened to his mother earnestly apologising once more on his behalf that they began to feel real.

When they left the school, his mother got out her mobile phone and called the house.

"We're just leaving," she said, her voice weak with exhaustion. Then she gasped. "What?! Okay, we'll be right there."

She seemed panicked, but once she'd put her phone away in her handbag, she regained her composure. For a moment she stood entirely still.

"Oh dear," she sighed.

"What?" asked the boy.

"It's the cat . . . Your dad's furious. He wants you to take it back today."

"Why, what did it do?"

"Turned the house upside down, it sounds like."

She wasn't wrong. They arrived home to find the living room in a complete state. A broken glass lay on the carpet, surrounded by a puddle of whiskey, the lace curtains had been torn from the railing and the tattered remnants of the morning's newspaper were strewn around the room. Almost all the video tapes had been pulled from their shelf onto the floor.

It turned out, though, that at least half the mess had been caused not by Koji but by his father's frantic attempts to stop him.

"Damn cat," he muttered angrily when they walked in. He was still panting, his shoulders heaving from the exertion of the chase. "Kept hopping about all over the place."

Apparently he'd tried to pick the cat up. When he'd gripped

the tailless rear – his father admitted he'd used "a little force", which probably meant he'd used quite a lot – Koji had gone completely berserk, kicking his father in the chest and stomach with his long rabbity legs. Enraged, his father had tried to catch him again, but he'd escaped – and escaped, and escaped . . . Right now, he was under the dining table, pawing playfully at one of his father's cast-off slippers.

"This weekend's been hell," said his father, seating himself on the sofa and deliberately avoiding their gazes. "Should never have rented that deformed thing. I reckon that's where it all started going wrong."

"No," said the boy, scarcely breathing the word. "That's not true."

"What? What did you say?" his father asked, turning towards him with a scowl. "It's too late for apologies. I'm too angry, Koji. If this bruise hasn't cleared up by tomorrow I won't even be able to show my face in the office. You see what you've done?"

"Yes, but it's not true what you said."

"What do you mean?"

"It's always been hell."

The boy felt his throat tense up with fear. He waited for his father to fly into a rage.

But he didn't. He simply turned away from the boy once more, gazed absently at the television and said, "Take that thing back to the shop."

Under the contract, the cat was theirs until tomorrow. The plan had been to take him back in the car after the boy's father finished work. But now he declared, "I don't want that damn thing around here another minute." Then, after a pause: "You know how to take a bus, don't you?"

In any case, the swelling around his father's eye would have made driving difficult. And there definitely didn't seem to be much chance of him changing his mind and saying, *Oh, alright, we can take it back tomorrow.*

"Ko-chan," said his mother. "Why don't I come with—?"

"I'll be fine," the boy interrupted, and he ran upstairs.

When the boy returned with the carrier, the cat wordlessly padded over and climbed in obediently, curling up on the blanket inside as if he'd understood the entire preceding conversation.

As the boy closed the hatch, his father murmured, "It's always been hell, huh?"

The boy felt a sadness in the voice. Not that the voice itself was sad. But when it reached the boy's ears it mixed with something inside him, and the result was sadness.

"The hell's inside me, Dad."

It wasn't something he'd been planning to say. The words simply came tumbling out.

Still looking away, his father smiled weakly. "No it isn't, Koji," he said quietly. "Even I can tell you that much."

The pet shop owner seemed a little surprised to see the boy returning a day earlier than planned.

"What, sick of him already?"

The boy wordlessly shook his head and set the carrier on the counter. The owner opened the hatch. Gracefully stretching his unevenly sized legs, Koji climbed out of the carrier.

"Something wrong? You seem a little down compared to yesterday."

That cheerful version of me was a lie. I was lying the whole time. Lying because I was scared of my dad.

The words wouldn't come.

It was just like when he'd been apologising in the meeting room. The moment he opened his mouth, he felt like he was going to cry again.

"Never mind. If you could just sign here for the return . . ."

The owner set the form and a pen down on the counter.

Koji was watching the proceedings with what appeared to be great interest.

Leaning on the counter with one elbow, the boy reached for the pen.

"What name did you give him?"

". . . My own."

"What, 'Koji'?"

"Yeah."

"Hmm." The owner nodded but said nothing more.

The boy wrote the date of the return and his name. When he reached the box marked ANY COMMENTS OR QUESTIONS? his pen froze.

Just then, Koji stretched his neck out, nuzzled the boy's right arm and gently licked the scratch he'd left the night before.

For a moment, the boy made as if to pull his arm away. Then he relaxed and smiled.

The cat, who appeared to have decided that one lick was more than enough, hopped gently down from the counter and away from him.

The boy gripped the pen and turned his attention back to the comment box.

He wrote: *Thank you very much.*

The owner peered at what he'd written, then smiled.

"You made it onto the Ark in time, then?"

The boy looked at him in confusion. He went on.

"Listen, I'm not sure what exactly you've got going on, but there are plenty of things in life that it's never too late for. Even if you lose your tail in the process."

The boy nodded silently. He smiled at the owner. But he could feel his eyelids growing warm again.

The Cat Who Knew How to Pretend

I

Two months of looking, and still we'd turned up nothing.

We're very sorry, but . . .

Each of the three pet shops had begun their response with these same words.

Even a kitten would be tricky, but an adult of that type . . .

To be honest, I'd been expecting as much.

At one shop, the owner had come straight out and told me: "You're not going to find one at a professional pet shop, trust me." I was grateful to them for even looking. Other pet shops had turned me down from the get-go, insisting I was asking for the impossible. When I'd explained *why* I needed the cat, one owner had even said: "You know, I don't think this plan of yours is a great idea."

We'd tried other channels too. My father had sent out an e-mail to his entire company, my mother had stuck up flyers at the local bank and shopping centre, and my little brother had tried the "wanted" section of an online auction website. *Looking for an adult American Shorthair*, they'd all written – to no avail.

"If it was just the breed," said the owner of the third pet shop I tried, "that would be one thing, but . . ." He'd handed me back the photo I'd shown him and added, with an air of finality: "I really don't think I can help you."

The photo was of our family cat. His name had been Ron-Ron.

An American Shorthair, with Brown Classic tabby patterning. About three months ago, at the age of twelve, he had passed away.

"A cat that looks exactly like this one? See, that's the problem. There just aren't many Brown Classics about in the first place. If it was a Silver Classic, I might have been able to find something, but . . ."

I didn't need him to tell me that. The most common patterning on an American Shorthair was the Silver Classic tabby, where the stripes were set against a base of silvery fur. Brown Classics were less popular, maybe because their fur made for a less beautiful contrast with the stripes.

"But I was thinking, with a brown one, surely you wouldn't be able to tell if the patterning was a little off . . .?"

The owner was having none of my desperate optimism. "I don't think that's how it works. When someone really loves a cat, they know it down to every last detail. One stripe in the wrong place, and, well . . ."

"I guess you're right," I said, sliding the photo back into my bag.

I remembered Ron-Ron's patterning vividly. So, I was sure, did the rest of my immediate family. But we weren't searching for his doppelganger for my sake – or that of my mother, father or brother.

Our family of four occasionally gained an additional member.

Actually, I don't know if she really counted as a "member", but in any case, it was for her that we'd embarked on our quest.

I bowed and made my way out of the shop.

"Oh, by the way . . ." came the owner's voice from behind. I turned. "There is one other place you could try." A pause. "Suppose I might as well give you the name. Not that I necessarily approve."

After this strangely drawn-out preamble, he finally revealed what he was talking about. "Have you considered a rental?"

He went on to tell me about the Blanket Cats – carefully trained animals that had grown up with their own special blankets. There was a shop, he explained, that rented them out to people for short stays.

"I can't guarantee they'll have an animal that matches your requirements, but it wouldn't hurt to ask."

"They . . . rent them out? For how long?"

"Three days or so, if I remember correctly. Maybe you could ask for longer."

"Three days," I found myself repeating in a low voice.

That could work. Three days was exactly how long the additional family member was going to spend at our house.

I turned back towards the counter and got out my mobile phone.

"Can I get their number?"

After that came two strokes of luck.

The first was that one of the "Blanket Cats" was an American Shorthair. A six-year-old adult – and a Brown Classic tabby to boot.

In fact, the cat was a little smaller than Ron-Ron, with slightly different patterning. When I first saw it, I wasn't exactly blown away by the resemblance. I took a photo of the potential stand-in with my phone and sent it out to my family. They all sent back slightly unconvinced-sounding messages along the lines of: *Better than nothing, I guess.*

I made a temporary reservation on the cat just in case, and headed home, worried we might need to rethink our strategy.

But then came the second stroke of luck. The following evening, my father got off the phone after a long conversation with my uncle and turned to me with a slightly pained expression.

"Mother's eyesight's gotten a lot worse. Apparently she can hardly see what she's eating at meals."

Okay, so it wasn't really a stroke of luck.

"And she's getting even more senile too, from the sound of things."

Nope. Lucky was *definitely* not the word.

But maybe for Grandma, in a way, it was. Or so I kept telling myself.

To an old woman with failing eyesight and a slightly tenuous grip on reality, what difference would a few minor discrepancies in the cat's appearance make? None at all, hopefully – otherwise we were in trouble.

"She's really looking forward to seeing Ron-Ron . . ." sighed my father.

That was enough to make my mother's eyes mist up. Even my brother – a no-nonsense science student who wasn't so easily triggered – was staring silently at the photo of Grandma that hung on the living room wall.

The photo had been taken in her sprightlier days – when, carrying her big suitcase and pointy umbrella around like Mary Poppins, she would shuttle between the house where she lived alone, my uncle's place, my aunt's and ours. It showed her beaming as she hugged Ron-Ron.

"Well, she *is* eighty-nine, I guess . . ." said my father, before returning to the glass of beer he'd abandoned earlier. It must have been flat and warm and bitter-tasting, but that didn't seem to be the only reason for the wince on his face.

Grandma always visited us towards the end of summer. When the mid-August Bon festival came around, she'd carry out the remembrance service for my grandfather, who had died when my father was still a child, then turn up in Tokyo with his memorial tablet in her suitcase. She'd impose herself – I hate to put it that way, but that's how it felt – on us for at least a month, and often until it was time to get the kotatsu blanket out for winter.

Our detached house had a spare room, meaning we could at least provide her with her own place to sleep. But from what I'd heard, she and my mother hadn't always gotten on that well.

When I was still a kid – and grandma was in her seventies– my impression of her could be summed up in one word: stubborn.

"Well, her husband died young, and she never remarried. She had to raise us all on her own," my father would say defensively.

In her moodier moments, Mum would reply: "Sure, and all that hardship has turned her into a right old grouch."

But shortly after her seventy-seventh birthday, that stubborn old lady had suddenly mellowed out – a transformation that coincided with Ron-Ron's arrival at our house.

Grandma adored the cat beyond words, and Ron-Ron seemed quite attached to her too. Whenever she left us for her house in the countryside, she always seemed far more reluctant to part with the cat than with me and my brother. Sometimes she even cried as she hugged him to her chest.

In the past few years, Mum seemed to be getting on much better with her. My father, who used to be so busy with work that he left it entirely up to my brother and me to keep her company, would now come home early with a box of fancy traditional cakes, which they'd nibble on over a cup of green tea while they reminisced.

I told myself this was probably because, as my parents entered old age themselves, they were starting to understand my elderly grandma's loneliness, her apprehension about the future.

She was visiting us this year too – the following week, in fact. She couldn't take the train by herself anymore, so my father was going to pick her up from my uncle's house. After staying at my aunt's last week, and then my uncle's, the plan was for her to spend a few of these late-summer days with us.

And after that, she would be moving into a home.

While she was at my aunt's house, my uncle had gone to her apartment in the countryside and emptied it of her belongings.

It was a tiny two-room place on a prefectural housing estate, and it still felt tiny, even after he'd cleared it out. Standing there alone in the empty apartment, thinking to himself that this was where his mother had raised him and his siblings, and where she'd spent the lonely decades after they'd all grown up and moved out, my usually stoic uncle had been surprised to find himself getting emotional. Meanwhile, when my father had heard all this over the phone a few days ago, he'd wept like a child.

Sometimes I wondered why, if they were finding all this so tough, they didn't just ask her to move in with them.

But it was a thought I kept to myself. I wasn't a child anymore; I knew that sometimes, voicing those sorts of naive ideas was the cruellest thing you could do.

It was the same when Ron-Ron died.

We'd discussed it as a family and decided that the best thing would be not to tell Grandma. If it could be helped, we didn't want her ever to find out.

Which was why . . .

"So," I asked, "do you think we should hire that cat I found yesterday?"

Mum, Dad and my brother all turned to look at me. They didn't need to say anything. Their expressions told me we had a consensus.

Dad was taking the whole of Friday off to pick Grandma up.

Mum, meanwhile, had bought her a brand-new feather quilt, saying, "This is the last chance we'll get to host her."

Even my brother, who normally stayed out late on weekends

with his university friends, had been sternly informed by my father that we'd all be eating dinner together while Grandma was staying with us.

Of course, I was required to make a few concessions of my own.

"Hiromi, I'm not asking you to take Friday off too," Dad had said. "But do you think you could come home early?"

"We're understaffed at the moment," I'd protested. "Everyone's taking their summer vacation late this year."

But he was adamant. "If your company won't let you put family first at a time like this, then I don't see why you're working for them in the first place."

It turned out Mum had a special request too. Someone she wanted me to invite for dinner.

"Grandma hasn't even met Mr Nagano yet. You should introduce him. It'll put her mind at ease. And anyway . . . we don't know if she'll still be around for the wedding."

Uh-oh, I thought. Here comes trouble.

"Mr Nagano" was my boyfriend. We'd been seeing each other for a while and, with marriage on the cards, he'd met my parents for the first time in June.

But over the summer, we both seemed to have arrived at the conclusion that maybe we weren't meant for each other after all. There'd been no formal break-up yet, but we hadn't exchanged a single text message or phone call in the past fortnight.

"Good idea," said Dad, nodding enthusiastically. "I'm sure Grandma would love to meet him. She was so worried about your prospects last time."

"Exactly," Mum replied triumphantly, before turning back to me. "You're almost thirty, Hiromi. You owe your grandmother a bit of good news."

I wasn't going to disagree with that. Still, it was *because* I was almost thirty that there were certain aspects of marriage on which I was completely non-negotiable.

"Right then," said Mum, as if it was a done deal. "Ask him to keep an evening free."

"Funny, isn't it . . .?" said Dad with an emotional sigh. "Mother moving into a home, Ron-Ron passing away, Hiromi getting married . . . Time really does fly, doesn't it?"

At this point my brother decided to butt in with a question that managed to be innocent, perceptive and insensitive all at once.

"Erm . . . you are, like, still seeing him, right?"

"Of course I am!" I replied, before I could stop myself. "Why wouldn't I be?"

When the Friday in question came around, I took the afternoon off from work, picked up Ron-Ron's stand-in from the pet shop, and brought him home.

After emerging from the carrier, he stretched lazily, then surveyed the living room with evident curiosity.

"Hmm," said Mum, cocking her head to one side. "He looks a little different from the photo you sent. You know, now that he's here and everything." She glanced up at the photo of the real Ron-Ron on the wall, then back at the stand-in.

I'd been thinking the same thing. Seeing him in the shop, I'd have rated the likeness at about seventy per cent. Now he was in our living room, the setting for so many memories of the real Ron-Ron, he was a fifty per cent match at best.

"But we've got him now, Mum."

"I know, but . . ."

"We'll just have to roll with it."

"But Grandma's always been pretty sharp at noticing this sort of thing. I'm really not sure . . ."

"It's too late now, Mum! She'll be here any minute."

And just then, the doorbell rang.

2

Grandma had aged more than I'd expected. It had only been eight months since I'd seen her over the New Year, but it was like she'd put on several years at once.

Her body had shrunk, the wrinkles on her face had spread, her hair had thinned and even her feet seemed smaller. More than anything, though, it was her eyesight that had deteriorated. My father had to guide her into the living room, wrapping an arm around her shoulders and leading her by the hand.

She appeared to have gone almost entirely blind.

The secret of the cat's true identity seemed safe for now – at least when it came to the difference in his patterning.

Grandma eased herself onto the floor, resting her back against the sofa. When "Ron-Ron" came over, mewing, she scooped him onto her lap with a delighted look on her face. The cat's performance was pitch-perfect, even if he wasn't aware he was acting.

In any case, the first meeting between the stand-in and Grandma had gone well. As the pet shop owner had told me, shy cats didn't get to become Blanket Cats.

"Grandma, I'm cooking ayu tonight," said Mum. "Your favourite."

Grandma had a soft spot for ayu sweetfish simmered in soy sauce, mirin and syrup. This time, Mum had stewed it for even longer than usual, resulting in a mush that she hoped wouldn't pose too much of a challenge for Grandma's weakened jaw. Watching Mum lean in and loudly repeat herself until Grandma understood, it occurred to me that we were probably past the point at which the old lady might complain about what she was served.

After the brief excitement at her arrival, the living room soon became quiet again. Grandma had never been particularly talkative, but having to say everything slowly, simply and loudly enough for her to understand turned out to be strangely exhausting.

Mum retreated into the kitchen on the pretext of getting dinner ready, while Dad had disappeared into the tatami room next door with Grandma's luggage and now said something – loudly, so that we'd all hear – about checking the television was working properly. The television crackled on and he didn't come back. It was just me and Grandma in the living room. I couldn't very well leave her here on her own – and it would be some time before my brother got back from university. Right then, I thought. Here we go.

"Grandma," I said. Not because I had anything to say in

particular, but simply to break the weighty silence that had descended.

She turned to me, Ron-Ron still on her lap, with a look that said, *Yes?*

"It's, erm . . . well, it's been a while, hasn't it?"

Of course it has, I thought.

There was no reply from Grandma, but her cheeks creased into a faint smile.

"Ron-Ron is so adorable, isn't he?" I said.

What am I doing?

Still smiling, Grandma stroked the cat's back.

"Hasn't changed a bit since last year, has he?" I went on.

Digging my own grave, apparently.

Still no reply. It wasn't like my comments merited much of a response – assuming she'd even heard them.

I felt the tension lift from my body, which was then immediately replaced by a strange anxiety. I found myself saying, "I'll go help with dinner." And with that childish excuse, I made my way into the kitchen. Now I'd run away from her too.

I found Mum busy making blanched spinach with katsuobushi and soy sauce.

"What are you doing in here?" she chided me. "Go keep your grandmother company while I make dinner."

Not fair, Mum.

Pursing my lips slightly, I opened the fridge, retrieved a flask of iced barley tea and poured myself a glass. It wouldn't be long before iced tea season was over. I wondered if Grandma would get to drink any next year.

Mum sighed as she squeezed the water from the blanched spinach. "Sounds like your uncle had a pretty hard time of it too."

"Hard how?"

"Oh, you know. Helping with her . . . needs."

"You mean, like . . . when she has to pee?"

Mum nodded silently and laid the spinach on the chopping board.

". . . The other type too?"

She didn't reply to that, but seemed to chop away at the spinach more vigorously than usual.

I took a sip of my tea. "What else?"

"She gets confused sometimes. Forgets where she is or who people are. Apparently when it was your auntie's turn to mind her, she found her wandering about in the middle of the night."

Her turn to *mind her.* Something about the phrase upset me. Deep down, though, I was probably just afraid of the responsibility it implied.

"Do you think she's okay with being put in a home?"

". . . I wonder."

When my uncle had explained it all to her, she'd seemed to agree it was a good idea. It was getting dangerous for her to live alone, but none of her three children were in a position to look after her. He'd shown her pamphlets and taken her to see the care home, where she'd even commented enthusiastically, "I'll have to make lots of new friends, won't I!"

But, just as my uncle was breathing a sigh of relief, a change had come over her. Suddenly, she was berating him, telling him she was going nowhere, and if they were going to try and toss her away like that she'd rather die in her own home and haunt them for the rest of their lives.

"Apparently that kind of thing is fairly common when people go senile . . . But still, it puts your aunt on the spot a little, to hear something like that. She's talking about going back to her family home, maybe even divorcing your uncle . . . It's been really tough for her, I think."

"Which do you think is the *real* Grandma, though?"

"Oh, who knows . . ." said Mum, brushing off the question with a bitter smile.

Going senile. It was something I thought I knew about from television and books, not to mention my boss, who lived with his slightly befuddled parents and was always complaining about them. But seeing it happen to my own grandmother like this, I felt less certain. Was the "normal" Grandma the one who'd agreed to move into a home, or the one who said she was going nowhere? Though, the longer I thought about it, the less "normal" it seemed to put your parent in a home in the first place.

"More importantly, Hiromi," said Mum as she retrieved a small bowl from the cupboard. "When's Mr Nagano coming?" Without waiting for an answer, she went on: "Tomorrow night would be best, wouldn't it . . .?"

"Hang on a second, Mum . . ."

"What, haven't you asked him?"

"Not yet."

"What are you waiting for? Tomorrow's the only chance he'll have to meet Grandma."

"But . . . he's a busy man, Mum."

"Yes, but you can get him to make an exception, can't you? You know how much she's been looking forward to you getting married. Go on, give her something to be happy about. Alright?"

She sounded like she was trying to coax an unwilling toddler into something. I downed the rest of my barley tea.

I still hadn't messaged or called Mr Nagano. I'd been planning on telling Mum he was on a business trip this weekend. But hearing her talk about Grandma like that, I'd felt a twinge somewhere deep in my chest. Lying seemed like a rather cowardly way out of the situation.

Okay, I'll give him a call. Just as the words were on the tip of my tongue, a strange growling sound reached us from the living room.

We exchanged a confused glance. I had a bad feeling. That did not sound like a happy cat.

My father emerged from his hiding place, beating us into the room. I heard him ask, "Mother, are you okay? What's . . .?"

Then he came into the kitchen, his expression rigid. He glanced at me, looked away awkwardly, then even more awkwardly turned to Mum.

"Sorry, but is there a . . . cloth or something I can use?"

"What happened?"

"Oh, Mother just, erm . . ." He paused and gave a forced chuckle. Then he went on, speaking quickly: "She's gone and wet herself."

*

Before dinner, I went into my room and sent my "boyfriend" a text message.

Could you call me if you have a moment?

I was half-expecting him to ignore the message completely, but a few minutes later my phone rang.

I hadn't heard his voice for a while. He didn't sound entirely happy to hear from me.

I told him Grandma was visiting for three days, that it was probably the last time she ever would.

But when it came to the actual reason for the call, I faltered.

"Okay, sure. But . . . why did you message me?"

"Actually, erm . . . I mean, this is just my parents' idea, and you don't even have to give it a moment's thought . . ." I was painfully aware how pathetic this disclaimer sounded, and yet I couldn't stop myself. "Personally, I don't even see the point."

"What is it, Hiromi?" He sounded faintly irritated.

"Could you, erm, come to dinner tomorrow night? . . . is what my parents were asking, anyway."

He fell silent.

"Erm, yeah," I continued, "they want you to meet my grandmother. It'll be the last chance she gets, so it would be sort of as a favour. To her."

Again, no reply.

He was probably pretty annoyed.

He probably wanted to say, *Why would I do that?*

Maybe even to add, *I mean, it's basically over between us at this point.*

But he said nothing.

"Sorry," I said, unable to bear the silence. "I'll make up an excuse." And with that I hung up.

We'd never actually talked about breaking up in so many words. But this exchange had felt like proof that things were well and truly over between us.

I could hear the television downstairs. Dad had turned the volume way up for Grandma. What was the point, I wondered, when she could barely see it either? Maybe he was just trying to fill the awkward silence with noise. Doing his duty as a son, in his own way. After Grandma had wet herself, he'd insisted on washing the soaked clothes himself. Then, watching my mother scrubbing away at the floor in the living room, he'd said *Sorry about this* so many times it had started to get annoying.

Dad was very fond of his mother. When Grandma was in better shape, Mum used to call him a mummy's boy. Now, after everything else she'd been through, he seemed to want his mother to be happy in her final years – an opinion his siblings shared. And yet . . .

Once my brother got home from university, things got a bit more lively in the living room. It was almost dinnertime.

For some reason, I found the idea of seeing Grandma's face again almost unbearable.

My phone started beeping. Not a message, but a call. The name on the screen was *Nagano*.

"Sorry, I think we got cut off. My signal's terrible."

Had he not realised I'd hung up? Or was he just pretending not to?

"About what you were saying . . . Actually, before we get

to that, have you really not told your parents about what happened with us?"

It was my turn to fall silent – though my silence told him all he needed to know.

"Right . . ." He chuckled. "What a mess. How did we end up here, eh?"

The truth was I didn't know. All this would have been a lot easier if there was a reason I could put my finger on.

If someone forced me to put it into words, all I'd manage was: "It just didn't feel right." For whatever reason, I couldn't see myself in a marriage – or starting a family – with him, and he felt the same way. A case of early-onset marriage blues? Or should that be "*family* blues"?

"I don't suppose you feel like, I don't know, giving it another go?"

I decided to lay out the painful truth.

"If I was going to get married, it would be with you, sure. But there's something about all that – getting married, starting a family – that I just can't seem to picture anymore." I sounded like I was admonishing myself.

"Sure," replied Nagano with disconcerting readiness. "I get it."

"Also, with Grandma here, I feel like I'm losing track of what family even means."

More than anything, I was beginning to wonder whether happiness was even possible by the time you got to her age.

Our conversation had fizzled out. Downstairs, the television was booming away.

"I'll be there tomorrow night," Nagano said all of a sudden.

"You sure? I'm really sorry about this . . ."

"Don't worry. All I have to do is sit there in front of your grandma and say we're planning to get married, right? It's not even really lying. That *was* the plan, we've just . . . lost sight of it somewhere along the way."

". . . Which makes it a lie."

"Well, even if it is, I don't think you should feel bad. If it means so much to your grandma, I mean. Anyway, I'll be there."

He hung up.

First a fake cat, now a fake boyfriend.

I kept telling myself all this was for Grandma's sake. But deep down it felt like a betrayal.

3

We ate dinner in the living room, not the dining room. We got the kotatsu table out from the upstairs cupboard, set it alongside the glass table in front of the sofa, and sat around them on the floor. This was how we always ate when Grandma came to visit.

The meal was a lively affair. Mum and Dad talked a lot. There was enough conversation that we didn't even need to turn the television on.

But there was something oddly high-pitched about my parents' voices, an exaggerated edge to their laughter. Dad's in particular. If I pointed it out, he'd probably claim it was just because Grandma was so deaf. If I stood my ground and told him there had to be another reason, would Mum back him up?

I tried to keep up with the conversation, but after a while, unable to match their energy, I fell silent and merely listened. Now that I had time to actually pay attention to what they were saying, I realised they were having two separate conversations. Dad was rehashing memories from his childhood, while Mum was chatting away about cooking techniques. Occasionally Grandma would manage a reply and there'd be a short back-and-forth, but for the most part Mum and Dad would just say their piece and that was the end of it. It reminded me of that shooting game at the arcade where all the bullets that missed the target were silently swallowed up by the background.

There was a loud chime from my brother's phone. A new message, presumably.

This was a common occurrence at dinner, but my father, irritated by the interruption, snapped, "Hey, turn that thing off while we're eating."

Mum was similarly indignant. "I mean, really – just when we're all sitting down for a meal together."

Suddenly it all made sense. At the same time, I felt a cold shiver run down my spine. So that's what the two of them were trying to stage. A peaceful evening together. The happy family gathered around the dinner table, with Grandma their honoured guest.

Why? Because they wanted to give Grandma a last happy memory to take with her into the home? Or, to put it in religious terms, was this their attempt to atone for what they were doing?

Either way, I couldn't shake the feeling that they were conning her.

Grandma was smiling merrily as she ate her dinner. But a transparent plastic sheet lay between her and the cushion she was sitting on. Apparently my uncle had handed it to my dad with the words, "You'll need this." Its purpose was to catch all the food that Grandma's poor eyesight made her spill. She was also wearing a disposable nappy under her tracksuit bottoms. My uncle had given Dad a box of those too, warning him that she was particularly prone to accidents at night.

I really don't want to live to that age, I thought. Not one bit.

There had been a time in my life when I'd been so scared of death that just thinking about it had been enough to make me cry. I'd even fantasised about a future in which there would be a cure for every illness and people would live forever. When did I stop thinking about all that?

Ron-Ron, who finished eating before us, mewed softly as he came up behind me.

"How was dinner, Ron-Ron?"

Miaow, came the reply. With the real Ron-Ron, slight variations in the tone of his voice had told me what sort of mood he was in. With his stand-in, though, I was clueless.

Even his dinner was different. The real Ron-Ron had loved it when we topped his rice with shredded strips of dried fish. But his stand-in was only allowed a specific type of dry cat food, to avoid any dietary disturbance caused by his frequent changes of abode.

Still, tickling the soft fur under his chin, it was impossible not to be reminded of the real Ron-Ron. Just as I was remembering how he used to lift his head at times like this, as if to say, *More of that, please,* the stand-in began doing the same thing. It made me happy, and at the same time a little sad.

Ron-Ron had died at the age of twelve. Not a bad run for a cat. The direct cause of death had been pulmonary oedema as a complication of acute renal failure, but in the six months or so before he passed away, he'd aged dramatically, his body suddenly growing weak. His movements slowed, his eyes gummed up, he kept drooling, and he lost control of his bladder. Looking back now, he'd probably been going a little senile too.

Cats do go senile. There are books that say this is just humans projecting, but my boss, Mr Harada the section manager, had already had four cats die on him and was adamant that they really did lose the plot, that he'd seen it happen. When it got really bad, they'd forget they'd eaten and keep coming back to their bowl for more.

Ron-Ron died before it got to that stage. In his final moments, he'd eaten half a spoonful of finely chopped tuna, seeming to relish each morsel, before closing his eyes for the last time.

I'd always thought of it as a happy death.

My brother was giving me a look.

My father was still rambling away, but my mother also seemed to have cottoned ont o something, even as she carried on chiming in with the conversation.

What? I asked my brother with my eyes.

In reply, he slowly mouthed the word: *Grand–ma.*

What about her?

She's–act–ing–weird.

How do you mean?

Her–food.

Then I saw what he meant.

Grandma was steadily working her way through the entire platter of sashimi, including the decorative seaweed garnish. She kept ferrying the raw fish into her mouth, not even bothering to dip it in the accompanying soy sauce.

"How about some salad, Grandma?" said my mother in an attempt to divert her from the sashimi. But it was the same with the salad: she began shovelling it straight into her mouth without adding any dressing.

By this point, even my father had fallen silent.

". . . Mother," he said, his voice turning oddly high-pitched as he attempted to sound casual, "that's enough salad, don't you think?"

There was no reply from Grandma. She simply pulled the salad bowl towards her and continued munching away at the lettuce in silence.

"Mother!" said Dad, his voice growing even more tense. "That's enough!"

This seemed only to strengthen Grandma's resolve – if she was even conscious of what she was doing, that is. She carried on chomping away at the lettuce.

"I said stop!"

Dad tried to grab the salad bowl. Then Grandma gripped it with both hands and yelled, "Thief!"

She was glaring at him – her lips trembling, her expression hostile, as if we were all villains from whom she had to protect the salad.

Mum, who had been leaning over in an attempt to stop Dad, now sank back to the floor and began to sob.

"Oh, come *on*!" yelled Dad, turning his frustration on her. "Why are *you* crying?"

Then, with impeccably bad timing, my brother's phone chimed again. This time it was Mum's turn to shriek, through her tears, *"I told you to turn that thing off!"*

This was a disaster. Just like that, our fake happy family had shattered into pieces.

There was a pause. Then, as if the spell had suddenly broken, Grandma let go of the salad bowl. She blinked a few times, rubbed her eyes and cocked her head doubtfully from side to side. She seemed to be having trouble seeing anything at all now.

All of a sudden, Ron-Ron, who'd been sitting next to me, ducked under the table before appearing at Grandma's side.

Miaow, miaow, came his soft voice.

For just a moment, I was reminded of the real Ron-Ron. Whenever he wanted to play, he would pester us in exactly this way.

"Here, you," said Grandma, beaming as she scooped the cat up in her arms. His body shape, weight, and patterning were all different from the real Ron-Ron's, but Grandma didn't seem to notice. She set him on her lap and began affectionately stroking him, just like in the old days.

But my relief was short-lived. Just then, another shiver went racing down my spine.

Just like in the old days.

In the old days, Grandma had always liked to share a bit of her dinner with Ron-Ron. If she tried that now, we were in trouble.

"Ron-Ron!" I called, panicking. "You're too heavy for her. Come here!"

But Dad was oblivious to the danger. "No, let him," he said, glaring at me. "She'd say if he was bothering her."

This was not good. Not good at all.

For a while, Grandma simply stroked the cat. Then she glanced at the platter of sashimi and said, "Ah."

She seemed to have remembered the old days – and the one dish Ron-Ron had loved more than any other.

She reached out, grabbed a slice of chutoro tuna with her fingers, then tore it in half with her teeth.

"Look, Ron-Ron, fish!"

She turned towards the cat, holding the tuna out in the palm of her hand.

Eat it, I prayed. *I'm begging you.*

Ron-Ron sniffed the sashimi, then stared at it dubiously.

Come on. Do it for Grandma.

If he didn't eat the tuna his cover would be blown. Even more than that, though, I just wanted our stand-in to accept this gesture of affection from Grandma, who had so adored the original Ron-Ron.

But the cat had already lost interest in the tuna and was looking off to one side.

I caught his eye.

Please!

For a moment, he stared right back at me.

I summoned the most pleading look I could manage. My only hope was what the pet shop owner had told me: *The Blanket Cats are all intelligent creatures. Sometimes scarily so.*

Ron-Ron mewed softly.

He turned around and eyed the tuna once more. Leaning forward, he gave it another sniff. He leaned even closer. He stuck out his tongue. It touched the tuna.

After that it all happened very quickly.

Suddenly, the fish was in Ron-Ron's mouth. Barely pausing to chew, he swallowed the entire slice.

"There we go," said Grandma, delighted. "Was that tasty?"

On her face was the gentle, carefree smile of a child.

Dad slept in the tatami room with Grandma that night.

This was so that he could change her nappy straight away if she had another accident. So that he could squeeze her hand if she had one of her bad dreams. And so that if she did start sleepwalking, he'd be able to stop her.

I stayed up reading. Around midnight, I heard something in the kitchen.

I tiptoed downstairs, wondering what to do if I found Grandma rooting around in the fridge, eating food with her bare hands again . . .

But it was Dad.

He was making himself a whiskey on the rocks.

Seeing me, he smiled weakly. "Sorry for all the fuss, Hiromi." He paused. "But it's only for one more night, and if it does get too much you lot can always stay in a hotel or something."

I shook my head silently.

Just before bed, Grandma had begun to panic, as if she'd forgotten where she was. "*I want to go home*," she'd shrieked at us in tears. "*Let me go home! Please!*" In the end, we'd managed to get her to calm down, but in her agitation it seemed she'd wet herself again. Dad had changed her nappy. Mum had tried to do it for him, but he'd insisted, clumsily attaching it to Grandma's body. Watching him from behind, I had the odd impression that he'd shrunk slightly.

"Dad . . ."

"Yeah?"

"Is there really no way she can move in with us?"

Dad gave another pained smile and shook his head. "Your mum would probably throw a fit." Then, as if trying to convince himself, he went on. "No, we have to be realistic . . ."

"So that's it, then?"

"What?"

"You're fine with that, are you?"

Rather than respond, Dad took a sip of his whiskey. "Your boyfriend's coming over tomorrow, then, is he?"

"Don't change the subject."

"You know, that cat's got a good head on his shoulders. Cosying up to Grandma like that. *And* he gobbled that tuna down for us, even though he's only supposed to have the dry food."

"Dad, you're not listening."

"I am."

"No, you're not. Seriously, are you really okay with the idea of putting Grandma in a home? How do you feel about it?"

"Hiromi . . . did you say your boyfriend has an older brother? Looking after your parents can be a tricky old business, so make sure his brother's clear about his responsibilities. You don't want him leaving you two to deal with everything later on." He gazed into space. "Yep, it's a tricky old business alright . . ."

As he murmured these last words, a tear trickled down his cheek.

4

Early the next morning, before the rest of us were up, my father took Grandma out for a drive. The original plan had been for us all to go together, but I could see why he'd changed his mind.

"Do you think he'll be alright on his own?" I asked my mother over breakfast.

"I imagine it won't be easy," she replied, "but it's probably better that way for both of them. They'll have plenty of time to chat about the old days."

"Or like, commit double suicide."

At this crude joke from my brother, the smile on our mother's face vanished. I grabbed the newspaper on the table, curled it up and thwacked him on the head with it.

"He said they'd be back by evening," my mother said, less to us and more as a sort of reminder to herself. "What time did you say Mr Nagano was coming?"

"We agreed five o'clock."

"Will sushi be okay?"

"I'd prefer yakiniku or something," interjected my brother.

"We can't have meat," snapped my mother. "How do you expect Grandma to eat it?"

"Anything'll do," I said quickly.

I had no doubt that my "boyfriend" would play his role perfectly. He'd make sure Grandma had a wonderful last night at our house. He was a good person. He would never do anything to upset me or my parents.

But . . .

I didn't know what came after it, but I could feel the word bobbing around in my brain. *But, but, but . . .*

My mother suddenly burst out laughing. "Look," she said, pointing at the sofa in the living room.

Ron-Ron had tunnelled his way under one of the large flyers that came with the newspaper. The real Ron-Ron used to love doing exactly the same thing.

"Really getting into the role, isn't he?" my brother said admiringly.

"You know," Mum replied, "when he first arrived I thought he was nothing like the old Ron-Ron. But the resemblance is definitely growing."

They carried on chatting.

"Imagine if his fur suddenly had the same patterns."

"Oh, that'd just be creepy!"

"You never know, Mum. Maybe he's been possessed by the spirit of Ron-Ron."

"What *are* you on about?"

I gazed absent-mindedly at the cat, now firmly ensconced under the flyer. Only his rear end was poking out and wiggling in our direction.

Renting him had been the right decision. As long as our Blanket Cat kept this up for another day, we'd be able to keep Grandma in a state of blissful ignorance.

But, but, but . . .

There it was again. That *but.*

"Anyway," said Mum, smiling. "I'll order the best sushi on the menu."

Dad and Grandma came back in the early afternoon.

"We went to the seaside," said Dad.

The care home was in the mountains, near a hot-springs resort. Once Grandma moved there, she might never see the sea again.

When she walked in, she failed to recognise us and started introducing herself politely. "Hello, everyone. Thank you for having me." Then she saw Ron-Ron in the living room and seemed to come back to her senses with a start.

"Your boyfriend won't mind if I'm a little red in the face, will he . . ." said Dad, helping himself to a can of beer from the fridge. He stood there in the kitchen, gulping it down. Then, as if finally coming round, he grinned and said, "Phew. I'm spent."

"How was it?" asked Mum in a low voice. "Was she alright?"

"Yeah. Slept most of the way."

"Did she like the sea?"

"She cried."

"Oh . . ."

"You know, when we were little, she took the three of us to the seaside. Just the once. I kept pestering her, begging her to take us, until one day she managed to get the day off work, and off we went. Made all these extra-large onigiri to take with us as a picnic. I can almost still taste them . . ." Dad drained the rest of his beer in one go, then went on. "Anyway, I told her all that, and that's what set her off."

I couldn't tell from his story whether Grandma had cried out of nostalgia or because she was sad about being separated from the children she'd spent all those years caring for. Dad himself probably didn't want to know.

Grandma had plumped herself down on the sofa and was cradling Ron-Ron. In a low voice, almost a whisper, she was singing him a lullaby. Ron-Ron had closed his eyes and lay there stock-still, as if absorbed in the song.

My "boyfriend" had said he'd call when he got to the station. Just after four o'clock, about an hour before he was supposed to arrive, my phone rang.

"I thought maybe we could get a coffee or something first. At the café by the station."

Yes, I thought. That sounds like a good idea.

I hurried out of the house and made my way to the café. When I saw him smiling and waving from a seat by the window, I instinctively glanced away.

I felt bad about all this – of course I did. But when I started telling him how sorry I was, he smiled and said, "You don't have anything to apologise for."

"But . . ."

"Tell me. Do you think it's a hundred per cent lie, what we're doing?"

Lost for words, I began a vague nod, turned it into a slow shake of the head, then abandoned that too.

"Here's what I reckon," he went on. "Even if it's fifty per cent acting, I'm okay with that. As long as the other fifty per cent is real."

". . . Right."

"I mean, us getting married – that's not *completely* off the cards, is it?"

The chances weren't quite zero, I'd give him that.

But I didn't know if I'd stretch to fifty per cent either.

I'd fallen silent. He went on, still smiling.

"Can I ask you a hypothetical question?"

"What?"

"Say we get married. And we stay together for our whole lives, and have kids and everything, grandkids even . . . And then I turn senile. What would you do?"

"What would I . . . do?"

"Because, I mean, you can just stick me in a home. I'd be fine with that. In fact, I'd prefer it. I'd hate to think I was an inconvenience to my wife and kids. I'd hate to watch the people I love suffering for my sake."

He's a good man Kind. And I can tell he means every word.

But, but, but . . .

That word was back, bouncing around in my head like a balloon, bumping into an invisible wall inside me, endlessly rebounding and colliding. I closed my eyes for a moment, then looked back up at him.

"Don't you think that's a little self-centred?"

He went blank with surprise.

"Why?"

"All that stuff you just said. You never stopped to think how your wife and kids and grandkids might feel."

"But that's the point. I *am* thinking about them. I want to save them the hassle of looking after me when I'm all old and doddery."

"Why do you get to decide?"

"Decide what?" he asked, his tone sharpening slightly.

"That looking after you is the worst thing that could happen to them. How can you know that? I mean, caring for someone like that can be really demanding, don't get me wrong. But some people would still prefer that to the grief of putting their parents in a home."

I remembered my father's face the night before. How small he had looked from behind as I watched him change Grandma's nappy.

"Tell me," I went on. "If one of *your* parents said they were going to put themselves in a home, you'd be alright with that, would you? You'd see them off with a smile?"

"Of course not. But . . . sometimes it's the only real solution, isn't it? In some cases, probably most cases, it works out better for everyone involved. I mean, just look at your family. You're putting your grandma in a home, right? What else can you do? It's what's best for your family – and for her too. I'm sure of it, Hiromi."

"*Sure*?" I said, raising my voice. "How can you be *sure*?"

Some of the customers sitting nearby started in their seats, turning to look.

Mr Nagano took a sullen sip of his coffee. "You're always doing that. Picking me up on my choice of words," he muttered.

Maybe it was just the way he'd said it that had upset me so much. Realistically speaking, I had to admit he was probably right.

But, but, but . . .

What I really wanted, I realised, was for him to seem *troubled* by all this. To worry and waver and fail to make his mind up. To tell me he didn't know what was right.

Of course, if you'd asked me what that actually achieved, I wouldn't have had an answer.

"Well, never mind," he said, gathering himself, the smile returning to his face. "Shall we get going?"

". . . Yeah."

"Don't worry, I'll play my part," he said, his smile broadening into a grin. "Just make sure you play yours too."

Back home, a large tray of sushi was waiting on the low table in the living room, surrounded by various side dishes my mother had made. Everything was in place for our last dinner with Grandma.

"Well?" asked my mother when I walked in, eyeing me suspiciously. "Where's Mr Nagano?"

I ignored her and sat down opposite Grandma, who was sitting on the sofa.

"Just you, is it?" asked Dad, who was getting the drinks ready. Again, I didn't reply.

I'd bolted out of the café while he was paying at the till. It wasn't my finest hour. In fact, it was downright cowardly.

But, but, but . . .

"Grandma?"

"Hello." She looked slowly up at me, smiling. There was something oddly transparent about her expression.

"Grandma . . . I'm sorry. See, I was supposed to bring my, er, boyfriend to dinner. But the thing is, I don't think we're getting married after all. Which is why I, er, decided not to bring him."

Mum, Dad and my brother were all staring at me open-mouthed.

Grandma, meanwhile, was still smiling at me. It appeared she didn't have the faintest idea who I was.

I turned to the others and, doing my best to sound casual, said, "So, yeah. I thought you should all know."

"It's good for young couples to fight," Grandma said all of a sudden. She spoke in a lilting voice, the words seeming to bubble up from somewhere inside her. She smiled her transparent smile. "If you're going to marry someone, make sure you have plenty of arguments first."

I wanted to reply, but I knew that the moment I opened my mouth I'd start crying instead.

Ron-Ron, who had been lying underneath the table, hopped up onto the sofa. With an attention-seeking mewl, he made his way onto Grandma's lap.

"Ah, Ron-Ron," she said. It was like someone had changed

the TV channel and she'd come back to reality. It was quite possible she'd already forgotten my confession. That was fine by me. In any case, it had probably been more for my benefit than hers.

"You really love having Ron-Ron around, don't you, Grandma?" I remarked.

She nodded emphatically as she stroked him. "Oh, he's a darling. Such a lovely little thing."

Ron-Ron mewed gently, almost as if he'd understood.

"You're so kind, aren't you?" she went on. "Thank you for everything you've done for me . . ."

I felt a sudden chill.

The others were giving me uneasy glances.

Had she known all along . . .?

Grandma held Ron-Ron up in her hands, then squeezed him to her chest again.

"Thank you, really . . ." she said to Ron-Ron. Then she looked at us and said again: "Thank you."

Now it wasn't just her smile that seemed transparent. Her voice, her entire body appeared on the verge of fading away before our eyes.

My father gave a low groan. I didn't have to look at him to know he was fighting back tears.

"You're all so . . . kind, aren't you?" she said, before looking down at Ron-Ron. "So kind."

Were we kind? Maybe. But we were also weak – too weak to stop Grandma leaving us.

Were we weak because we were kind, or kind because we were weak? Kind *in spite of* our weakness, weak *in spite of* our kindness? I didn't know. Still, I felt as though the "but" that had been bobbing around in my head had finally receded below the surface.

My phone started ringing. The ringtone told me who it was. I felt around my pocket and turned it off.

Then I turned towards the kitchen where the others were still standing motionless, like a video in freeze-frame, and said, "Let's eat!"

Dad was still too busy fighting back tears to respond, but Mum managed a smile in my direction. "I'm guessing you'll be wanting a beer too?"

Our last evening with Grandma.

When we parted ways the next morning, I wouldn't tell her "Goodbye", I decided. I'd tell her "See you soon".

Still sniffling slightly, my father retrieved a bottle of umeshu from the fridge. He'd bought it especially for Grandma, whose only luxury, in the days when she was rushed off her feet with work and childcare, had been a small glass of the sweet plum wine before bed.

"Right, well, I'm going to sit down," said my brother.

"Don't eat the kappa-maki, alright?" warned my mother. Whenever we had sushi with Grandma, no matter how high-grade the fish was, we had to order an extra portion of kappa-maki. For her, the cucumber rolls had always been the highlight of the meal.

Ron-Ron jumped down from Grandma's lap, made his way over to me, and started mewing and nuzzling at my legs.

He really was a darling. And, it seemed, incredibly intelligent to boot.

I reached into my pocket again and gripped my phone.

"Mum, I'm just going upstairs to make a call, okay?"

She didn't reply. She was busy getting plates out from the cupboard, so she must not have heard.

Just as I was about to repeat myself, I saw that she had already set out a total of six glass plates on the kitchen counter, and realised I didn't need to.

"I want us to argue," I said, secretly grateful that he hadn't turned his phone off. "It doesn't matter which of us is right. Let's just . . . have lots of arguments from now on, okay?"

"From . . . now on?"

"Yeah. Tonight, for instance."

"You're sure?" he replied. I could hear a smile in his voice.

"Yeah. Grandma's waiting."

". . . You want us to argue in front of Grandma?"

"Well, we don't *have* to. Only if it comes naturally." Then I burst out laughing at what I'd just said.

He was chuckling too. "I'll be there in five."

It was at least a ten-minute walk from here to the station.

"Wait. Were you already on your way?"

"Er, yeah. I figured being chased from your doorstep would be better than nothing."

"Did you hesitate?"

"What?"

"Before you decided to come here. Did you hesitate and wonder if it was the right thing to do?"

"Well, yeah," said Nagano, a slight edge to his voice. "Obviously. Had a nice long sulk first."

That was good to hear. If you were going to argue with someone, they'd better come armed with plenty of doubts and worries of their own.

And if you were planning on making up afterwards, they'd better be the kind type too.

When I hung up, I could hear Dad laughing downstairs. He was talking about Grandma, except instead of calling her Grandma or Mother like he usually did, he was calling her Mum.

You used to really lay into us, didn't you, Mum?

You could be pretty scary when you were mad, Mum.

Oh, Mum, what are you like . . .?

I put the phone down on my desk and slowly made my way downstairs.

I walked towards the living room where my family – my kind, weak family – was waiting. Soon we'd be joined by the man who was supposed to become our newest member. Something told me Grandma would greet him with a smile.

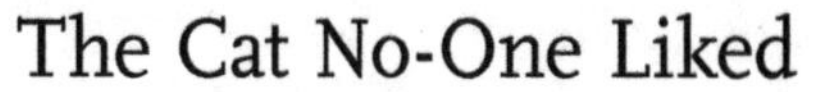

The Cat No-One Liked

I

I could hear the cat again. The low, piercing, openly hostile growl.

Number 104, probably. The young office worker who'd just moved in last month. Clearly she didn't know how terrifying our elderly landlord could be. The kinds of tricks he was capable of.

I made my way out of my second-floor apartment and down the stairs to the first floor where, from the end of the corridor, I peered cautiously over at number 104. My guess had been on the money. The landlord was standing there by the door while the young office worker apologised profusely from inside.

But if the old man had been the type to be satisfied with a simple apology, he wouldn't have resorted to a ruse like this in the first place.

"Those are the rules." The same line as always. "Your contract was clear enough, young lady. Or didn't you read it?"

Young lady? Really?

After that he just started laying into her.

"I want you out by the end of the month, you hear? Nope, rules are rules. It's not complicated – a kid would have known better . . . No excuses! You broke the rules, and that's that . . .

It's not like I'm forcing you to leave tomorrow. I'll be inspecting the apartment. You might not get your deposit back, but what did you expect? I'll have to change the wallpaper and everything . . . What? It's the smell. Cats *stink*. Their owners never seem to notice, but they stink alright . . . The end of the month, you hear? I'll be listing the place tomorrow. If you try and overstay, I'll just have to get in touch with your guarantor."

I've never been the most well-spoken guy, but recently the old man had been doing wonders for my vocabulary. Just watching him was enough to make words like "imperious" or "overbearing" or "disdainful" spring effortlessly to mind.

The old man carried on with his spiel. By the end of it, the woman had retreated into a sulk. When she closed the door, it was with a furious slam.

I knew how she felt. There was something about the guy that really got to you. Even as a bystander I was feeling pretty riled up. If it had been me he was lecturing, I'd have been in half a mind to stab him.

Just then, he turned in my direction.

I tried to hide, but it was too late.

Our eyes met. All I could do was grin awkwardly and bow in his direction.

"Hello," he said, still frowning, then gave me the briefest of nods. "Perfunctory", I guess you'd call it. Or was it "peremptory"? I could never remember the difference.

At his side dangled the pet carrier. A cranky old man in his seventies walking around with what almost looked like a picnic basket. You couldn't really say it suited him. But this carrier was one of the main reasons why nobody liked him.

Inside it was a cat. Once a month, on a Saturday, the old man rented it from a pet shop for a couple of days, then used it to check whether any of his tenants were breaking the "no pets" rule. He would pace up and down the corridors with the carrier, and any pets hidden in the apartments would, without fail, start miaowing, or barking, or tweeting in response. If it was an animal that didn't make a noise – a turtle, say, or an iguana – then the cat in the carrier would start growling instead. It was like a carbon monoxide alarm or a metal detector or something.

I made my way down to the ground floor and out into the street, then turned and looked back at the building.

It was a three-storey structure containing twenty studio apartments plus the landlord's. The old guy must have been well off, because apparently he used to live in a large house on the same plot of land. For whatever reason, he'd flattened the house and dug up its garden and replaced them with this low-rise block of apartments, setting one unit aside for himself. I guess there's no knowing where life will take you.

As rental properties went, it was a decent setup. In fact, it was almost perfect. A three-minute walk to a major station from which express trains could whisk you to Shinjuku in fifteen minutes – or, if you changed there, Shibuya in twenty. Good metro connections to the rest of the city too, and just a short drive to the nearest expressway onramp. The building itself was only five years old and was hooked up to cable television, and the studio apartments felt more spacious than some two-bedroom places. Well-fitted kitchens, separate bathroom and toilet, and a secure entry system on the ground floor. Despite all this, the rent was way below market rates. In fact, it was so absurdly cheap that you'd be forgiven for thinking one of the previous occupants must have committed suicide or something. Prospective tenants flocked to the property: as an estate agent might put it, it was a "real find". Provided, of course, that you were willing to overlook the landlord's personality.

On my way to the station, I passed the local letting agency just in time to see a young employee putting up a new listing in the window.

There it was. Apartment 104. AVAILABLE FROM NEXT MONTH, the listing said. The old guy moved fast. And ruthlessly. Remembering the forlorn look on the woman's face as she stood there bowing in the doorway, I let out a sigh.

The old man would say it was her fault for breaking the rules. He had a point, I guess. The new advert made things just as clear: PETS STRICTLY PROHIBITED, it said.

I guess rules *are* rules. I let out another sigh.

As I gazed at the advert, the bunched-up strokes of the kanji for "strictly" started to resemble the landlord's wrinkled features.

"What kind of cat is it?" asked Etsuko, looking mildly concerned.

"I've only seen it a couple of times," I frowned. "But it's got this really nasty look about it."

"Seriously?" said Etsuko. "But . . . how can you tell what it's like just from looking at it?"

"You just can, I'm telling you. There is *no* way that cat is the friendly type."

I wasn't exaggerating. I knew next to nothing about cat breeds, but this one looked exactly how I'd always imagined the nasty ones in fairy tales.

"Is it fat?"

"Yeah, and sort of flabby looking. Long fur too. With this real uppity look on its face."

Just as some humans can't help rubbing people the wrong way, some cats are just inherently *annoying*. That probably explained why the secretly kept pets in our building couldn't help crying out whenever the cat drew near – somehow, they knew, and that was why they always sounded so genuinely upset. It wasn't the sound of one animal greeting another through the door, but a sort of angry goading that seemed to mean something along the lines of *The hell is wrong with you?*

"I can't really picture it . . ." Etsuko said, cocking her head to one side.

"Trust me. It's the worst cat ever."

Of course, the cat hadn't chosen to be rented out to the old man. What really irked me was the way it happily went along with his sneaky tactics.

"I guarantee you'd say the same thing if you saw it."

"You reckon?" Etsuko said, her head still tilted. "I *love* cats, though." And she went on stroking the kitten on her lap.

She'd found it the previous evening, lying in a cardboard box together with a message from whoever had abandoned it. *Looking for a kind owner.* Pretty outrageous thing for them to write, now that I thought about it.

"You planning on keeping that thing?" I asked.

She hesitated. "Erm, yeah. If I can."

"Are you even allowed pets in this apartment?"

"Nope."

"Right. So . . . what's the plan?"

"Um . . . Actually, I was wondering if we could keep it at your place."

"No way."

"I'd move in too."

"Not happening," I said dismissively. Then her words sunk in. "Wait, what?"

Etsuko smiled shyly. "Well, it's way too early to be thinking about marriage or anything, but I thought we could at least try moving in together."

"You serious?"

She blushed. "I mean . . . That's what you want too, isn't it?"

Yes yes yes, I nodded, like some kind of spring-loaded doll. Before I knew it, I'd even thrown my arms up in celebration.

It was half a year now since I'd first persuaded Etsuko out on a date. We'd had our fights, but I'd been steadfast in my devotion. Now it seemed all my efforts were paying off.

"But," she sighed, interrupting my celebrations. "I guess if you're not allowed cats at your place either, then . . ."

"Wait – no, it'll be fine. We'll work something out."

"Yeah? Like what?"

"Oh, I don't know. Bumping the old guy off or something."

Etsuko snorted. "You're such an idiot."

It was true – I could be a bit of an idiot. Still, if at that moment Etsuko had turned to me and, in all seriousness, told me to kill the guy, I might well have gone out and bought myself a knife. There was another phrase I'd been really getting to grips with recently: "blind devotion".

"You could always live here," she said.

"Or we could move somewhere new, I guess."

"But it's so hard to find a place that lets you have a pet. And if you did I bet the rent would be through the roof."

"True."

"Do you have much money saved up?"

I hung my head and shook it from side to side.

Embarrassingly enough for a 25-year-old, I was still what they call a freeter, hopping endlessly between casual jobs. I cleaned an office building by day and worked at a convenience store by night, and that was just about enough to keep me in my current digs. Etsuko was a temp worker who only had a placement about a third of the time, so money was tight for her too. Even if we split the rent, it was hard to see how we'd be able to afford anywhere nearly as comfortable as my current place.

"We could move out of the city," I said. "Somewhere like Chiba or Saitama, where the rent's lower."

"Seriously? You really think you could stand it out there?"

"I guess not."

"Yeah, thought so," she said bluntly, before adding: "I don't think I could either."

Play over work, the present over the future: those were my priorities. Not the most responsible approach to life, I know, but that was who I was. Once you'd grown used to the bustle of the city, how could you ever be happy out in the sticks?

Can't we just get rid of it?

I swallowed the words before they could get out. A comment like that might be enough to put Etsuko off me in a flash.

I didn't want to lose Etsuko.

Etsuko didn't want to lose the kitten.

Cats weren't allowed in my apartment.

I couldn't move out.

And Etsuko wanted to move in.

It was enough to make my head spin. I wasn't good with dilemmas like this. In fact, I hated them.

At times like this, there was only one thing to do . . .

We had sex. Afterwards, we lay there naked in each other's arms while the kitten looked blankly on.

A rather pathetic scene, all told.

Still, with *that* out of the way, my head felt a lot clearer.

"Hang on," Etsuko said as she pulled her clothes back on. "I've just had an idea."

"No way. Me too."

"Really?"

"Yeah. So, what we need is for the kitten to keep quiet whenever the landlord rents that cat."

"Right, right. That's what it all comes down to."

"And the kitten will only make a noise if it doesn't like the other cat."

"Exactly. Which means . . ."

"We just have to make sure they're friends first. Right?"

"Right!"

"The old guy doesn't own the cat, he hires it. Which means there's nothing to stop *us* from hiring it either."

"Exactly."

"Right? So we take it home, we introduce it to the kitten. We make sure they're all friendly, and then next time the landlord does one of his little patrols, the kitten stays nice and quiet. Easy-peasy, right?"

I ended with an "okay" sign. Etsuko smiled, nodded and made one back.

It just might work, I thought.

Etsuko cocked her head to one side. "But I thought you said it's a super grumpy cat?"

"Probably just looks that way," I said. "I bet it's friendly once you get to know it. Some cats are like that."

"Someone sounds very optimistic all of a sudden."

"Seriously, it'll be fine," I said, throwing my chest out and making a peace sign this time. "Trust me."

I went to see the landlord the very next day.

It was our first real conversation since I'd moved in the year before last.

The old man opened the door and, in the unfriendly tone of someone trying to repel a door-to-door salesman, barked, "What do you want?"

The guy really was something else.

"There's something I'd like to ask," I said, desperately contorting my face into a smile. I asked him for the details of the cat rental agency, emphasising that it was for a friend.

For what felt like an age, the old man glared at me with

what appeared to be the most suspicious face he could muster. Then, as if screwing up a ball of paper and hurling it in my direction, he told me the name of the pet shop.

He really was unbearable. Maybe it *would* be easier to bump him off.

Still, I beamed at him as I thanked him and made to leave.

"Wait a minute," he said. "I wanted a word, actually."

"Yes?"

"You're not sorting your recycling properly, are you? I keep finding plastic bottles mixed up with the cans."

I felt like shouting, *That wasn't me, you old tool!*

Still, the important thing was that our plan had been set in motion.

2

The pet shop turned out to be a surprisingly clean place, with almost no noticeable noise or odour. Perhaps because the "products" – the animals – were all sitting in glass cases.

I'd been expecting it to smell a bit more feral, like a zoo or something, with lots of dogs and cats and birds and whatnot all trying to make themselves heard over the din.

"That'd be ridiculous," said Etsuko in disbelief when I told her. "How would they manage to sell anything?"

Ok, she had a point, but still.

The glass-panelled display cases were divided into a criss-cross of individual enclosures. Like see-through baggage lockers, or a bigger version of those little plastic organisers you could buy at hundred-yen shops. The cat section was almost all kittens, and the dog section almost all puppies.

"Erm, Etsuko . . ." I murmured, squeezing her elbow.

There was a young woman behind the counter, scribbling away at something. Worried she might set a Tosa or a Doberman or something on me if I offended her, I kept my voice low.

"There must be some animals that no-one buys, right?"

"Oh, definitely."

"What happens to them?"

I'd heard about people with a penchant for older men or women, but that didn't seem to be a thing with pets. It was always the younger, the better. What was with the collective Lolita complex when it came to animals?

Etsuko cocked her head pensively. "Maybe they discount them."

"But pets aren't really the kind of thing people try to bag on the cheap, are they? Plus the old ones would like, take up more space."

"I don't think space is the issue . . ."

"Seriously, though. Say these animals grow up and get all old and still don't find a buyer. What happens to them?"

They get put down. I could only grimace as the answer to my own question flashed through my mind.

Now that I looked at the cages again, the puppies and kittens all seemed sort of desperate, like they were acting as cute as they possibly could. Even the ones who weren't wagging their little tails or pushing their cheeks up against the glass seemed to be silently crying out, *Pick me!*

I'd always thought pets had it easy. Three meals a day, naps aplenty. But now I realised that to even get to that point, they had to emerge victorious from this cruel contest – a literal fight for survival. I felt like telling them, *Hang in there, guys.*

"Etsuko . . ."

"Yeah?"

"If a pet was twenty-five, they'd be like, way past it, right?"

"Are you talking about yourself?"

I nodded silently. Since leaving school, all I'd done was dodge and scrape my way along, bumbling from one part-time job to another without ever working out what I wanted to do with my life. It wasn't a situation that seemed likely to change anytime soon.

Was I really fine with that?

Clap-clap-clap! Like a dance instructor beating out time, Etsuko brought her palms together in front of my face.

"Snap out of it, mister mopey face. We've got a cat to rent. Here goes . . ."

She strode up to the counter on her own. After a pause, I reluctantly followed.

"Erm, excuse me!"

It was only as I watched her leaning over the counter and calling out to the clerk that I realised I'd made a glaring oversight.

"Crap," I murmured.

I'd forgotten to ask my landlord the most important detail: the cat's name.

It was always this way with me. My attention span was close to zero, I was terrible with maps, and I struggled to follow simple instructions. I was the lord of lost property, the master of misspellings, the king of careless mistakes. My middle-school teacher's prediction – *At this rate you'll never be a respectable adult!* – was turning out to be alarmingly accurate.

Though, if we ever had a school reunion, there was a part of me that wanted to turn to him and say, *Hey, teach, when you say "respectable adult", what do you actually mean?*

"How can I help?" asked the clerk, arriving at the counter.

"Well," said Etsuko, "we'd like to, er, rent a cat. We can rent them here, right?"

"Absolutely," said the clerk, nodding politely. Then she glanced up at me, and then at Etsuko, each time for just an instant.

There it is, I thought, clenching my teeth.

When you'd dropped out of high school after just a year and been in casual employment for almost nine, you knew what that glance meant.

"And which of you will be renting the cat?"

"Him," said Etsuko, pointing at me without a moment's hesitation.

Inside me, a little voice cried out, *Oh. My. God.* Why the hell hadn't we talked this through in advance?

Etsuko was only trying to avoid bruising my ego. But as someone in semi-regular employment, she had no idea how hard situations like this could be for a freeter like me. And when she found out, who was to say she wouldn't just turn around and dump me on the spot?

She made way for me at the counter.

"Is this your first time?" asked the clerk. Here we go, I thought. "Sorry, but we require any customers renting animals to register first."

"Right."

"It's a very simple process, really. It's just, you know, what with them being living creatures and everything . . ."

"Sure."

"So do you have some form of ID you'd be able to show me?"

"Will my health insurance card do?"

"Sorry, we need something with a photo."

"How about my driving licence?"

"It really needs to be something with your workplace on it."

Always the same old story.

"I've got a Marui store card . . .?"

The clerk gave me an incredulous look. It seemed jokes weren't really her thing.

"My Tsutaya Books card, then. Or is that no good either?"

It was like talking to a brick wall. But I couldn't stop now. My pride was at stake.

"Petrol station card?"

Nothing.

"Tower Records card?"

The silence was deathly – in fact, death might have been preferable.

"Blood donor card?"

The clerk looked imploringly at Etsuko.

Time for the punchline. "Ah, here we go," I said, digging around in my wallet and eventually sliding a card out from one of the pouches. "How about this?"

It was a Pokémon card.

This was normally the point in my little routine at which people cracked. Even the most stern-faced clerks would finally get the joke – and even if we'd done nothing to solve the actual problem, at least we'd have broken the ice.

But this one was something else. She was still staring at me as if to say, *Just stop it, would you?*

Etsuko scrambled to intervene. "Okay, okay, you've had your fun," she said to me placatingly. Then she turned to the clerk. "We'll put it in my name. I assume that'll be fine?"

"Well, yes, I suppose . . ."

Etsuko got out the card her temp agency had issued her. This was still pretty low on the identity-card ladder, but after my Pokémon card it was like manna from heaven. To put it in baseball terms, it was like following a deliberate slow pitch with a regular one: to the batter it looks like the fastest thing they've ever seen. An unexpected switch-up, a surprise change of tack. In a way, I'd set Etsuko up perfectly.

In any case, things went a little more smoothly after that.

Etsuko filled out the rental form, and the clerk typed her name, address and phone number into the computer.

"And do you have any specific requests regarding the cat?"

Again, Etsuko made way for me at the counter. "One–nil to me," she whispered with a grin.

Uh-oh. When she finds out I forgot to ask the cat's name, she'll be two for nothing and laughing all the way out of here. Looks like I'm paying for dinner . . .

*

It turned out I was overthinking things.

When I asked if I was supposed to tell her the name of the cat I wanted, the clerk told me their names weren't important. During the course of the three-day rental, the cat's temporary owner usually gave them one of their own choosing. The same cat might be called "Elizabeth" by customer A and plain old "Whiskers" by customer B.

"It's a way of establishing a bond with the cat."

"Right . . ." I nodded.

"Doesn't that get confusing for the cat?" put in Etsuko.

"No. They know it's only temporary," said the clerk. Then, in what appeared to be her first attempt at a light-hearted comment, she added, "Well, who knows what they're actually thinking!"

"Huh," said Etsuko in an impressed voice, before grinning at me. "I guess they're either incredibly smart or incredibly stupid."

I smiled back at her. But my mind was elsewhere.

They're just like us, I was thinking. The drifters and temp workers of the cat world . . .

"Now, these are the cats that are currently available," said the clerk, taking a file from the shelf and opening it on the counter.

Inside was a list of the cats together with their photos. There were no kittens. The clerk, apparently convinced we'd be disappointed by their absence, began hastily explaining why. Kittens couldn't cope with constantly moving from one owner to the next, which meant special training was necessary before they could be rented out. The Blanket Cats had been raised to sleep comfortably anywhere – as long as they had their favourite blanket.

Yeah, I thought, that sounds about right. For people like Etsuko and me, hopping from one workplace to the next, the ability to adapt to new environments was vital.

And if you think our inability to stick at any one job for long means we're weak-willed, think again. What about the determination to keep throwing yourself into one new situation after another, huh?

Something must have been up with me that day. I mean, there I was, comparing my life to that of a rental cat.

"Hey," urged Etsuko. "Which one is it?"

I looked down the list. Next to each of the photos was the cat's age and gender, plus their type or breed or whatever you call it. Calico, American Shorthair and so on. Instead of names they had numbers. It reminded me of the menu at a Chinese restaurant.

I found the landlord's "accomplice" on the last page. There he was, the plump thing, openly glowering at the camera. It was enough to make even the cat-loving Etsuko gasp and frown.

The accompanying text read: *Six years old. Male. Mongrel.*

"Why does it say 'mongrel'?" I asked.

"Oh, that just means he's a mixed-breed," replied the clerk. "What's known as a domestic or household cat."

Jeez, I thought – why not just write "domestic cat" then?

Mongrel . . . It reminded me of those surveys people hand out in the street where there are three options for your occupation: employee, student – and "other". I couldn't shake the thought that these cats and me had plenty in common.

"So the other ones are pedigrees, are they?" asked Etsuko.

"That's right. They're mainly cats from the shop who never found an owner, which is why there are so many purebreds."

Seriously, "purebreds"? Surely, when it comes to breeding, there's no such thing as pure. I mean, two different people got together and made every single one of us. We're all mongrels, lady!

Wow. I really was in a funny mood today.

"Can we get this one?" I asked, pointing at the photo.

"Oh," said the clerk, with a strange gulp. "Well, sure, but . . ."

"Is there something wrong with it?" asked Etsuko.

"No, not exactly. It's just that, well . . . in all honesty, I wouldn't recommend him to a first-timer."

"Why?"

"Well, he's got a bit of a temper. A little . . . unpredictable, if you know what I mean. Not the friendliest of cats. A bit of an acquired taste."

"But he's been through the same training as all the others, right?"

"Oh yes. It's just . . . he can be a bit picky when it comes to his host. And if he decides he doesn't like you, he can get a little wild . . ."

Yikes, I thought, thinking of the old landlord – himself the very picture of crankiness. If that was the level of grouch it took to earn the cat's respect, we might be in trouble.

Still, it was this cat or no cat at all.

"That's okay," I said. "We'll take him."

". . . Are you sure?"

"We'll be fine."

"Right, but . . . you're really sure?"

The clerk's sceptical tone was starting to bug me.

I wouldn't write us freeters off so easily, I wanted to tell her. *When it comes to the number of jerks we have to deal with on a daily basis, we'll give any full-timer a run for their money. In fact, generally speaking, the only workplaces that'll have us are the ones that are overflowing with jerks. So how about getting down off your high horse?*

"He'll be alright with us," I said, puffing out my chest slightly. Etsuko was looking at me admiringly. "I'll set him on the straight and narrow," I added with a chuckle.

Three minutes later.

My triumphant grin was nowhere to be seen. Instead, I was fighting back tears with a plaster on my nose.

The clerk had set the carrier down on the counter and opened the hatch. Within seconds of seeing my face for the first time, the cat had apparently decided I wasn't cut out to be his owner.

Like some deranged jack-in-the-box, his right paw had shot out of the carrier and scratched me right across the nose.

Still, the two of us – me and the mongrel – were going to have to learn to get along.

3

When we got back to Etsuko's place, the first thing I did was pick a name for the damn cat.

"Let's call him 'Mongrel'," I said.

"That's a bit harsh, isn't it?" said Etsuko with a slight frown.

"Why? That's what he is."

"I know, but . . . What about his feelings?"

"Oh, come on, it's just a name. Don't get so worked up."

Etsuko had called the kitten she'd rescued "Charmy". Like the brand of washing-up liquid. Personally, I thought that was a much more offensive thing to name a cat, but if I told her that she'd probably hit me, and I'd already suffered enough violence for one day. So I just set the cat carrier down in the middle of the room in silence.

For some time now, loud hissing sounds had been issuing from inside. Mongrel, it appeared, was not a happy cat. So much for what the clerk had said about him calming down once he was in the carrier.

"You sure about opening that?" said Etsuko anxiously, clutching Charmy to her chest.

"We have to at some point, right?"

"What should I do if he comes over here?"

"How should I know?"

Keen to avoid a repeat of earlier, I leaned back as I crouched by the carrier, keeping my face as far from it as possible. Etsuko was slowly backing into one corner of the cramped room.

"Here goes."

I opened the hatch. This time, Mongrel emerged lazily from the carrier. Slowly, he turned his thick neck, taking in his new surroundings, before letting out a series of low, threatening grunts. A bit like a rugby player doing the haka.

Then, all of a sudden, he whipped round, snarled and dived at my belly. His claws tore right through the faded cloth of my T-shirt, leaving a series of rising welts. Dark blood began to seep from them.

"Ouch!" I cried out. "You bastard!"

I lashed out with a foot. Mongrel dodged it effortlessly and began pacing slowly towards Etsuko.

"Aargh!" she shrieked, squirming on the spot. What was she doing?

Mongrel came to a halt.

He sat down with his back almost straight – a bit like one of those maneki-neko figurines with one paw raised, except both his were on the ground. His eyes were fixed on Etsuko – or rather, the kitten clasped in her arms. Charmy was peering back at him too. Eventually, she let out a feeble *miaow*.

Huu-uuu, growled Mongrel.

Myaa, Charmy responded softly.

Shuu-uu, snorted Mongrel.

Miii, said Charmy.

Wrao, wrao, said Mongrel.

Were they . . . having a conversation?

Charmy slipped out of Etsuko's arms and tumbled onto the floor. Like any cat, she knew how to nail a landing.

Mongrel took a languid step forward, and then another, edging closer to Charmy, who was padding over to meet him.

This is not good, I thought. I started hearing the tense music they used in TV dramas.

But in the end, Mongrel didn't attack Charmy, and Charmy didn't wail in terror.

Instead, she rubbed her cheek against Mongrel.

Then she extended one of her tiny forelegs and gently pawed the hulking cat in the shoulder.

Mongrel didn't move. He was back in his squatting position, a grumpy look on his face, doing absolutely nothing.

Myaa, wheedled Charmy, pushing her face up against Mongrel's belly. Then she burrowed right underneath it. Like a kangaroo cub or something.

Mongrel didn't move a muscle. He just gazed moodily off into space and let Charmy do as she pleased.

"So, er, what I'm trying to say is," Etsuko began as she pumped disinfectant onto the back of my hand, "I don't think you and Mongrel are very compatible."

". . . Whatever."

"Okay, he has a grumpy face, but he's actually really nice. To me and Charmy, I mean. Deep down, I reckon, he has a heart of gold."

"Oh, sure!"

"See, this is what you do, Tak-kun – you get all defensive. Mongrel's clocked that, which is why he hasn't taken to you. I think you've got to be a bit more . . . open-minded. You know, like, really try and get to know him."

"The hell I do!"

I wrenched my hand away from her and started blowing on the still-tingling wound.

Mongrel had attacked me. Again.

Even now, on day two of his three-day stay, a single glimpse of my face was enough to make him lash out. The previous evening, he'd clawed the top of my foot just after I'd got out of the bath – of course, the hot water having done wonders for my circulation, blood came gushing from the wound. In the middle of the night, he'd jumped onto my belly and begun scratching away furiously before scarpering off to the other side of the room. In the morning, when I was washing my face, he'd managed to rip a hole in my pyjama trousers. And when, early hour be damned, I'd decided to calm myself down with a beer, he'd spotted the open can on the table and knocked it right over.

Still, my magnanimity knew no bounds. I'd been gracious enough to heap an extra-large portion of cat food into Mongrel's bowl for lunch.

"Go on, eat up," I'd said, sticking the bowl in front of him.

And the bastard had scratched me on the back of the hand.

"I really like him, you know," said Etsuko. "And he's so good with Charmy. Look," she went on, jerking her chin towards the corner of the room. Charmy was following Mongrel about, pawing playfully at him. Mongrel wasn't exactly reciprocating the affection, but it didn't seem to bother him either. He just sort of sat there in silence and let Charmy do her thing.

"Don't they make a great pair?"

"Nope."

"I've never seen her so relaxed. Abandoned kittens can come across as needy, but they're normally really wary of other cats. Mongrel must have some special aura!"

I nodded vaguely, watching him. Our eyes met. He looked away haughtily.

Was it really possible that he just . . . hated me?

It was infuriating. But also oddly depressing.

"You've got work tonight, right?" Etsuko asked. "Are you coming back here after?"

I thought for a moment. "Nah, I'll sleep at my place. Mongrel's happier with me out the picture, right?"

Etsuko laughed. "Oh, come on, stop sulking."

"I'm not *sulking*."

"Spoken like a true sulker."

She was probably right. I should just admit how I felt.

Even Mongrel – the least popular of all the rental cats, the one nobody liked – had decided he didn't like me. It was pathetic, it was humiliating, it was frustrating, it was . . .

"Etsuko."

"Yeah?"

"Do you know the word nekomatagi? As in, 'ignored by cats'. Normally it means a fish that's so unappealing even cats won't eat it, but where I'm from it means something a bit different. Not a fish, but a person. Someone so devoid of value that even the cats just walk right on by." I paused. "Etsuko, do you think that's me? I mean, look at me. Still messing about with part-time jobs at this age, no hopes for the future, like *at all*, nothing I really want to do with my life, I mean I really am just . . ."

I hadn't been planning on venting like this, but the words just kept coming.

At the beginning of my little speech, Etsuko just laughed and said, "Uh-oh, here comes mister mopey again!"

After a while, though, her expression turned serious and she began nodding encouragingly.

"How about finding a full-time job, then?"

"Etsuko, I'm a high-school dropout. Who's going to hire me?"

"So you're just going to carry on like this, then?"

"Oh, I don't know . . ."

I got up and edged towards the door. When I got to the entrance, I saw that the laces had been pulled out of one of my trainers.

"Oh, sorry. Mongrel was playing with that just now."

Never mind, I thought. I'm over it. I'm a nekomatagi, after all.

I turned up for my night shift at the convenience store in a lousy mood. I watched the customers come and go. People who seemed to have no real reason for being there in the middle of the night, standing around reading magazines off the shelves, checking out the latest additions to the snack and drink sections, squatting outside the shop to eat their ice creams and text on their phones, then clambering to their feet, chucking the wrappers onto the street, and ambling off into the night. Watching people like that, I began to feel all sorts of miserable.

What are we doing?

We, I thought, automatically using the plural. Five years down the line, what will have become of us?

If we stayed put, that would be it. Our lives would be one slow shuffle to the bottom. But where the hell were we supposed to go from here?

It was the kind of thing no-one had ever taught us at school. Rappers and rockstars were always telling us to "break things".

But break what? And why? More importantly, where were we supposed to find the hammer that would get the job done?

It was four in the morning, and I was arranging a fresh delivery of bento boxes on the shelves. It was my last task of the night. As I lined them up neatly, I glanced up at the curved mirror designed to prevent shoplifting. Reflected in the convex glass, my forehead alone was enormous, and my hands and feet were pathetically small.

At five a.m. the morning team took over and I made my way out of the shop.

When I arrived in front of my apartment block, a recently expired bento dangling in a plastic bag at my side, the front door slid open before I'd even reached for my key. Startled, I looked up.

It was the landlord.

"Morning," I said reflexively, bobbing my head, but the old man simply glanced suspiciously at me and made his way over to the rubbish collection area by the entrance.

Today was food waste collection day. People were always breaking the rules – taking their rubbish out at night rather than in the morning, or not sorting it properly. Even at this early hour there were various plastic bags stuffed with rubbish lying around.

The old man was opening them up one by one and sifting through their contents. Now that I thought about it, a sign had been posted by the entrance last week that read: RUBBISH MUST BE CORRECTLY SORTED.

The old guy really was going above and beyond.

Speechless and slightly repulsed, I tried to make myself scarce. But he stopped me.

"Oi."

Oi? Really? If I was some juvenile delinquent having a bad day, I might have whipped a knife out right there and then.

"Yes?"

"This your rubbish?"

"What? No. I've literally just got back from work."

". . . Right then. Never mind."

I'll give you never mind, I thought.

I glared angrily at the old man as he turned away and started rummaging through the bags again.

"What, you want something?" he asked. "We're done. You can go now."

I felt my blood pressure inching up.

I remembered the time I was summoned to the careers office at high school. The teacher had asked me what I planned to do with my life, seeing as I didn't have a university or job lined up. When I told him I'd "just sort of work it out as I go along", he let out an exaggerated sigh, flapped the back of his hand at me like he was swatting away a fly, and said, "Alright, we're done. You can go now."

I decided I had to get this off my chest. "Actually, can I ask you something?"

"What?" replied the old man, retying the bag he'd just looked through.

"Well, see, we're all paying rent to live here, right? Which means we're sort of, like, your customers."

"And?"

"It's just, the way you treat us, you wouldn't really think that was the case, would you?"

The old man turned to look at me.

He didn't seem particularly angry, but then the guy was always scowling, so it was impossible to know what he was actually thinking.

"If you don't like it, leave," he said quietly.

It was a pretty infuriating line, but there was also a sort of mysterious, powerful aura emanating from his tiny frame.

"Well, no, I'm not saying I don't *like* it here, exactly . . ."

The old man simply grunted and nodded slightly, then began gathering up the rubbish bags, his inspection complete. He picked them up, a bundle in each hand, and walked into the building. I hurried after him.

"What are you doing with those, then?" I was beginning to suspect he might be one of those stalkers who sift through people's rubbish.

"Keeping them until six o'clock."

"Why?"

"Why do you think? Because that's when you're allowed to take rubbish out."

"Keeping them, like . . . in your own apartment?"

"Where else am I going to keep them?" he replied in an irritated voice as he marched off.

I watched him go. Somehow, he seemed slightly more human than he had a moment ago. What he was doing made a strange kind of sense.

"Erm," I called out.

He stopped and turned as if to say, *What is it now?*

"You know how I asked about that rental cat the other day?"

He grunted in acknowledgement.

"Why do you always rent that one in particular?"

"Because that's the one I want. Why else?"

I decided to take the plunge. "Is it because no-one likes him?"

I refrained from adding: *Just like you, I mean.*

The old man simply stared at me.

4

"Come here a minute," said the old man, walking off without waiting for my reply. That bossy tone drove me mad – and yet I felt like I had no choice but to follow him.

His apartment was on the ground floor, right at the end of the corridor.

"Come in," he ordered, opening the door.

I went in.

The apartment was bigger than mine, but much more sparsely furnished. In the corner of the room, bleakly devoid of any decoration, there was a Buddhist altar. For his family, I guessed. As I peered at it, unable to restrain my curiosity, the old guy set the offending rubbish bags down on the kitchen floor and called out to me: "At least offer some incense."

"How do I . . .?"

"You telling me you've never offered incense at an altar before?"

"Erm, yeah . . ."

In fact, I'd only ever seen an altar like this on TV. This was my first sighting of one in the wild.

"Young people these days . . ." he grumbled. He took my place in front of the altar, lit the candle and a stick of incense, then struck the bell so that it let out a piercing chime.

I watched the old man press his hands together in prayer, then imitated his pose as best I could. I found myself gazing at the photo on the altar.

It showed five people all standing together.

A young mother and father. Their two young children. And . . . the old guy.

Wait, why was he in the photo?

When he'd finished praying, I found myself pointing at the photo and saying: "Is that, like, okay?"

"What?"

"It's just, well, you're still alive, right? I thought it was bad luck to put a photo of someone on an altar before they die."

The old man stared at me in baffled silence. He seemed to have been expecting a different question.

This was the problem with older people. They didn't get the convoluted way our young minds worked.

Yeah, I know what you want me to ask. And that's precisely why I'm not asking it, you dummy.

I mean, seriously. Did he really expect me to turn around like a little kid and ask what had happened to the happy family in the photo?

The old man went and sat by the low table in the middle of the room. I stayed in front of the altar. I felt more at ease with him out of my line of sight.

The kids in the photo appeared to be two sisters. The older one looked like she'd be in the first year of school. The younger one had probably just started nursery.

"Was it . . . an accident or something?" I asked the question in a deep, solemn voice, one I didn't even know I was capable of.

"A fire," replied the old man, in a voice even deeper and more solemn than mine.

". . . Seriously?"

"The house that used to be here."

The house in question had, in fact, consisted of a pair of separate dwellings, enabling the old man to live alongside his son and his family. The fire had started in his son's home. It was the middle of the night. The wind had been strong. In no time at all, the blaze had spread from the kitchen, where it had started, through the entire building.

For some reason, I started hearing the old man's muttered explanation in the grave tones of the narrator from the hard-hitting documentary series *Project X*.

This was my problem. I could never take things seriously. Now I realised why: because I was scared. There were so many things in my life I'd been scared to take seriously.

The old guy had made it out of his house. So had his son and his family.

But I thought they died in the fire?

Before the question could form on my lips, my eyes landed on the older sister in the photo.

She was holding a pale brown object in her arms, so tiny that at first I'd thought it was some sort of leather pouch.

In fact, it was a little kitten, about the size of Charmy.

As if sensing what had caught my attention, the old man said, “They left the cat behind, see.”

The older sister had rushed back into the blazing building. The younger one had followed her in. The mother had gone shrieking after them, and the father after her. And that was when . . .

I imagined a piercing scream ringing out. The whole scene was straight out of a weeknight police drama.

Sorry.

I really was scared of taking things seriously, see. And at that moment, there was nothing I hated more about myself.

“Is that why you hate cats so much?”

“They ruin the apartments.”

“Is that really why you hate them, though?”

“They keep people up at night with their miaowing.”

“. . . Never mind, then.”

The two of us seemed like complete opposites. But when you really got down to it, maybe we weren’t so different.

“You hate cats, and yet you rent one just so you can find other people’s pets. Don’t you think that’s a bit weird?”

The old man didn’t reply.

“Anyway, why *do* you always choose that cat?”

I was back to the same question I’d asked him earlier.

“Is there a reason it has to be him? Apart from that pet-detecting trick of his, I mean.”

Still no response.

The old guy really was hard work. Just as I was thinking I

might as well clear off, I glanced at the photo on the altar one last time and realised there was something I'd forgotten to ask.

"So . . . did the kitten die in the fire too?"

Finally, the old man spoke.

"He wasn't inside."

"What?"

"He'd escaped on his own." He paused. "He came back the next morning."

"What? No way! That's . . ."

I wanted to find this cat and grab him by the scruff of the neck. *What the hell were you playing at,* I'd shout. *A whole family died because of you!*

"So what did you do?"

"What did I do?"

"With the damn cat, I mean. Did you have it put down or what?"

"Watch your mouth, kid," he snapped. "My granddaughters loved that cat."

". . . So you kept it?"

"For a while. But he reminded me too much of my family. I ended up giving him to someone I knew."

"And that was that?"

"He still comes back here every now and then."

I stared wordlessly at him.

"I figured my granddaughters might miss him, so once a month I arrange for him to visit."

Wait.

Let me get this straight.

That cat was . . . Mongrel?

That grumpy thing?

This time I didn't hear the usual tense music in my head.

All that happened was that the old guy, sitting at the low table on his own, facing away from me, suddenly looked incredibly frail.

"Well, that makes sense," said Etsuko, nodding deeply when I'd finished telling her the story.

"What do you mean, it makes sense?"

"Well, if Mongrel used to be his family's cat, then all sorts of things add up."

"They do?"

"Yeah. Mongrel still thinks of that plot as his territory, right? If he finds another cat living there, of course he's going to flip out. I mean, they're on his turf. Right?"

"Ah. Yeah, I guess."

"And you probably smell like that place to him, which would explain why he hates your guts."

"Nice detective work. You're like Nagisa Katahira or Azusa Mano or something." I chuckled.

"Oh sure, that's me," said Etsuko in a terrible Kansai accent, before suddenly turning serious again. "But it's only natural that Mongrel turned out all moody. I mean, going through something like that when he was still a kitten . . . it must have really affected him."

"Sure. Bet it turned him *cat*-atonic."

That earned me a slap on the head.

What made me come out with stuff like that? Was I that afraid of the conversation turning serious?

Etsuko, exasperated, turned her attention to Mongrel, who was entertaining Charmy in the corner.

"I wonder," she murmured, "if all this playing with Charmy is bringing back memories from when he was a kitten . . ."

My countless scratch marks aside, our three days with Mongrel passed without incident.

"I reckon we're in the clear. Even if Mongrel smells Charmy, he's not going to start growling or anything."

A relieved-looking Etsuko was already working out how and when to move into my place.

"I'll take him back to the shop," I said.

When I put Mongrel back in the carrier he scratched the back of my hand again. But now that I knew what he'd been through, I found it hard to get mad at him.

I closed the hatch.

Just then, Charmy starting mewing. *Myuuu, myuuu, myaaa, myaaa,* came the reedy little voice. Like she was lamenting Mongrel's departure.

Etsuko and I looked at each other.

"I don't know much about cats," I began, "but won't Charmy remember what Mongrel smells like?"

"It . . . looks like it."

"And what do you think she'll do next time she smells him?"

"Start . . . miaowing. Like she is now."

"Oh no . . ."

*

There was no turning back now.

"If the old guy does catch us, I'm sure we'll think of something," said Etsuko, more to herself than me. "We'll manage."

"And you never know," I said, "Charmy might stay quiet. Yeah, I reckon she'd do that for us. Definitely."

Any sensible adult would have said we were both being hopelessly naive about all this. Really, though, there was only one of us who was living in la-la land – and that was me. Obviously.

And so Etsuko and Charmy moved into my apartment, and the fateful Saturday rolled around.

The day when the old landlord rented the cat. Mongrel's monthly homecoming.

We decided to sit it out in the apartment, scarcely daring to breathe while the old guy did his rounds. By a stroke of good luck, Charmy had just gobbled down her lunch and was dozing away.

Were we actually going to get away with it?

We heard footsteps coming down the corridor. Slow, erratic footsteps – the sound of them alone confirmed that this was no youngster.

The footsteps got closer, and closer, and closer.

Then they stopped.

Mongrel didn't make a sound.

Then, just as I was clenching a fist in triumph . . .

Myuuu.

Charmy. The idiot!

Panicking, I flung a bath towel over her. Etsuko started stroking her in an attempt to quieten her down.

But there was no stopping her.

Myuu, myuu, myaaaa, came the forlorn appeal. The sound of an abandoned kitten wailing for her surly old friend.

She wriggled out from under the towel and scrambled over to the entrance, miaowing relentlessly.

Myuu, myuu, hyaa, hyaa, myuuuu . . .

Now she was scraping at the door with her claws.

Maybe Mongrel knew what was going on, or maybe he was just being his usual unfriendly self. In any case, there was no response from the other side of the door.

Myaa! Myuu! Hyaa! Waaa!

Charmy's cries were increasingly shrill and urgent. Now she was practically body-slamming the door, clawing frantically, mewling all the while.

Etsuko got to her feet, gave me a sad smile as if to say, *The game's up,* and made her way over to the entrance.

She opened the door.

The old man was standing there with Mongrel in his arms, framed in the doorway with the daylight at his back. I couldn't make out his expression.

He silently set Mongrel down on the floor in the corridor. Charmy rushed excitedly over. As always, Mongrel gave no reaction. Even as Charmy climbed onto his back, then began burrowing into his belly, he simply gazed off into space with his usual grumpy expression.

Before Etsuko could say anything, I made my way past her and stood there in the corridor facing the old man.

"Sorry," I said, bowing my head. "I . . . have a cat."

I'd been steeling myself for this moment. I'd told myself

I'd have to face it, and here it was. It might sound funny, but just then, I felt a little proud of myself.

The old man stared at me, then at Etsuko, and then down at Mongrel and Charmy at his feet.

"I'll be back for him this evening," the old man said in a low voice.

"You'll . . . be back for him?"

"He could do with a bit of playtime."

Seeing my confusion, Etsuko took over. "Thank you so much!" she exclaimed, bowing as deep as she could. "Erm," she went on, as though sensing a glimmer of hope. "Does that mean we're allowed to—?"

"Nope," interrupted the old man. "No pets."

". . . Right. Of course."

"I want you out."

I bit my lip in silence. But the old man hadn't finished.

"Once you've grown up a little, that is. Get a real job, save some money up. Then I want you out."

And with that he was off.

I knew nothing I could say would make him turn around, so I simply watched him go.

He walked slowly. From behind, he seemed somehow larger than a moment ago. Then he was small again, and then large . . . and now he'd shrunk again, and then he turned a corner and was gone.

The Cat Who Went on a Journey

I

Tabby had a bad feeling about her from the off. Six years on the job and you learn to see these things coming.

He'd been moved from his cage to the carrier, which had then been set on the counter. And the moment the hatch opened, and he came face to face with the human who would look after him for the next three days, he knew she was trouble.

The young woman peering at him stank of perfume. She had long nails and oversized rings on her fingers.

"*This* is an American Shorthair?"

The disappointment in her voice was palpable.

Yep. Trouble all the way.

Tabby was what they call a Brown Classic. Compared to what most people pictured when they heard "American Shorthair" – the Silver Classic tabby, with vivid black stripes against silver fur – he made a rather mediocre impression. He knew this. It was probably why he'd never found a buyer during his days in the shop.

Still, when it came to working as a Blanket Cat, Tabby was a natural.

Humans were straightforward creatures, when it came down to it. He'd thought this ever since he was a kitten. He was smart, and level-headed to boot. He knew not to get attached to his temporary owners. And he knew just how to act – and miaow – in order to make them happy. After all, acting friendly was all part of the job.

Whenever he saw a new cat struggling to get to grips with the role, he'd tell them, *Don't take it so seriously.*

After all, it was basically play-acting. For three days, the customer got to pretend they lived with a cat, and the cat got to briefly enjoy the luxurious life of a pet. That was all there was to it. Sure, the change of environment could be stressful, and things got a little more taxing when your new owner turned out to be some joker. But you can't have everything in life. After all, even if no-one talked about it, Tabby had a pretty good idea of what befell the other kittens who failed to attract a buyer.

We're the lucky ones.

All they had to do was find a sort of happiness in that good fortune. As long as they did their job, they were guaranteed food and a place to sleep. What else could you ask for? There was no point in hoping for more – either for humans or the animals they carted around at their leisure.

"Don't they come in any other colour?" asked the woman, loudly chewing her gum. Just last month, one of the other cats had accidentally swallowed an old piece of gum and got into all sorts of intestinal trouble.

There was no doubt about it: Tabby had drawn the short straw. This woman would make an awful owner. She was probably the type to pour milk all over the dry cat food, or to give him one of those dreaded baths and then blast him point-blank with the hairdryer . . .

There *was* a Silver Classic at the shop, but she'd been ill with a cold for the past week or so. Their owner was probably reluctant to rent her out – especially to a customer like this, where anything could happen. Rather than tell the customer to wait and have to entrust them with the barely recovered Silver Classic, it would be easier just to palm her off with the other American Shorthair.

Here we go, Tabby thought as he looked up at the woman. Luckily, the woman had just stood up straight again and was blocking the sun. Humans liked a cat whose eyes were big and round, rather than squinted against the light.

Pointing his tail up, he nuzzled himself against the woman, then let out a soft little *miaow*.

"Ooh," said the woman with a delighted grin. "I think he likes me!"

"He's very affectionate," said the owner without missing a beat.

"I can tell!"

"Well, he seems fine with you . . ." The owner still looked a little hesitant. But when Tabby gave another emphatic *miaow*, he nodded and took the form the woman had filled out. "Take good care of him."

The woman reached down and tried to pick Tabby up. He nonchalantly ducked out of the way and hopped back into the carrier.

"No way. He got back in all by himself. *A-ma-zing*."

"He's a clever cat, this one."

It was true. Even for a Blanket Cat, Tabby was exceptionally intelligent.

And that was probably why, every now and then, a certain thought would make itself known. Though you'd never be able to tell from his calm exterior, a shadow would sweep through him, and he'd hear an inner voice murmur:

Is this what you were born for?

The question didn't come from his head. It had been assembled somewhere else, somewhere deeper inside, his heart maybe, or some other part of him. In any case, from that place deep within him would come the voice.

Is this enough?

Is this all you want to be?

Then the voice would go on.

Never forget.

Never forget the role you were born to play.

Whatever that role was, it wasn't faking affection for one temporary owner after another, and Tabby knew it.

He was six years old – forty in human years. His youth already behind him. He'd reached the halfway mark. It was time to look back and reflect.

There aren't many people who, after taking a long hard look at their life, can simply conclude that all is well and carry on as they were. Most of the time there's a sigh of sorts, followed by a reluctant tramping onwards. Some people are so disheartened by what they find that they can't even bring themselves to take another step. In other words, they have what is known as a mid-life crisis.

This, it seemed, was precisely what was happening to Tabby.

*

The woman walked out of the shop with the carrier, set it down on the passenger seat, and drove off. There was a loop through which she was supposed to pass the seatbelt, but that didn't seem likely. She hadn't even bothered with her own.

The carrier bounced. It shook. It vibrated to the bass of the car stereo. The window must have been slightly open, because Tabby could hear the deafening rush of the wind.

Tabby pressed a cheek up against his blanket, closed his eyes, and stuck it out. Patience and hardiness were crucial qualities in a Blanket Cat, and Tabby had them in spades. As long as he told himself it was part of the job, he found he could put up with almost anything. Whether it was hot or cold, his appetite was always hearty, his bowel movements regular, his sleep sound. He never fell ill. He recovered from injuries quickly, and in his youth had always held his own in scraps with other cats.

Sometimes, the pet shop owner would say, "It's a shame all you get to do is sit around and be petted, isn't it?" To which Tabby always wanted to respond: *Well, we're pets – it sort of comes with the territory*. It was their job, after all. What else was there to do?

Recently, though, Tabby had been having other thoughts.

Memories had been returning to him. Vague, fleeting memories from some deep, dark part of himself.

He remembered a lurching motion. A bit like this car, in fact – but even more severe, so that he couldn't quite lie still.

A reeking darkness. The smell of rust and mould and dust – and something else. Something salty, almost bitter – what was it . . .?

Whatever the smell was, it signalled danger. He mustn't let it envelop him, that much he knew. But it was also strangely nostalgic.

The car went up a sharp incline. As it reached the top, it slowed ever so slightly, then there was a beep before it abruptly accelerated again.

That must have been a toll gate. They were on a motorway. Pushed up against the wall of the carrier by the sudden burst of speed, Tabby let out an exasperated sigh.

Don't lock him in the carrier for longer than half an hour. If you must, then give him five-minute breaks every so often. Motorways can be physically taxing for the cat, so avoid them where possible.

It seemed the woman was intent on ignoring every single one of the pet shop owner's instructions.

Tabby curled up in the blanket and closed his eyes again. At times like this, sleep was the only solution. These days he seemed to spend more time nodding off than in his bright-eyed youth. Presumably, as he got older, the naps would only get more frequent.

He didn't mind. In fact, he preferred sleeping lightly to being out for the count. That was another thing he'd only realised in his middle age.

Lolling around all day in some warm, comfortable nook – that was no way to be. He needed to stay alert. Ready to twitch his whiskers at the slightest sound or sniff of danger. Recently, he'd been reminding himself of this on a daily basis.

That's right. That's who you really are.

The voice again.

What, have you forgotten?

It seemed almost to be chiding him.

But what was it trying to tell him?

Who *was* he, really?

With a screech, the car swerved from one lane to another and then into a sharp curve.

The force flung the carrier's hatch open. His scatter-brained owner hadn't even bothered to secure it properly. It soon flapped shut again, but it was open long enough for a gust of air to rush in, together with the dazzling afternoon sun.

There it was. The smell.

The one from his memories. So familiar, and yet impossible to place.

The car came to a halt. The woman cut the engine and hopped out.

"Phew. I'm thiiirsty!"

She seemed to have entirely forgotten about the food and litter tray that Tabby had been provided with, which she'd thrown into the boot of the car. Instead, she simply walked off on her own.

This wasn't good, thought Tabby. Not good at all. If she carried on like this, his very life might end up on the line. Tabby nosed the hatch open, peered around to check the coast was clear, then slipped right out of the carrier. He stretched, groomed himself – and there was the smell again, tickling his nostrils.

Then he looked out the window, and it all made sense.

The ocean. The woman had pulled into a car park that overlooked the ocean. That was what he'd been smelling.

Various owners had brought him to the seaside when he was younger, but that was a long time ago now. It must have smelled the same back then, and yet it had never triggered this intense feeling of recognition. *No, it was different back then. It didn't seem so familiar. I didn't think it was something I needed to remember.* Just as those earlier days as a Blanket Cat had slid quietly by, so the salty air had passed in and out of his lungs almost unnoticed.

Now was different. Feeling the tug of some invisible force, Tabby jumped onto the driver's seat and pressed his nose to the top of the window, where it was open just a crack. He took a deep breath. He felt the briny air rush into his nose and fill his lungs.

That's right, came the voice again. *Never forget.*

We travelled for weeks across the ocean. We guarded the travellers on their voyage. We ploughed west through the wilderness. We stayed at their side. We crossed rugged mountains, forded rivers, pushed through sandstorms, watched the dawn rise over lakes.

And you are our descendant . . .

Tabby's heart was thumping in his chest. He could barely sit still. It was almost the same thrill he'd felt in his youth, that time of adventures and mischief – and yet different. Back then, he'd been constantly setting out to discover new worlds. Now it was the opposite. He felt as though he needed to get back to where he used to be. To where he really belonged.

The woman returned with a soft drink. Tabby crawled

under the driver's seat. The door opened. The smell of the ocean rushed in, thicker than before, enveloping him.

He jumped out.

"*Hey!* Wait! Hey, stop!"

He ran as fast as his legs could carry him, pursued by the woman's shrieks.

2

When Tabby had put enough distance between himself and the car, he stopped running. His nose twitched as he surveyed his surroundings. His gaze came to a rest on a pickup truck whose driver had just climbed inside. The truck's bed was covered with a tarpaulin, but he could see an opening at the rear.

He ran over to the truck, its engine already rumbling, and boarded it with a decisive leap. Or rather, a series of leaps. He really was showing his age. Clinging to the small step above the number plate, he climbed up onto the truck's body. Then, just as he slipped down into the bed, the vehicle pulled off.

It was dark under the tarpaulin. The truck bed was filled with cardboard boxes, but they weren't too tightly packed. It looked like he'd be able to find himself a decent hiding place.

He waited for the truck to join the motorway and reach a steady speed. Then, just as he began making his way towards the front of the bed, he glimpsed a faint, flickering light.

Startled, he paused and held his breath. The light was coming from the other side of a wall of boxes. He'd assumed the front of the bed was packed tight, but maybe there was some kind of cavity back there.

Flattening his body, he slowly inched forward, his every whisker bristling, his tail bushed out. He hadn't felt tension like this in a long time. In fact, the memory of it seemed to well up not from his own past but from some other, distant time, long before he was born . . .

Just before he reached the wall, he spotted a wide opening on one side. It wasn't just that the boxes had been stacked that way either. Someone appeared to have created a sort of tunnel.

Dropping his body even further, he crawled warily down it. He could still see the light flickering between the boxes. It seemed too low and dim to be some kind of built-in lighting. Its movements were irregular and didn't match the truck's vibrations.

Tabby came to the end of the tunnel. His whiskers felt it before he saw it: he had emerged into a sort of clearing.

Just then, the light was turned on him. He flinched in the dazzle.

"Look!" came a little girl's voice. "A cat!"

Panicking, Tabby scurried back the way he had come and into a space that would be too small for humans to reach.

"There was a kitty cat! I saw it!"

"Shhh!" came a boy's voice. "Keep quiet, Emi!"

"But there *was*!"

"I know. I saw it too."

"Where did it come from?"

"How should I know?"

"Do you think it jumped in when we stopped just now?"

"I don't know, Emi, okay?"

The girl – "Emi" – spoke so cheerfully she could have been sitting in a playground. But the boy's manner was gruff.

"*Miaow! Miaow!*" called the girl, waving her torch about. "Where are you hiding, kitty cat? You can come out now! *Miaow!*"

She's alright, thought Tabby. He had a sense for this kind of thing. All those years as a rental cat hadn't been entirely wasted. He'd listened to enough humans cooing over him to know, instinctively, whether or not their intentions were pure.

Yes, this was the voice of someone he could trust. Someone who really wanted to be his friend. From the slightly lisping way she spoke, he put her age at six or seven, maybe even younger.

"Emi, I said shut up!"

"But . . ."

"Do you *want* them to find you? You're on your own if they do!"

The boy, who Tabby guessed to be the girl's older brother, was growing more and more irritated. He sounded about ten or eleven.

You're much louder than she is, you know, thought Tabby in exasperation. Humans really could be idiots sometimes.

But it wasn't just anger Tabby detected in the boy's voice. It quivered with the strain of leadership, with the pressure of having to protect his little sister.

In fact, there was something oddly familiar about both their voices. This guileless little girl and her nerve-wracked brother.

Using a splayed stack of boxes as an impromptu staircase, Tabby made his way to the top of the wall they formed. Peeping down, he could see brother and sister sitting on the other side, in a space big enough for them to lie down. In the corner two backpacks lay side by side.

Remember, came the voice again.

We were always at their side.

And you are our descendant.

Tabby leaped down from his perch. Not because he consciously chose to, but because the voice seemed to urge it.

He wasn't as nimble as he used to be, and it was a long time since he'd last dived off one of those climbing frames for cats. And yet he jumped. His body rotated in mid-air. The pads on his paws had grown hard and tough in his middle age, but they still managed to soften his landing.

"Wow, did you see that?" exclaimed Emi in delight. "Look, the kitty's back!"

Tabby gave a shy little snort. Now that he thought about it, it had been a long time since he'd had the chance to show off like that.

Emi was stroking him on the back. He could feel her hand shaking nervously – it seemed she'd never had a cat of her own – but the sing-song voice in which she repeated *kitty-cat, kitty-cat* was kind and warm, as though she'd been reunited with an old friend.

Was she lonely? Anxious?

The two of them weren't here to play hide-and-seek – that much was clear. They seemed to have run away from home.

But why?

Mewing softly, he padded away from Emi and towards her brother, who was sitting with his back against the wall of boxes. Tabby rubbed a cheek against the boy's foot. In his shorts, socks and sports shoes, he looked like he'd just stepped out of the house to play. He even still smelled faintly of soap. In other words, it couldn't have been long since the two had left home.

The boy glanced at him, then said, coldly, "Get lost." Instead of stroking him, the boy started biting his nails, gnawing at them with what appeared to be growing restlessness.

SATORU, read the name badge on his backpack.

Satoru was staring off into a corner where the torchlight couldn't reach, as if deep in thought. In his shadowy features Tabby saw anxiety and regret.

"Hey, I said get lost. You're not supposed to be here." He shuffled around on the spot so that he was facing away from Tabby and Emi.

But Tabby stayed there at the boy's feet. He didn't decide to do so – it just sort of happened, like it was the most natural thing in the world. Why, he didn't know. It was almost as though his mind and body were no longer his own.

"Hey," Emi called to her brother, "what type of kitty is this?"

Satoru glanced at Tabby again and muttered, "Shorthair. American Shorthair."

"Oh. So it's American?"

"Originally."

The lad knew his stuff. If Satoru could recognise even a plain old Brown Classic, then maybe he was more of a cat person than Tabby had given him credit for.

"Actually," he went on, "not if you trace them *all* the way back."

"Really?" said Emi, though Tabby was just as surprised. If he'd been able to speak human, he would have echoed her question.

"Yeah. If you go way, way back, they're British."

This was news to Tabby. He found himself thinking of Churchill, a British Shorthair at the shop who sat around looking like he owned the place and was always trying it on with the Scottish Folds. Could he, Tabby, really be a compatriot of that libidinous creature?

"Then why is it called an American Shorthair?" asked Emi, her face blank with confusion.

"Well, it was the British who made America into a country in the first place," said Satoru. "They sailed all the way across the Atlantic Ocean in ships and made it their new home."

"Really?" asked Emi. Tabby chimed in with an inquisitive *miaow* of his own.

"Yeah. And the cats they took with them are the ancestors of the American Shorthair."

"So they were pets?"

"Not exactly. More like . . . companions. They kept the food safe from mice on the ships. When they got to America they protected humans from all the nasty animals. Snakes and spiders and things."

"That's so cool!" exclaimed Emi, her eyes widening.

Tabby felt his cheeks puffing with surprise too.

It was all beginning to make sense. If his forebears had crossed the Atlantic in ships, then no wonder the smell of the ocean was so familiar. And the voice that seemed to emanate from deep within him must belong to those ancestors.

That's right, came the voice. *We travelled with those ancient pioneers. We are the cats who helped create a path where there was none. Your sturdy legs, your jutting jaw, your strong neck, large head and broad chest, your fearlessness . . . They were all formed in that wilderness, and honed in the bleak alleyways of settler towns.*

You are our descendant . . .

"What a special kitty," said Emi, squatting down by Tabby to stroke him. Thanks, he thought, but there's this other spot I'd really like you to . . . But when he stretched his neck out, it was Satoru who, for the first time, reached out and petted him.

The boy knew how to stroke a cat too. Just the right spot, and just enough pressure. Of the two of them, it seemed only Satoru had looked after a cat before. But how was that possible if they were brother and sister?

So many questions. For now, though, with Satoru scratching him under the chin and Emi stroking his back, Tabby simply closed his eyes and purred.

"He really likes this, doesn't he?" said Emi.

"Yeah . . ."

"Such a cute kitty cat."

But Satoru had fallen silent, and now withdrew his hand.

"What's wrong?" asked Emi.

"Don't get too attached," said Satoru, turning away. "We're getting rid of him at the next stop, okay?"

"What? We can't do that!"

"Why not? Nobody asked him to jump in here."

"But . . ."

"Cats are no good, Emi. They're selfish, they scratch you, they play tricks on you, and their fur gets everywhere. And their poo and pee stinks."

Tabby felt oddly calm in the face of this sudden wave of abuse. Maybe this was because, behind Satoru's harsh words, he sensed a terrible sadness.

"But . . ." said Emi imploringly. "*Please* don't get rid of him."

"He'll only slow us down."

"But we can't just abandon him!" Emi's voice was shaking, her hand frozen halfway down Tabby's back. "If we do, he'll end up like us."

"No, Emi!" shouted Satoru, turning away so he was facing the darkness. "He's *nothing* like us!"

Such sadness in their voices, thought Tabby. In the countless homes he had visited as a rental cat, he had encountered plenty of kids their age. But none of them had ever sounded like this.

"It's different with us, Emi," said Satoru, still facing the dark corner. "*We* abandoned that woman, not the other way round." He spoke as though he was trying to persuade himself just as much as his sister.

That woman?

Who could he mean?

Instead of replying, Emi began to stroke Tabby again. He felt the palm of her little hand running down his back, over and over.

A long silence followed.

"Sorry, Emi," Satoru muttered eventually. "We don't have to ditch the cat."

He was looking away, so Tabby couldn't tell what sort of face he was pulling. But there was no mistaking the sob that had caught in his throat.

3

The truck carried on down the motorway.

Tabby had climbed onto Emi's lap. This wasn't something he did with just anyone, even in his capacity as a professional.

Satoru seemed to be slowly warming to him too.

"He's pretty tame, that's for sure," he said.

"Do you think someone abandoned him?"

"Nah. Ran away, I reckon."

"Really?"

"Yeah. Just look at his little face. Doesn't look scared or sad or anything."

The kid was sharp. Tabby wasn't entirely happy about the "little face" part, but he decided to take the rest of the comment as a compliment.

"American Shorthairs are really tough. I mean, like, strong-willed. Good at fending for themselves."

"What about Chestnut? Was she like that?"

"Well, she was a mixed-breed . . . She was really needy."

"With who? Mum?"

"With everyone."

"I wonder if she would have been like that with me too."

"Definitely. She was always like, *Pleeease. Feeeeed me.*"

"Silly," said Emi, laughing at the goofy voice Satoru had put on. Then she murmured, "I wish I could have met her . . ."

"Well, she was already old by the time I was born."

"I wish Mum had got us a new cat."

"She always said she was still too sad about Chestnut."

Ah, so that's why it's only Satoru who's used to cats.

"Do you think Mum's sad now?" asked Emi.

"About Chestnut?"

"No . . . About us. Do you think she sits there in her new house and gets sad when she thinks about us?"

Her new house? This was getting confusing again.

Satoru had fallen silent.

"What do you think?" Emi prompted. But her brother didn't reply. "Hey, do you think she—?"

"Emi . . ."

"What?"

"How about we have a bite to eat?" Satoru pulled his backpack over and reached into it, producing a packet of crisps.

"Can we give some to the kitty cat too?" asked Emi excitedly, leaving the question about their mother hanging – not because she'd forgotten, Tabby thought, but because she was pretending to. As proof of this, he noted how she avoided Satoru's eye when he handed her the crisps.

"Here you go, kitty cat," she said, holding out a handful for him.

I don't normally go in for this kind of thing, you know, Tabby grumbled as he leaned towards the hand. *But I suppose I can make an exception* . . . All Emi and Satoru heard, though, was what sounded like a miaow of delight.

He scooped up some of the crisps with his tongue. They were fish-shaped little things – salty and completely insubstantial, dissolving the moment he bit into them. A little disappointing, but he couldn't drop the act now. He licked Emi's fingers as if hungry for more.

"Hey, that tickles!" she giggled, pulling her hand away. Her smiling face kept being plunged momentarily into darkness. At first Tabby thought this was just the torch wobbling, but no – it was flickering. The batteries must be running out.

"I'm going to turn it off," said Satoru.

"What? But it'll be pitch dark!"

"We don't have a choice. We'll need it tonight."

"No . . . don't . . . please . . . I'm scared . . ."

"That woman must have put old batteries in it. Urgh, I hate her guts . . ."

That woman?

Presumably the one he mentioned earlier, Tabby thought.

"You'll be alright. Your brother's here. Look, I'll hold your hand."

He reached out and took her hand, gripping it with such force that she almost toppled over sideways. Tabby, perched on her lap, had to scrabble to keep his balance too.

What's up with me? Why didn't I just jump right off her? Emi's lap was too small for him to sit comfortably anyway.

But something had stopped him. Some momentary impulse had made him vow to himself that he wouldn't leave her side.

That's right, came the voice of his ancestors. *Stay by the young traveller's side. Protect her. That has always been our duty.*

Satoru turned the torch off.

The truck bed was plunged into darkness. Tabby could make out Emi's hand tightly gripping her brother's.

He stared into the gloom. Now they were in his world. The world of darkness.

He twitched his whiskers, strained his ears, puffed out his tail.

If anyone dangerous shows up . . . if anyone tries to harm Satoru and Emi . . . well, they'll have to go through me first.

He gave a low growl. His fur was standing on end.

I have claws and fangs so that I may fight.

I am brave so that I may protect the travellers.

I am the descendant of cats who crossed an ocean. Of cats who survived the wilderness.

At first, Emi froze up completely. But as her eyes adjusted to the dark, Tabby felt the tension in her legs ease slightly.

"It's not actually *that* dark, is it?" she said.

"See?" said Satoru, his triumphant tone also tinged with relief. "Told you."

With the amount of light that was seeping in, it seemed even Emi and Satoru could discern the boxes silhouetted against the tarpaulin.

Tabby, meanwhile, could see perfectly in the gloom. The coast was clear. No threats in sight.

"I wish we could keep him," said Emi as she petted him. Rather than stroking his back, she had followed her brother's example and was now scratching him gently under the chin. *There we go,* Tabby purred in response. *That's the spot.*

Satoru sighed. "Well, you're out of luck. That woman hates cats."

There she was again.

"Really?"

"Yeah. I reckon."

"But the other day, there was an advert on TV with a kitty cat, and our new mum was saying how cute it was!"

Our new mum?

"Hey," snapped Satoru all of a sudden. "I told you not to call her that."

". . . Sorry. I mean . . . Mum."

"No!" he yelled, then clicked his tongue. "We only have *one* mum, Emi, and it's not her."

"But . . . Dad gets mad if we don't call her Mum."

"Who cares? She's not our mum. She's a phoney." Satoru was speaking faster now. "She didn't give birth to us, did she? So how can she ever take Mum's place?"

Right. I need a minute to get this straight . . .

While Emi was distracted, Tabby hopped off her lap, then smoothly clambered back up to the top of the boxes, where he began grooming himself. There was nothing like gaining a bit of altitude when you had some thinking to do.

He'd just about grasped who Satoru meant by "that woman". And why the two kids were hiding in this truck in the first place.

The human heart really is a delicate thing, he thought.

Sure, there were cats who, well into adulthood, kept suckling away at their blanket or burrowing themselves into the chests of older cats in search of a teat. But the attachment of humans to their Mums was in another league altogether.

Tabby remembered nothing about the "Mum" who had brought him into the world, or even how many siblings he'd had. He'd been at the breeder's for barely three months when he was taken to the pet shop. The shop's owner and the other staff had all taken good care of him, but that wasn't the same as having a Mum. When he failed to attract a buyer, he'd been kept on as a rental cat, and so the endless three-day excursions with his blanket had begun . . . As for the many, many customers who had rented him, their faces and smells were all a blur by now. He'd certainly never felt like calling any of *them* "Mum". Never had, and never would.

Hey, you two, he would have said if he could speak their language. *Listen up, okay?*

We're all alone. We go through all this on our own. If life is one long journey, then we all travel solo. Friends, couples, families – at some point, sooner or later, they're all torn apart. So it doesn't matter whether you think your mum is "real" or "phoney", "new" or "old". That's right – even you two, sitting there clutching each other's hands, will one day go your separate ways . . .

Tabby blinked.

Where did that come from?

He began hastily grooming his forelegs in an attempt to calm down.

What am I thinking? What's wrong with me?

A wave of sadness hit him. His chest felt strangely hot and tight. His ears drooped.

Just then, the truck suddenly slowed.

Before Tabby could work out what was happening, the vehicle went into a long, sharp curve, then came to a stop.

Then it moved off again.

"We've come off the motorway," said Satoru.

"Does that mean we've reached Mum's house?"

Ignoring the question, Satoru flicked on the torch. "Emi, put your backpack on."

"Why?"

"We're getting out. The next time we stop at a junction."

Satoru had risen into a squat, his own backpack already on his shoulders.

Satoru lifted one corner of the tarpaulin and peered outside.

"What can you see?" asked Emi, squinting over his shoulder. "Where are we?"

At her feet was Tabby. Satoru hadn't said anything about taking him with them. And Tabby had no idea what he was going to do next.

But when Satoru lifted the tarpaulin and Tabby saw the kind of landscape that surrounded them, his first thought was *I know this.*

Before them, golden in the late-afternoon sun, lay a large swathe of reclaimed land, a semi-wilderness still awaiting development. It was dotted with the occasional builder's yard or warehouse, but other than that it was simply weeds as far as Tabby could see, a wide expanse of grassy nothing.

A long, long time ago, we crossed a land just like this.

We, Tabby found himself thinking. Not *I*, but *we*.

As the travellers crossed the wilderness, we were always at their side.

This time, it wasn't the mysterious voice that Tabby could hear. It was his own.

The truck came to a halt.

"Is this a junction?" asked Emi.

"Shh!" Satoru hissed, holding a finger to his mouth as he crouched, waiting, barely moving a muscle.

It wasn't a junction. The driver opened the door, hopped down from his seat and, muttering something about "when nature calls", made his way to the side of the road and unzipped his work trousers.

Satoru turned and looked at Emi. "We're getting out."

"Here?"

"If we get off in the town someone might see us."

"But . . ."

"Don't worry. Look, I'll go first."

Satoru clambered nimbly over the tailgate and hopped down onto the ground. The driver, whistling as he urinated, hadn't noticed a thing. In a stroke of luck, the wind was strong enough that the tarpaulin was flapping around noisily anyway.

"Right," whispered Satoru. "Your turn!"

"I'm scared . . ."

"You'll be alright," said Satoru, standing below her with his arms spread wide. "I'll catch you. Come on!"

But after Emi managed to get one leg over the tailgate, she

froze. Though Satoru gestured wildly for her to hurry, she seemed unable to move a muscle.

"I can't," she said, clearly on the brink of tears. "I'm scared."

The driver had stopped whistling.

There was no time.

"Come on, get a move on!" Satoru urged in a whisper, his face contorted with worry. "I'm here, alright? Just jump!"

Rearing up on his back legs, Tabby reached out a paw and scratched Emi's backpack.

As she turned to look, he jumped up and began really digging his claws into it.

Satoru must have got the message, because he gestured at Emi to put the backpack down first.

"It'll make it easier to jump!"

"Right," murmured Emi, letting it down from her shoulder. Tabby was ready. He bit into the shoulder strap. The weight was nothing he couldn't handle. He had as strong a jaw as any cat he knew. After all, his ancestors had never struggled to carry all the mice and rabbits they'd caught back home.

Leaning over the tailgate, Tabby let the backpack drop from his mouth and into Satoru's waiting hands. Nice catch. The boy seemed dumbfounded by all this, but managed to grin up at him as he clutched the bag.

Tabby felt a surge of joy. This had to be what his ancestors meant about never leaving the traveller's side. Not just sitting around and looking pretty, but actually serving a purpose. A working cat – deep down, that's what I am, he thought. No matter how many years had passed since his ancestors had first done their duty, the blood pulsing through his body was still that of an American Shorthair, steeped in the sweat and tears of those brave pioneers.

But this was no time to get emotional. The truck rocked slightly as the driver climbed back into his seat. The door slammed shut. He'd left the engine running. Once he released the handbrake, put the truck into gear, and pushed down the accelerator, Satoru and Emi would be torn apart.

Tabby stared up at Emi. How he wished he could speak her language! Still, he decided, there were some things even a cat could communicate.

Watch, Emi. I'll show you.

For him, the drop was nothing. A quick hop and he'd be on the ground in an instant. He wouldn't even have to jump – he could plunge headfirst towards the ground and still land on his feet.

Instead, though, he descended feet first, carefully lowering himself down the tailgate. That way, Emi would know just what to do.

She watched him, then nodded and, just as he'd shown her, turned around so she could cling to the tailgate as she descended. Gingerly she lowered her feet. The tips of her toes reached the rim that ran around the body of the truck. Good, good, that's it, thought Tabby, watching intently from below.

If she falls and Satoru can't catch her, I'll get between her and the ground, he decided.

If his body were a little bigger he could have borne her weight, but there was nothing he could do about that. Let her fall on him if she needed to. Let her body crush him. If he could cushion the blow, then at least Emi would escape unscathed.

Bring it on. I'm not afraid. What else is this sturdy, well-built body for? This thick, soft fur? These healthy bones? What else did I eat all that dried fish for, if not in preparation for today? For this very moment?

Emi was slowly drawing closer to the ground.

"There we go, that's it," whispered Satoru encouragingly. "Almost there, Emi."

The truck rocked slightly again. They heard the handbrake being released.

This is it, Emi, the final stretch. You can do it. Quick. But not too quick.

Then, just as the truck lurched off, Emi let go of the hook at the bottom of the tailgate.

Satoru was waiting for her. She fell into his arms. He clutched his sister tight.

4

The siblings and the cat began to make their way through the barren expanse of reclaimed land.

They set out briskly enough, but before long had slowed to a weary trudge.

The road that led from the motorway junction to the town was long and straight. It had looked long to begin with and, now that they were walking down it, felt even longer.

The sky was growing dark.

If they didn't make it to the town by nightfall, they'd probably have to sleep out here somewhere. Tabby glanced up at the children's backpacks. No tent or sleeping bags, of course. What about food, he wondered – did they even have any, apart from the crisps they'd eaten earlier?

This is not good, thought Tabby, his gaze dropping to the ground. There would be plenty of bugs in this weedy expanse, not to mention mice. But even if he were to catch and bring them something like that, he couldn't imagine them being very pleased about it. He felt his tail droop as he walked.

Emi seemed to be struggling to keep up.

"Satoru . . ." she said, her face and voice trembling as though she were on the verge of tears. "My legs hurt."

"It's just a bit further."

"But I'm so tired. I can't walk."

"Don't say that."

"But . . ." Gripping the crash barrier, Emi squatted down at the roadside.

"What are you . . .? Emi, come on!"

But she shook her head weakly and showed no sign of getting back to her feet.

The truth was that even Tabby was exhausted. He hadn't walked this far in a very long time. Maybe even his whole life.

"Fine," said Satoru, his voice sharpening. "I'll go on ahead then."

At this, Emi finally burst into tears.

The distance separating them began to grow.

Tabby dashed after Satoru, then stopped in his tracks and turned back towards Emi. Then he stopped again. He found himself helplessly caught in the middle, unable to move an inch as he glanced desperately between the two.

Satoru! Emi! Satoru! Emi!

What am I supposed to . . .?

His mind had gone completely blank. This had never happened to him before. Tabby had always been the most unflappable and decisive of cats, but now his heart was pounding and he had no idea what to do. All he knew was that he had to help them – but how?

"Satoru, wait," said Emi. "Hey, don't leave me all alone . . ."

All alone.

Tabby had always been on his own.

It didn't matter if you were a human, a cat, or something else entirely – in the end, we all had to go it alone.

But now he realised something. *Going it* alone and *feeling* alone weren't the same thing.

One day, Emi would have to set out on her own in life, that much was certain.

But that didn't mean her life had to be a lonely one. There would be times in the future when she needed company. When she deserved it.

Never mind the future – what about right now? Wasn't Emi feeling lonely *right now*?

Tabby started running after Satoru. He would scratch him in the calves if he had to. The sharp claws that had once cleared a path through the wilderness were always ready. If he still didn't stop, Tabby was even prepared to bite him.

But just as he was closing in, Satoru came to an abrupt halt by himself.

"Urgh," he sighed, "you have to be kidding." Then he turned and shouted to Emi. "Okay, let's take a break."

He began walking back over to her.

His expression was angry, but there was a kindness in his eyes, a sadness about his mouth. When Emi looked up at him, he forced a smile and called out, "I'm pretty tired too."

There we go. There we go!

Feeling another wave of irrepressible joy, Tabby puffed out his chest slightly and walked in front of Satoru, leading him back to his sister.

"Hey, shorthair," said Satoru. Bit rude, thought Tabby, but the boy spoke gently. "You can run off now, if you want."

Not happening, kid.

Tabby had made his decision. Or maybe it had been made a long, long time ago. In any case, he had a duty to escort these inexperienced travellers safely to wherever they were going.

But . . . where *were* they going?

Satoru and Emi were sitting by the roadside, taking turns to sip from the plastic bottle of tea that Satoru had produced from his backpack.

"Let's give the cat some," said Emi, who had stopped crying now. Still sniffling slightly, she picked up a discarded bento tray lying nearby and poured some of the tea into it.

"Funny old cat, this one," said Satoru. "You'd think he'd have run away by now."

"He must like us," she said, stroking Tabby. "Ooh, I know," she went on excitedly. "Why don't we give him to Mummy as a present? It'll be such a nice surprise for her. And that way we'll be able to go and see her all the time, because the kitty will be there. And then, maybe, even though Mummy's moved far away, we can still live with her like we used to!"

Emi spoke breathlessly, as though convinced of her plan's brilliance. But Satoru gave no reply.

"What's wrong?" asked Emi. Her brother turned away.

A shadow of unease passed across Emi's features. Still, she smiled and went on: "It's not far to Mummy's house, is it?"

Satoru bit his lip, glumly eyeing the setting sun.

". . . Emi."

"What?"

If her voice was shaking just then, Tabby reflected later, it must have been because deep down she already knew. It was also only later that he realised why Satoru still hadn't said a word – no, had been *unable* to say a word.

"Mum's house is . . . pretty far away."

"How far?"

"Like, really far."

"You mean we can't walk there?"

"Nope."

"What about taking a bus?"

". . . It's too far for that. So far that we might not be able to see her, Emi."

"But Mummy's waiting for us, isn't she? She must be wondering where we are."

Still glaring at the setting sun, Satoru shook his head and said, quietly, "She's already got a new cat."

"Really?"

"Yeah."

"Oh. Well, she'll just have to show us the new one, then."

Satoru shook his head again.

Sorry, he mouthed. *Sorry I lied.*

He didn't say the words out loud, and from where Emi was sitting she couldn't see his lips. And yet her eyes were welling with tears.

"Mum has a new family now," he said. "She's divorced Dad and married someone else, and so has Dad. It's never going to be like it was before, Emi. The four of us living together, me and you and Mum and Dad."

Now it was Emi's turn to bite her lip in silence. As she stared down at her feet, a single tear fell from her cheek to the ground.

"I'm sorry, Emi. I . . . I knew all along, but . . . you missed Mum so much, and you were so excited about seeing her . . . so I lied. I'm . . . really sorry . . ."

From Satoru's eyes trickled the tears he'd bottled up for so long.

What should I do?

Tabby found himself glancing between Emi and Satoru once again.

What *could* he do? How could he help? He didn't know. But he had to do something. Anything, anything at all, to help these two – not his customers, not his owners, but his *companions* on this strange journey – to smile again.

A car was approaching from the direction they'd come.

Tabby ran out into the road, deliberately veering this way and that, sitting down, rolling around, doing whatever he could to get the driver's attention.

Just as he'd hoped, the car slowed, honking as it crawled towards the cat sitting in the middle of the road. But Tabby didn't move. He was scared, but he wasn't going anywhere.

The car stopped right in front of him.

Here goes, he thought, and leaped up onto the bonnet. Then he began jerking his head urgently in the direction of the roadside, as if to say, *Look. Over there.*

The driver was a middle-aged woman. Following Tabby's gaze, she glanced down at the roadside and spotted the two tear-stricken children.

"Oh my!" she said, scrambling out of the car. "Are you two okay?"

As a species, Tabby had never rated humans all that highly.

If he was honest, part of him still felt that way.

But another part of him was learning to see these creatures in a slightly different light.

The driver who had taken Satoru and Emi to the local police station. The two officers from the missing children unit – a young woman and older man who hadn't uttered a single harsh word. Tabby wanted to say to them: *You lot can be a pretty decent bunch sometimes.* Not that praise from a cat would mean much to them.

Emi was taken to one side by the woman, who gave her a mug of hot milk and a jam bun. Satoru sat with the man, who took notes as he explained why and how they'd run away from home.

"It's all my fault. I forced her to come with me. Emi didn't do anything. So please don't arrest her. Just me."

"Nobody's arresting anyone," said the man with a smile. "You're a very kind brother, Satoru."

A younger uniformed officer came into the room. "I managed to reach their parents. Their mother said she'd be here right away. The father too, if he can."

Their mother. Their *new* mother.

The young officer turned to Satoru, his expression severe. "Your mum's been looking for you two all afternoon, you know. Searching the whole neighbourhood. She was about to file a police report!"

"Oh . . ." said Satoru in a quiet voice. His expression was sullen, almost irritated. Presumably because it was "that woman" they were talking about.

But the young officer had more to say.

"She was crying on the phone, you know. At first she just kept saying how relieved she was. Then it was: 'Tell them I'm so, so sorry.'"

Satoru's features contorted slightly.

"Your mother must be very kind too," chipped in the older man. At this, Satoru finally cracked. He began sobbing, his face flat against the desk in front of him.

Out of the two siblings, it was Satoru who was beginning to look like the real crybaby.

The female officer had a reward for Tabby too.

"The guy on night duty gave us this from his bento. A special treat just for you."

It was chikuwa – a whole stick of the fish-paste cake,

deep-fried with seaweed flakes. Sure, why not, thought Tabby. And he tucked in gratefully.

"That cat is quite something," said the older male officer admiringly.

"I know!" replied the woman. "You don't often hear about cats saving their owners, do you? Reminds me of Hachiko or something."

Comparing him to a dog famed for his faithfulness – it wasn't the most flattering compliment you could give a cat. But Tabby would take it.

"But, erm," interrupted the young male officer, "it's a stray, isn't it? Or someone's lost cat. Shouldn't we call the pound or something?"

Ugh, thought Tabby, here we go. Hastily spitting out the chikuwa, he began scanning the room for an escape route.

But just then, Emi shouted, "He isn't!"

"He isn't what?" said the young officer.

"He's not a stray! He's not lost!"

"But . . . he's not *yours*, is he?"

To this Satoru and Emi gave two different replies at the same time.

Satoru said, "He's moving in with us!"

Emi said, "He's not our pet, he's our friend!"

The young officer was lost for words. The older man patted him on the shoulder, grinned and said, "Think you'd better admit defeat."

Tabby returned the chikuwa to the plate and began nibbling away again. It was too much to fit in his mouth, really, but he managed to get it down. He was glad of the distraction, the excuse to simply munch away. Otherwise, he might get that strange, hot tightness in his chest again, and then he really wouldn't know what to do.

There was a knock at the door. Then, before anyone could respond, it flew open.

"Emi! Satoru!"

In swept their "new" mother, her eyes red and wet as she scooped the children into her arms. "You silly – little – things!"

Even after their father arrived and began thanking and apologising to the officers, their new mother simply clutched them to her chest. After a while she began apologising, just like she had on the phone. "I'm so sorry," she said, over and over again.

Emi hugged her back, while Satoru simply stood there. But when his new mother collapsed, sobbing, to her knees, he laid a hesitating hand on her back and began crying just like his sister.

They'll be alright, thought Tabby. They were already starting to see her not as "that woman", but as their new mother. In time, the "new" would fall away too, the way a cat's claws drop out once they're too old to be of use.

While the police officers were occupied with the family, Tabby slipped out of the room.

Outside, he looked up and saw the moon, a perfect circle in the night sky.

How was that, then, he asked his ancestors. *Did I do okay?*

There was no reply from the voice. Still, Tabby felt strangely satisfied, as though the countless selves that swirled within his body and mind had been fused into a single whole.

Right then, he thought, glancing back at the police station.

Farewell! he mewed.

And he trotted off into the night.

Their new mother had agreed that they could keep the cat. But by the time Emi turned and called, "Kitty cat! Let's go home," Tabby had already set off on his next journey.

Of course, this was enough to send Emi into fresh floods of tears, but Satoru was there to console her.

"I reckon he was sent by the gods or something," he said. "You know, to protect us." Though still hiccupping, Emi gave several deep nods of agreement.

If Tabby had been able to write in human language and leave her a letter, it would have gone something like this:

Our journey together has ended. Tomorrow you'll set out on a new one – one that'll bring you closer and closer to your new mother.

Take care of yourself, Emi. And give Satoru my regards.

Where Tabby went after that, nobody knows.

But with a brain that sharp and a body that tough, the odds are good that he's still going strong. In fact, he's probably helping someone else along on their own journey right now.

A middle-aged Brown Classic. He might look a little coldly on the world of humans, but whenever he spots a lonely-looking child, he'll prowl over and offer his help. If you ever come across a cat like that, there's always a chance it's Tabby.

Maybe he's in your neighbourhood right now.

The Cat Dreams Were Made Of

I

If his family was going to lose everything, surely he could make at least one of their dreams come true?

He would get them a cat.

Adopting one would be tricky. But a rental – that could work.

"There's this shop that rents them out," said Ryuhei, rubbing the cheeks that had grown so gaunt over the past month or so. "Three days at a time. Surprisingly cheap too."

"Wow, now you've really lost it," said his wife, Harue, sighing as she stared at the floor.

"Come on," Ryuhei grinned. "Surely we're allowed to do at least *one* of the things we always said we'd do."

I mean, we worked so hard to get here, he wanted to add. But he could already hear how pathetic the words would sound coming from his mouth.

"Do you really think it's a good idea?"

"How do you mean?"

"Well, what if it stinks the house up, or scratches the walls or floor? Our asking price is low enough as it is."

"Oh, come on. It's just a couple of days. And at this point, what's a hundred thousand yen here or there?"

They'd read the real estate magazines. They were already depressingly familiar with the going rate for a place like theirs.

A ten-year-old detached house. Four bedrooms with a kitchen and "combined living and dining area". Ninety square metres, the plot itself measuring just shy of a hundred. A three-minute walk to the bus stop, a five-minute bus ride to the nearest station. From there it was a forty-five-minute schlep into Shinjuku on one of the slow local trains that actually served the station.

Even if they went out swinging, they were looking at an asking price of twenty-two million yen. They'd probably be happy to sell it for anything upwards of fifteen.

Fifteen million plus Ryuhei's eight million in severance came to twenty-three million – barely enough to cover the balance on their mortgage. They'd be left with nothing.

"It's a fresh start," Ryuhei said in the sunniest voice he could muster, avoiding Harue's gaze. She seemed to have a lot more white hairs these days. "Remember that one-bedroom apartment we lived in after we got married? We're just going back to the starting line, that's all."

From next month they'd be renting a three-bedroom with no living room. That was still two more bedrooms than they'd started out with, but he didn't want to force the point. It would have sounded too pathetic.

"Yes, but we're not young anymore, are we?" Harue said bluntly.

They'd married when they were both twenty-seven. Now they were forty-three.

"And there are more of us."

Specifically, a daughter in her second year of middle school and a son in his fifth year of primary.

"*We're just going back to the starting line* . . . I don't know how you can be so flippant about this, Ryuhei."

She had a point, he'd give her that.

"If you don't find a new job soon, it's going to be really disruptive for Miyuki and Yota."

This was true too. Whenever the topic of their children came up, all Ryuhei could do was hang his head and bite his lip.

But *they* were the ones who'd always told him they wanted a cat.

"If I'd known things were going to turn out like this, I would have got them a cat when we first moved in here," he murmured.

He'd kept putting it off, telling his children an animal might damage the house and that they could get one when they moved somewhere bigger. It was a decision he regretted now more than ever.

"But if we did have one, we'd be stuck now, wouldn't we?" said Harue. "I mean, it's not like we're allowed pets at the new apartment."

"I guess . . ."

"We'd have had to get rid of it. Better not to have had one at all."

"Sure . . ."

When *would* he be able to fulfil the promise he'd made his kids, though? How many years would it be before they moved back out of the rented apartment, slowly worked their way up the ladder and found themselves living in a detached house again, one where they could have as many pets running around as they pleased? Maybe it wasn't a matter of time, he thought. Maybe the real question was whether that was even possible anymore.

He glanced around. The "combined living and dining area" he was sitting in was so cramped it barely seemed to merit the name. If it were a Japanese-style room you'd struggle to lay ten tatami mats on the floor. There wasn't really space for both a dining table and a sofa, as his family had pointed out, but Ryuhei, who had always dreamed of kicking back on his very own couch, had squeezed them in anyway. The result was that you couldn't walk three paces without banging into something. When he found himself squatting in pain after stubbing his toe on a table leg, Ryuhei would tell himself that he needed to be a better provider. But now even this modest home was being taken away from them. It seemed unlikely that either the dining table or the sofa would fit into their new apartment.

He turned his gaze back to Harue.

Sorry.

He only mouthed the word, but Harue understood. She smiled sadly back at him.

"It is what it is," she murmured in a barely audible voice, which made him look away again. If anything, this sort of telepathy between the two of them was more painful than if they had to spell it all out with words.

"So, we're giving up on the cat idea, right?" said Harue. Ryuhei nodded vaguely. "I mean," she went on, "it's not like

Miyuki or Yota actually wanted one that badly. And if they did get attached, it would just make it harder to return it."

Ryuhei looked up at the ceiling in silence. Directly above this room was Miyuki's, and next door to it was Yota's. It was way past their bedtime, though whether they were actually asleep was another matter. Recently they'd been arriving at breakfast with bleary-eyed faces.

"Do you think Miyuki's already told her friends?" he asked.

"Yeah. The close ones."

"Did she just tell them that she's moving schools?"

"Not sure. But knowing her, I doubt she's told anyone the whole story."

Unlike her happy-go-lucky brother, Miyuki was competitive, proud, strong-willed. In her first year of middle school, her stubbornness had got her into a spot of trouble with some bullies. Ryuhei really couldn't imagine her turning to her friends and telling them her dad had been laid off, or that they had to sell their house because they couldn't keep up the payments on the mortgage.

"Do you think she holds it against me?"

"Why would she? Like I said, it is what it is."

"She must think I'm a pretty useless dad, though."

This time, Harue didn't reply. Ryuhei sensed that pressing her would only invite some stinging retort, and so he too went quiet.

The windows rattled in the night wind. The house was a cheap, built-to-order structure. Five or six years after they'd moved in, the fittings had suddenly begun to deteriorate.

"Yota was crying earlier," murmured Harue. "Before you got home. He really doesn't want to move schools. Said he didn't want to leave his friends. That he'd been really looking forward to their school trip next year."

The windows rattled again. The wind was picking up.

It was the end of autumn. The end, maybe, of the happiness they'd spent so many years trying to build and protect.

Now the wind howled.

To Ryuhei, it sounded oddly like the angry mewling of a cat.

The next morning, he headed into town to visit the job centre. He browsed through the list of vacancies on the computer, but found almost nothing that matched his profile. The few positions that did appear were hardly tempting in terms of location or pay.

Out of curiosity, he tried adjusting the age setting to 20–29. Of course, the number of vacancies increased dramatically, but that only left him feeling more dejected.

If I'd only known, he thought. It was something he found himself thinking a lot these days.

If he'd only known, he would have changed jobs when he was still young – back during the bubble era, when the country was strong on its feet.

He'd made the mistake of thinking they were getting their house cheap. But if they'd waited another three years, it would have been a lot cheaper. In fact, all things considered, they'd have been better off just staying in the comfortable rented apartment they'd lived in before. That way, they could have postponed moving until they'd put Miyuki, at least, through high school – even if it meant eating through the severance package to pay the rent.

It wasn't like he'd committed some terrible blunder at work. Sure, he wasn't a hotshot working wonders for the company, but he'd never let his boss and colleagues down and had been climbing the ranks at a decent pace. He'd been on good terms with clients and subordinates alike, and smoothly carried out the tasks assigned to him.

And yet they'd cut him loose.

They'd called it a "painful decision", one that it "broke their hearts" to make. What they really meant was that, for the company to survive, several employees were going to be ditched like so much dead weight.

Why me?

What did I do wrong?

A few nights ago, he'd dreamed he was grabbing the HR manager by the lapels and shouting these very questions at him. He'd really laid into the guy, screaming himself hoarse.

Screaming – and sobbing.

He didn't linger at the job centre. It wasn't like vacancies were going to start popping up while he waited.

In the afternoon he met up with an old university friend. The friend worked for a large corporation, one less vulnerable to economic headwinds. From the moment he walked into the café he seemed to be on his guard. He nodded along as Ryuhei gave him a rundown of the situation, but his eyes kept darting around restlessly.

Does he think I'm going to try to tap him for money? I haven't fallen that far yet.

A bit of help landing a new job. That was all he wanted.

"I don't suppose you've heard of anything?" he asked with a grin once he'd finished explaining. "Your place has plenty of subsidiaries, doesn't it? Or sub-subsidiaries. I'll go anywhere, do anything, you know?"

His friend sipped his coffee in silence.

Ryuhei counted to five in his head.

His friend still hadn't said anything.

". . . Don't worry." Ryuhei looked out the window and recrossed his legs. "I'm just kidding."

His friend set his cup down on the saucer, his features finally relaxing. "It's pretty tough going for us these days too."

"Seriously? But you're listed."

"Sure, the company is. But the way we're treated it might as well be a microbusiness. We're basically subcontractors."

". . . Right."

"Looks like they're going to switch me out into the sticks in the spring too."

"Really?"

"Yeah. They weren't too impressed with my performance this autumn, so I think my days at head office are numbered. There's the kids and school to think about, so I'll probably have to leave the family behind. Move out there on my own."

"How long would you be stuck there? Two, three years?"

His friend shook his head. "Five at the least. Five years of living away from my wife and kids. And that's if I'm lucky. If

I mess up they might keep me out there for good. I'll be stuck in the middle of nowhere until retirement."

Better than being let go completely, though, isn't it?

Ryuhei let the words form quietly in his mind, then swilled them back down with his coffee.

His friend's mobile went off, bringing their conversation to a close. Ryuhei's own phone hadn't made a sound all day. In the month since his dismissal, he'd practically stopped using it. If he didn't find a new job soon and money got even tighter, he was going to cancel his contract. His own little version of ditching the dead weight.

When it came to the bill, his friend tried to pay for both of them. Ryuhei stopped him and dropped a five-hundred-yen coin into the tray by the till.

His friend looked at him as if to say, *You sure about that?* In that brief moment, his face seemed to fill with a mix of concern, sympathy – and pity.

Ryuhei took the change, then walked out of the café ahead of his friend.

"Hang in there, okay? . . . And look after yourself," he heard his friend say from behind him as he made his way to the metro station. But he didn't turn around.

He jumped on a train home from Shinjuku just before the evening rush hour kicked in. He opted for the slowest of the local trains and found it pleasantly empty. He had nothing left to do in Shinjuku, and nothing to do at home once he got there either.

All those days of riding the rush-hour trains, so jam-packed you couldn't even use the hanging straps. What had it all been for?

Those days of pounding the pavement, of sweating so much his shirts turned see-through, of drinking himself sick just to keep his clients happy, of forcing smiles, stroking egos, conjuring apologies, unruffling feathers, skipping lunch, giving up Sundays, flicking through gift catalogues with his calculator, the nerves, the anxiety, the endless hustle and bustle, the sheer exhaustion of it all . . . After all that, what had he actually gained? What was there for him to keep?

In the windows of the train, he saw his children's faces. Harue's too.

I want a cat. That was what Miyuki and Yota had told him.

When they'd bought their current house, even the specifications on the advert had made it sound quite cramped. Then they'd gone for a viewing, and it had turned out to be even smaller than they'd expected. Once they'd moved in and began filling the house with their things, it only seemed to get smaller and smaller.

He still remembered Miyuki's face on the day of the viewing, when she'd seen their new house for the first time.

She'd only been three at the time, and had probably been expecting something like one of the castles in her picture books. She'd taken one look at it and declared, "It's tiny," eliciting an awkward grin from the estate agent.

He wasn't asking for much. All he wanted, while they were still living at the house, was to make just one of his kids' dreams come true.

He imagined the looks on their faces when he turned up with the cat. Wide-eyed with surprise, gasping with delight. That's what he wanted to see.

Surely he was allowed that, if nothing else?

2

"Got you a little present," he said as he walked into the living room.

He held up the carrier for them to see. Just then, a soft *miaow* came from the cat curled up on a blanket inside.

Yota was the first to turn around.

"What is it?"

It seemed the noise from the television had drowned out the sound made by the cat.

"Take a guess," said Ryuhei, still standing in the doorway with a half-suppressed grin. Harue was staring at him as if to say, *Did you really have to*, but he pretended not to see.

"What, so the present is inside that basket thing?"

"It's called a carrier, and yes."

"Oh. So, what is it?"

"Like I said, I want you to guess."

"You want me to guess?"

He hated to say this about his own son, but Yota could be a little slow on the uptake. The nice way of putting it was that he was a laid-back, good-natured kid. The harsh way of putting it was that he was, well, dopey. A personality like that probably came in handy when you were trying to process the fact that your father had lost his job and you were being forced out of your home.

"Give me a clue, Dad."

"Alright, here's the first clue. It's something you two really wanted."

At this, Yota turned excitedly to his sister. "Miyuki! It's for you too!"

But Miyuki's eyes were glued to the television. Just like they had been the whole time.

Ryuhei felt something sinking inside him. Still, he summoned up a smile and called out, "What do you think it is, Miyuki?"

"Who knows," she said abruptly, without so much as a glance in his direction.

Instead, it was Harue who shot him a look, shaking her head as if to say, *Let it go. You'll only make things worse.*

His felt that sinking feeling again. Miyuki had been moody enough the night before, but this evening she seemed to be in an even fouler frame of mind. Had something happened at school?

If Yota was like a steering wheel with too much play in it, Miyuki was the complete opposite. The nice way of putting it was that she was sharp. Independently minded. The harsh way of putting it was that she was a stubborn kid who demanded too much from everyone, including herself. What would someone like that make of a father who'd failed to hold on to his job and home? Just thinking about it gave him the shivers – which was why he'd been doing his best not to.

"Go on," he said to Yota. "Take a stab."

"What's the second clue?"

"Err . . . Alright, I'll give you a super special clue because I'm nice. It's an animal."

"An animal?"

"Yeah. A real live animal. The one you and Miyuki kept saying you wanted. I've basically given it away now."

He glanced at Miyuki, desperate for her to join in. Though, given how pathetic he must have looked, it was probably a good thing she didn't look over just then.

"Hmm . . ." said Yota, crossing his arms to think. "And it's in the basket right now?"

"That's right."

"What noise does it make?"

"Come on," Ryuhei said with an incredulous chuckle, "that really *would* be giving it away." Inside, though, he was beginning to feel disappointed. Shouldn't that hint about them wanting one have done the trick? Was this how little it meant for kids to want something these days?

"A baby spotted turtle! Wait, no . . . they live in water."

"Since when have you wanted a turtle?"

"I saw one on TV the other day. They're so cool."

Ryuhei felt his disappointment curdling into despair.

If he let that despair turn into anger, he'd probably lose sight of the reason he'd rented the cat in the first place. Better to just get this over with, he thought.

"Yota . . ."

"Yeah?"

"Don't you want a cat anymore?"

"Sure I do. Cats are fun."

"Right. So you *do* want one."

"Yeah, I guess," said Yota nonchalantly. "Like, if spotted turtles are number one, cats would be like, fourth or fifth? Anyway," he went on, as if impatient to get back to the matter at hand, "come on, Dad, tell us what it is. What's the next clue?"

Yeah, Yota was a dopey kid alright. Still, at least he was playing along. Right now, that was all Ryuhei had to cling to.

"Alright, alright. Come have a look."

He opened the carrier's hatch and retrieved the cat.

A Russian Blue, its glossy grey coat almost shimmering.

"Wow!" exclaimed Yota, scrabbling over to get a closer look. "Can I hold it? Let me hold it!"

The grin on his son's face was a little idiotic, yes, but it was also carefree. There was something soothing about his cheerful approach to life, his almost infantile innocence.

Soothing. Ryuhei had always found the word a little annoying. But it was the only one he could think of to describe the faint warmth that had stirred in his chest recently whenever he saw Yota smile – as though he were sinking into a pleasantly lukewarm bath and letting out a deep sigh.

Yota took the cat awkwardly, barely managing to contain it in his arms. Just as the man at the pet shop had said, it didn't seem to mind this in the slightest, and patiently let itself be held.

"Well then," teased Ryuhei. "Still rather it was a turtle?"

"No way!" said Yota, predictably unembarrassed by this sudden change of opinion. "Cats are number one!"

Ryuhei grinned back at him. "Told you."

Miyuki still hadn't looked over. The television was on an ad break, and she hadn't so much as turned her head. Ryuhei, for his part, was doing his best not to look at her as he smiled.

Harue got up from the sofa and walked towards the kitchen.

"Mum, look!"

"Later, Yota. I have to heat your father's dinner up."

"I really don't think this is a good idea," said Harue, once the children had gone up to their rooms.

"Oh, it'll be fine." Ryuhei lay down on the sofa and gazed vacantly up at the ceiling. It was almost eleven, and yet noises were still coming from Yota's room.

He was playing with the cat – or Meowth, as he'd decided to call it. Apparently it was the name of a Pokémon, a cat-like creature on the rival team that followed Pikachu and friends around. Ryuhei didn't quite see why the cat had to be named after one of the bad guys, but in any case, Yota had taken Meowth off to his room, insisting that the cat would sleep there.

From the sound of things, though, he wasn't planning on going to bed any time soon. Probably not ideal for the cat, but it *was* Saturday tomorrow. Best to let him have his way, Ryuhei thought.

"But you have to take it back in a couple of days, don't you? Yota'll get attached, and it'll all end in tears."

"It's fine, really. I've told him what the deal is. He gets it."

When he'd explained that the cat was a rental, Yota had pulled a face. "What? We don't get to keep it?" But when Ryuhei had suggested that three days was better than nothing at all, he'd seemed convinced. There was also the fact that they wouldn't even be allowed a cat in their next apartment, but it seemed unlikely Yota had been thinking that far ahead.

"It'll be one of our last memories of this place," Ryuhei went on. "I thought I could take a bunch of photos and videos tomorrow."

That reminds me, he thought, I need to charge the camera batteries. But as he got up to do so, Harue's voice came at him like a right hook out of nowhere.

"Who's this all for, though?"

"What?"

"These memories. Who are they for?"

Isn't that obvious, he wanted to reply. But then came her next jab.

"They're for you, aren't they?"

"What – no! Yota and Miyuki said they wanted a cat, so I thought I could . . . you know . . . seeing as it's our last chance and everything . . ."

"Well, did Miyuki seem happy to you?"

And there was the uppercut.

He didn't know what to say. It was true that Miyuki had retreated upstairs without a word – in fact, without even a glance.

"And when you take the cat back in a couple of days, do you think Yota's going to be happy? You think he's going to turn around and say, *Gosh, Dad, thanks for all these wonderful memories?*"

Again, Ryuhei was lost for words.

"You know what I think?" she went on sharply. "I think memories aren't something you can just magic out of thin air. Telling them they'd better make some happy ones while they still can . . . It's not our business what they choose to remember, Ryuhei! We wanted a cat, but we couldn't have one – isn't that enough? Isn't that a memory too?"

"But we want to make their dreams come true, don't we? As their parents, I mean."

"Sure. And if we could actually get them a cat, maybe we would have. But *renting* one? I don't think that counts."

"I know, but . . ."

"In fact, it's worse than not getting one at all. I hate to say it, but I can't help thinking you're just trying to make yourself feel better about all this."

He didn't hear her words so much as feel them pierce his chest.

There were things he could have said back. But by now something hard and heavy had lodged itself somewhere between his chest and his throat, and Ryuhei found himself unable to speak.

"The estate agent called earlier," Harue said. "About the valuation on the house."

"Well?" he asked. "What did he think? Can we get twenty-two for it?"

"He said no-one would ever buy it for that much."

". . . Then what was the valuation?"

"He said even eighteen was unrealistic."

"Well," said Ryuhei, an edge coming into his voice, "then what does he think we should be asking?"

Calmly, as if absorbing his exasperation, Harue told Ryuhei

the estimated value of the little kingdom he had fought so hard to build and protect.

"He said if we ask for fifteen, we might just about get someone coming in at thirteen . . . And that if we're okay with going down to twelve, that would probably help."

His kingdom in tatters, and nothing to be done.

"Well, what do you think? Should we ask around, try someone else?"

Ryuhei thought about nodding, then shook his head. "They'll probably just tell us the same thing."

"Yeah. Probably."

"We won't be able to pay off the mortgage."

"I can work something out."

"With your dad, you mean?"

"Yeah. What else are we going to do?"

"Oh, I don't know. Stick it out until they send someone to seize the place."

He was only half joking. Without an income, the mortgage payments would be crushing. Maybe he could just stop making them until the bank was forced to take drastic measures . . .

"Let's *not* do that," Harue said with a sad smile. "Can you imagine how Miyuki would take it?"

She went on to explain why their daughter had been in such a bad mood that evening.

One of her classmates, who she'd never gotten on well with anyway, had apparently told her, "I heard your parents are so in debt they're planning on doing a runner."

Ryuhei clamped his eyes shut, stifling the groan that threatened in his throat.

Renting a cat to create some final, happy memories – now that he thought about it, that did sound a lot like a desperate father trying to make himself feel better about things.

Even if they managed three days of bliss, he thought, there was no way that Miyuki and Yota would ever look back on their time in this house with anything but sadness.

When he knocked on the door, a sleepy "Yeah?" came from inside.

"It's your dad. Can I come in?"

"Sure." Yota opened the door and, yawning and smiling, said, "I was just dozing on the floor."

"Try your bed next time. You'll catch a cold."

"Okay . . ."

"How's the cat?"

"Asleep already. Look." Yota pointed at the carrier on the floor. Meowth was curled up in his blanket, fast asleep.

"It's just like you said, Dad. As long as he has the blanket, he can sleep anywhere."

"Yeah. But it has to be *that* blanket. They're trained up like that from when they're kittens." Ryuhei was repeating what he'd been told at the pet shop.

"What, so no other blanket will do?"

"Yeah. They told me if there's one thing we shouldn't do, it's lose the blanket."

It was a simple, beige affair, the kind you could find at any bedding shop. He felt a sudden wave of pity for these rental cats, travelling from home to home with only their blanket for comfort. Then he felt the pity morph into envy.

I wish we had something like that, he thought with an inward sigh. A blanket to soothe us to sleep, wherever we find ourselves.

3

The next morning was a sunny one.

Perfect weather for a photoshoot. If they *were* going to make memories – and at this point, Ryuhei thought they might as well give it a shot – what better stage than a house bathed in sunshine?

Alternating between his digital camera and camcorder, Ryuhei set about creating a record of their brief life as a cat-owning family. Meowth curled up on the stairs, Meowth trotting down the hall, Meowth hiding under the dining table, Meowth on the balcony, Meowth in the wardrobe, Meowth in the bathroom . . .

"Do you think he used to be a model or something?" asked Yota admiringly.

"I wouldn't be surprised," nodded Ryuhei. Wherever they took him, he obliged them with the exact poses they'd been hoping for. He really was a good-natured cat – and sharp-witted too.

"He was so calm last night too," said Yota. "He looked really cute all curled up in the blanket."

"He slept well, I bet?"

"Yeah."

"And you stayed up all night watching him?"

"Yep." Yota grinned sheepishly, then gave a gaping yawn.

I don't know about sharp-witted, Ryuhei thought, but I do have a pretty good-natured son.

"Hey, Dad, shall we take some photos with him outside? We could go for a walk or something."

"Sounds fun. But how about staying inside for now?"

Before the house slipped from their grasp, he wanted to furnish it with as many memories as he could. Whatever Harue might say – that he was just meddling or trying to make himself feel better about things – surely it was his duty, as a parent, to ensure that a few years or decades down the line, his kids could flick through their photo albums with a smile and say to themselves, *Oh yeah, I remember that.*

He went up to Yota's room, where he took a few more photos and filmed the two of them playing together.

Yota had already posed for plenty of pictures with Meowth – more than enough, in fact.

But what about Harue and Miyuki? Harue had set about sorting through the kitchen ahead of their move, and when Ryuhei turned the camera on her she just glared at him. *Don't film me tidying up.* Miyuki, meanwhile, had shovelled down her breakfast before retreating to her room. On her door she'd hung a sign that said: STUDYING! KEEP OUT.

Still, even if they didn't see the sense in it right away, he felt sure they'd thank him for it one day. If he gave up now, they'd be left with nothing but the sad reality that he, the man of the house, had been laid off and forced to sell their home.

"Right, I'm going to take a break. Have a think about where

else you want to take photos and I'll come and get you in a bit, alright?"

He left Yota playing with Meowth in his room and went downstairs.

Harue was sitting on the kitchen floor, sorting through the pots, pans, dishes and storage shelves in the cupboard below the sink, deciding what to take to their new apartment and what to discard.

"When you go through everything like this," she said with a sad chuckle when he walked in, "you realise how much of it we don't actually need." She didn't turn around.

"Harue . . . just one photo. That's all I'm asking."

"What will that achieve?

"Well, the cat's here and everything, and once we really start packing up, this place won't look the same anymore. I just feel like we need some more evidence of our life here . . ."

"I don't think we do, Ryuhei."

"Well, I do. If we don't make an effort, we won't have anything to remember this place by."

"Yeah. And I'm saying I don't think that's something we need to do."

Their conversation was turning in circles again. This time, though, Ryuhei sat down on the floor next to her, sighed, and managed to say the words he'd been unable to get out the night before.

"Do you remember that TV show, *Album on the Shore*? Taichi Yamada wrote the script. You know, with Naoki Sugiura, and Kaoru Yachigusa, and . . . that's right, Tomiyuki Kunihiro."

"Yeah. I think I caught the re-run. Where their house gets washed away in a flood?"

"That's the one. Do you remember the last scene?"

"Doesn't it end with the flood?"

"Sure, it ends with the flood. But . . . there's this family album that survives."

Even before the flood, the family had been falling apart, its members growing increasingly distant from one another. And then their house, symbolic of the modest happiness they *had* shared together, had been destroyed forever.

But still, they had their album.

The drama didn't show what happened to the family afterwards.

"I like to think they managed a fresh start somehow. I reckon it's the same with us. As long as we have something to remember our life here by, we'll get through this together. We'll make a fresh start."

Harue didn't reply. But her hands, which had been sorting through a set of tableware they'd been given at someone's wedding, had stopped moving.

"You know how I'm the younger son," he said abruptly.

". . . I thought we were talking about memories."

"We are. See, because I was born second, there are way less photos of me as a kid. There are two whole albums of my brother before he even started school, and just one of me all the way up to the end of it."

"Yeah. I guess that's how these things go."

"Sure, and I'm not, like, sour or jealous about it. But you know how I'm always saying I don't really remember my childhood? I think that's why. If you have photos, you can remind yourself that such-and-such happened. But I don't, which is why I barely remember anything. I just think it's sort of . . . sad . . ."

Someday – it didn't have to be anytime soon – he wanted them to sit around, gazing at an album or a video, looking back fondly on the time they'd had a cat in the house. They'd smile and say, *Those were tough times, huh?* And then their smiles would widen. *But everything worked out in the end.*

Ryuhei waited in silence for Harue to reply. But their conversation had fizzled out.

She began wordlessly sorting through the tableware again, without even a glance in his direction.

"Harue . . .?"

"Sorry, but there's a lot to get done today. The junk collectors are coming first thing in the afternoon."

"One photo. That's all I'm asking. If you agree, Miyuki might change her mind too."

Harue let out a deep sigh. "What, so you can pretend we've always been happy here? Just stop it, Ryuhei. You're only making this harder."

And here they were again, back where they'd been the previous evening. Ryuhei clicked his tongue and sighed.

"I know you don't want to hear this," Harue went on, "but aren't there more important things you could be doing? If you want to put a smile on my face, or Miyuki's, then you could actually act like you're serious about getting a new job, for one thing."

"The job centre's closed today."

"I thought it was open on Saturdays?"

". . . I'm not sure."

"Anyway, seeing as it's the weekend, won't your friends be at home? If it was me, I'd be going door-to-door asking for leads."

Ryuhei thought about the friend he'd met up with the previous day. The blend of wariness, repugnance and pity on his face. The supercilious smile. It was an expression that came back to him more vividly now than perhaps it had ever appeared in reality.

"You know, I never asked to be laid off," he said, an edge coming into his voice.

"Well, no," replied Harue, still facing away from him, also bristling. "Of course you didn't."

Ryuhei got to his feet, feeling his temper about to flare.

Then the phone rang.

It was the estate agent. Someone was interested in the house.

"He says they want to come for a viewing now," Harue said, so bewildered she forgot to press the hold button or cover the mouthpiece.

The potential buyers had been in the neighbourhood to view a different property, which they'd decided against. As they were leaving, the agent had mentioned that there was another house nearby he'd just valued the day before.

"What shall we do?" asked Harue. "We haven't signed a contract with the agent yet or anything, so it's not like we have to. He's just asking if we'd consider it seeing as they're already in the area . . ."

"But we haven't tidied up or anything."

"He says that's fine. They're planning on renovating, so they just want to see the layout and how much sunlight the place gets."

Never mind tidying up, thought Ryuhei. Are we really ready for this mentally?

If the buyer liked the house and agreed on a decent price, that would be it. Their home wrenched away for good. But wasn't that what they wanted? If they let this chance slip by, there was no guarantee there would even *be* another viewing.

"Alright," he said. "Let's do it."

Harue nodded. "Yeah. It's for the best."

She looked vaguely distraught. So must I, thought Ryuhei.

Maybe this was how they were going to say goodbye to their house. Without any fanfare, or even a flood to sweep it away – just the arrival, in thirty minutes' time, of the estate agent's little van.

And with their photo album still a work in progress.

"What about the cat?" asked Harue.

"What?"

"We haven't told the estate agent we have a cat. And they say houses with pets attract fewer buyers."

"Shall we take him outside, then?"

"What if he runs away?"

"Yota can take him."

"No, that's too dangerous. What if the cat runs off and Yota chases it and gets hit by a car or something?"

"I could go with him."

"What? No, we're the sellers. We both need to be here."

It was beginning to look like there was only one solution.

Harue glanced up at the ceiling. "I might as well ask her, I guess," she said, more to herself than to Ryuhei. "Though I'm pretty sure she'll say no." And she went up to Miyuki's room.

Please . . . Ryuhei stared up at the ceiling, praying that she'd agree to take the cat out. This wasn't just about Meowth. He'd prefer it if both Yota and Miyuki were out of the house. He wanted to spare them the sight of these strangers ruthlessly sizing up their home – and of Ryuhei and Harue smiling meekly as they did so. If she insists on staying in her room, I'll just have to explain the situation to her myself, he decided.

He heard footsteps coming down the stairs. The conversation had ended sooner than he'd expected.

"Well?"

"She's just getting changed. Yota's putting the cat in the carrier."

"Oh. Right . . ."

"She said she doesn't want to see their faces anyway."

Ryuhei nodded in silence – though it was really more of a downcast hanging of the head.

He and Miyuki hadn't seen eye to eye about much recently. Now, it seemed, they'd finally found something they could agree on.

The potential buyers turned out to be a family of four. The parents looked to be in their forties, like Ryuhei and Harue, while the children – an older sister and younger brother – must have been around the same age as Miyuki and Yota. In other words, a family that was nearly identical to theirs had come to snatch their house away from them.

I really am glad Miyuki isn't here to see this, Ryuhei thought. The other family began walking around, inspecting every corner of their home even more brazenly than he'd expected.

"It's not quite how I imagined it," said the daughter, who seemed to Ryuhei to be a self-absorbed, nasty little girl. The son, by now bouncing around on the sofa in the living room, was chubby and spoiled-looking.

Of course, the parents made no attempt to curb his rude behaviour. They were too busy tapping surfaces, running their fingers over the various scars on the walls, murmuring to each other.

He couldn't hear what they were saying, but it was clear from the wife's expression, and the way she kept cocking her head, that they weren't impressed.

"You have to take a bus from the station, right?" the husband asked Harue.

She nodded. "It's five minutes, and—"

"You can actually walk it in ten," said Ryuhei, cutting her off.

"The garden looks a bit gloomy. Kind of . . . damp," said the wife. "Does it get much sunlight?"

"Oh, plenty," Ryuhei replied. "In the morning. We just had the sprinkler on earlier."

This really is pathetic, he thought. But every extra yen he could add to the price would help – though first he had to persuade them to actually buy the place. This, he thought, was his final duty as the house's owner.

The daughter elbowed her mother and jerked her chin in the direction of the stairs.

"Could you show us upstairs?" asked the mother. "She's dying to know what her room would be like."

Once again, Ryuhei breathed a sigh of relief that Miyuki wasn't here to see this.

They all went upstairs. When the daughter saw the STUDYING sign Miyuki had hung on the door, she laughed and muttered, "Lame."

Ryuhei felt like slapping her on the back of the head, but he restrained himself.

The girl carelessly flung the door open. At his side, he could feel Harue struggling to contain herself.

But as they stepped into the room, their expressions froze.

The wall by the bed was covered in thick felt-tip scrawl:

A CURSE ON WHOEVER BUYS THIS HOUSE!

4

The family left in a huff.

"'Selling your house isn't something you do every day," the estate agent said as he was leaving. "Maybe you need to sit down with the kids again – you know, really talk things through?" He'd mustered a salesman-like smile, but what he was really telling them was *I don't think I can help you.*

When the front door closed, Harue sank onto the step just inside the entrance. It seemed all the exhaustion of the viewing, all the fake smiling and friendliness, had suddenly caught up with her.

"What a disaster," she murmured weakly, a faint smile on her face.

"We'll never get that writing off." Ryuhei's voice seemed strangely hollow, his words hanging pathetically in the air. "We'll have to repaper the wall."

Another blow to their bank account. But more than money, what bothered Ryuhei was the sadness and frustration that must have driven Miyuki to write those words. It didn't even bear thinking about.

"What should we do?" asked Harue.

"What do you mean?"

Harue paused. "Never mind."

"We have to sell. You know that."

"Of course I do!"

"Whatever Miyuki might say. We don't have a choice."

"I know, Ryuhei. I get it."

"We'll find another estate agent."

Harue gave no reply.

"It'll cost a fortune to get someone in for the wallpaper," he went on. "I'll do it myself. I can pick some up at the hardware shop."

But Harue remained silent.

Ryuhei sighed and went back into the living room.

They heard a truck pull up, followed by the *beep-beep* of it reversing.

The junk collectors had arrived.

Harue rose lethargically to her feet with another weak smile. "What with all the fuss, I barely got any sorting done in the end."

And yet Harue seemed confident enough as she gave instructions to the junk collectors, telling them to remove this or that from the kitchen. Even after they'd worked through the pile she'd accumulated in the morning, she began handing them things straight from the cupboards. She seemed to be growing a little reckless.

Never mind, Ryuhei thought. However frustrating this might all feel, there was a limit to how much they could fit in their new place. They would never be able to take *all* their memories with them.

Harue asked the collectors to come back the next day too. "You can go through the storage cupboard in the living room. Oh, and . . ." She turned to Ryuhei. "They can take the sofa too, right?"

He hesitated.

It would still be a while before they moved. And if they really tried, surely they could squeeze it into their new place somehow? No, that would never work.

He nodded silently.

"Right then," said Harue with unnerving readiness. "The sofa tomorrow too, please," she told one of the workmen.

"Tomorrow – you sure?" asked the man.

"What do you mean?"

"We can take it today if you like. There's still room in the truck."

"Really?"

"Yeah, no problem. It's not that big. We can take the coffee table too, if you like." He seemed ready to haul the sofa away the moment they gave him the word.

Harue glanced at Ryuhei, but he looked evasively away.

He'd let her make the decision – if only because he was too scared to make it himself.

"What do you think?" pressed the man.

Harue turned back to him. "Sorry. I think it'll have to be tomorrow . . . Actually, let me get back to you on whether we need you over tomorrow at all. I'll call you, okay?" Apologising again, she bowed deeply in the man's direction.

"Oh, er, sure," said the man, bewildered by her excessive politeness. "It's fine with us either way."

From outside the front door came Yota's voice. "Do you think the other family's gone now?"

He was talking to Miyuki.

"Yeah, I reckon. I mean, that can't be their truck."

"Do you think Mum and Dad sold the house?"

"How would I know?"

"We're in trouble if they don't, right?"

"Who cares? Ugh – you can be so annoying sometimes . . ."

After that, the junk collectors finished their work in silence. Harue and Ryuhei did their best to avoid looking at each other. When Miyuki walked into the living room, they didn't say a word to her.

*

Of course, Meowth had no way of knowing what had been discussed in his absence, but the sofa appeared to be swiftly becoming his favourite spot.

"Don't you think it's weird?" said Yota. "He only got here yesterday, but it's like he's lived with us for years. He's so relaxed around the house."

He had a point. There was something weirdly familiar about the sight of Meowth stretched out on the sofa. Like he'd always been there. Like they might open up their old photo albums and find his face among their faded images.

I must be losing it, Ryuhei thought with a wry smile as he gazed vacantly up at the ceiling.

Harue was up in Miyuki's room and had been there a while. They were having a long conversation. Ryuhei knew what it was about, which was why he was trying not to think about it.

"Hey, Dad," said Yota.

"Yeah?"

"Miyuki said this thing to me earlier."

"What did she say?"

"She said it's Meowth's job to stay at lots of people's houses, so he'll forget all about us. Like, right away. Is that true?"

Well, it probably wasn't *untrue,* thought Ryuhei. Still, he wished Miyuki hadn't said it.

"Oh, you never know," he replied, forcing a grin. "I mean, cats are clever animals, and only the cleverest ones get to become Blanket Cats. So yeah. I think he'll remember."

"Really?"

"Yeah. I reckon."

"But Miyuki also said that when you're clever, you get better at forgetting stuff."

Apparently she'd told Yota a person's mind was like a rice bowl. You couldn't just keep filling it with memories. Unless you forgot things too, there was no room for the new ones and they'd all spill out.

"She said the really clever kids don't just know how to remember stuff. They're good at forgetting too."

"Right . . ."

"And stupid kids remember lots of pointless stuff, which is why they have no space left to remember the important things."

"That's . . . true, I guess."

"She said she's going to forget all about this place."

Ryuhei had the sensation of something cold trickling down his spine.

"And that she won't remember the new apartment either."

Now the back of his throat seemed to contract. He could hardly breathe.

"And – well, you know how I'm not very good at school? She said it's because I remember too much, and if I keep thinking about this house or the next one I won't be able to remember anything important, and life will be really hard for me."

Yota spoke casually, as if all this were someone else's problem. It wasn't clear if he'd really grasped what Miyuki had been trying to tell him.

Right now, that was probably a good thing.

"Don't worry about forgetting things," said Ryuhei, reaching for the digital camera on the table. "We'll take plenty of photos to help you remember."

"I won't forget," said Yota sullenly.

Ryuhei chuckled. "I bet you won't." And he set the camera back down on the table.

As a parent, not being able to give his kids memories they could cherish made him sad. It frustrated him. Infuriated him.

But there was something else on his mind, something that came to him now in his capacity as an adult, albeit a sorry excuse for one. As someone who'd been around a little longer than his kids had.

It was this: that trying only to remember the good stuff smacked of wishful thinking.

He reached for the camera again, but this time he turned the lens on himself. He looked at his face on the liquid-crystal flip screen. He wasn't smiling. That couldn't be helped. That was a memory too, he thought – not being able to smile. And he pressed the shutter.

Yota had gone up to his room, cradling Meowth in his arms. But that evening, just before ten o'clock, he came running back into the living room, his face pale.

"Dad! Mum! Help . . ." He was on the brink of tears. "His blanket's gone. I tried to put him to bed, but when I opened the carrier it wasn't there. And then Meowth saw it was gone and got all panicked and started running around and scratching me and stuff . . ."

Yota had scratch marks on his arms and the backs of his hands.

"Well, you took him out this afternoon, didn't you?" said Harue. "Did you take the blanket out of the carrier then?"

"No, no," said Yota, shaking his head over and over.

"Then it must be somewhere."

"But it's not!"

"Was it in the carrier the whole time?"

"Of course!"

"And you didn't take it out when you got home?" Ryuhei asked.

"Dad, I'm telling you, I haven't even touched the carrier!"

Ryuhei and Harue glanced at each other.

They could think of only one explanation.

"Wait here," said Ryuhei to Yota. But as he got up to leave, Harue stopped him.

"I'll go."

"Alright, let's both go," said Ryuhei.

"You stay here. Help Yota with those scratches."

"But—"

"You'll only make her more upset."

There wasn't much he could say to that.

"I'll manage," Harue said emphatically as she made for the door. But just then they heard footsteps coming down the stairs.

Harue stopped in her tracks. Ryuhei froze too.

Miyuki appeared in the doorway.

"Is this about that blanket?" she said coolly, her face and voice bristling with defiance.

"So you know what happened?" asked Harue.

Miyuki nodded casually, as if to say, *Oh yeah*. Then, with an even more nonchalant smile: "I threw it away."

"You . . . threw it away? Where?"

"The park. You know that wood at the back? Just sort of chucked it in there. Whoops."

She giggled. It wasn't just that she was refusing to apologise – she seemed to be deliberately trying to provoke a reaction.

Ryuhei took a deep breath, trying to control his emotions. "Why would you do a thing like that, Miyuki?"

"Well, it stank."

"That's . . . the cat's smell," he replied. "I told you when we got him, didn't I? That he'd get upset if he didn't have his blanket."

"Who cares if he gets upset?"

". . . Miyuki, do you hear yourself?"

"I'm just saying maybe he should try getting through life without his stupid blanket."

"*Miyuki!*"

"Hey, calm down," Harue said to him. But he couldn't stop himself.

"If you're upset about moving house, I get it. If you want to hate your dad, well, fine. But taking it out on the cat just because he's weaker than you, well, that's just not fair."

"But that's what *you're* doing!"

". . . What?"

"You got fired because you were no good at your job, and now we have to sell the house. You think that's 'fair' on me and Yota? And then you go and rent a cat. Like that's going to help!"

Ryuhei was dumbstruck. But Miyuki wasn't done yet.

"You're our dad, so start acting like one. Stop making us live with your failure!"

He turned his gaze downwards, biting his lip, feeling all his frustration and anger turn on himself, on his inability to even manage a reply.

"What's the point in renting a cat? You only did it to make yourself feel better. Don't go patting yourself on the back, Dad – that's not good parenting!"

Then there was a dry *clap*, and Miyuki fell silent.

Harue had slapped her across the cheek.

"Just *stop*, Miyuki."

"Isn't he the one you should be slapping, Mum? Go on, why don't you? I'm the victim here."

Harue slapped her again, harder.

This time, Miyuki didn't say anything back. Her eyes had opened wide. She put a hand to her cheek and stared at Harue.

Harue let her own hand drop to her side. She sighed, all the tension going out of her shoulders. "We don't have a choice, Miyuki," she said in a calm voice. "We're a family. This is how it is."

Neither Miyuki nor Ryuhei had seen this coming. Miyuki still hadn't said anything.

"It's just how it is," repeated Harue.

"Whatever," said Miyuki, looking to one side. But glancing at her face in profile, Ryuhei had the impression that something had eased within her.

"You wanted to see what that cat would do without its blanket, didn't you?" asked Harue.

". . . No."

"Well, your mother does."

Miyuki turned her gaze back to Harue.

"Yep," she went on, nodding in agreement with herself. "What will Meowth do when he loses his precious blanket? It's an intriguing question, I'll give you that."

Miyuki didn't reply. But Ryuhei detected a sort of tacit understanding in her gaze.

"The thing is," continued Harue, "I think all that'll happen is he'll get upset. Really upset."

". . . You think?" asked Miyuki.

"Yep. That's where cats and humans differ."

"What's that supposed to mean?"

"When a cat loses something precious, all it can do is get upset. But when *we* lose something precious, we get to keep the memory of it. And then we find something new to cherish. That's what humans do."

Miyuki opened her mouth, her jaw trembling as she tried to think of something to say, before closing it again.

"So, tell me, Miyuki, do you think it's fun? Making a cat get upset when that's all it knows how to do?"

Miyuki looked down at her feet, then shook her head slightly.

"Meanwhile, you're not a cat. So are *you* just going to sulk?"

Miyuki shook her head again.

Harue smiled. "Let's go find that blanket."

Meowth took the loss of the blanket even worse than they'd been expecting. Growling, occasionally hissing, he stalked restlessly around Yota's room, jumping about and scratching the walls.

They wanted to take him to the park with them in the carrier, but at this rate it was going to be a challenge to even pick him up.

"I'll stay here and look after him," said Yota. But if Meowth grew any more agitated, it seemed unlikely he'd be able to cope on his own.

"Alright then," said Harue, "I'll stay with you."

In other words, it would just be Miyuki and Ryuhei going to the park.

Miyuki frowned at her mother's words.

But she didn't say she wasn't going.

"Let's go, then," said Ryuhei. Now that he thought about it, this was the first time they'd been alone together since the decision to sell the house.

Things could get awkward, he knew. Miyuki seemed to have finally opened up slightly, but there was every chance she'd retreat right back into her shell.

Still, finding the blanket together felt like something they needed to do.

Miyuki walked out first. She got as far as the gate, then turned to look back at their house and chuckled, as if she'd noticed something funny.

Ryuhei slipped on his sandals, then paused and opted instead for the jogging shoes he barely ever wore. Best to have a spring in his step, he thought. This might be the last thing he and Miyuki remembered from their life together in this house.

"Right. Off we go."

He set off down the street, Miyuki trailing a few paces behind.

"Dad . . ."

"Yeah?"

"Have you taken any photos of this place from *outside*?"

She had a point.

He'd spent the whole weekend taking photos of the house's interior, but none of its exterior.

"I'll . . . take one tomorrow," said Ryuhei. He paused, hesitating, then went on. "We can stand outside and take one in front of the house. All together." Meaning Miyuki too, of course.

"Who cares about tomorrow?" she said bluntly. "Just don't forget, okay?"

Instead of replying, Ryuhei looked up at the night sky.

The stars were out.

Ryuhei didn't know much about constellations, but whenever he looked up at the stars, he felt able, even if just for a moment, to see things on a slightly grander scale.

He thought forward, to ten, twenty years from now.

When they looked back at the photos they'd taken at this house, would they do so with a smile?

That was his one hope. That was what this was all for.

"Miyuki," he said, still looking up at the sky. "Your dad's going to try a little harder from now on, okay?"

There was no reply.

He looked back down in confusion – and saw that Miyuki had already marched off again.

Hey. Just when I really nailed my line.

Pouting ever so slightly, he followed Miyuki down the street. When, after one, two, three . . . ten paces, he caught up with her, Miyuki pointed at the wooded area at the back of the park. He could make out a shopping bag lying among the trees.

"I wasn't *really* throwing it away, Dad. I was just hiding it."

Ryuhei didn't say anything for a while after that. The two of them walked along in silence, their shadows merging and diverging, trapped in an endless game of catch-me-if-you-can.

Somewhere off in the distance a stray cat mewed.

Ryuhei thought of all the strays out there tonight without blankets to curl up in. What dreams would they dream?

For some reason, the thought made the backs of his eyelids suddenly warm. He closed his eyes and watched as blurry constellations formed on that inner night sky, pale streaks against the dark.

KIYOSHI SHIGEMATSU was born in 1963 in Okayama Prefecture. After studying at Waseda University in Tokyo, he began a career as an editorial writer. His literary work has been honoured with four major prizes, including the prestigious Naoki Prize in 2000. *The Blanket Cats* was adapted for television in 2017.

JESSE KIRKWOOD is a literary translator working from Japanese into English. His translations include *The Kamogawa Food Detectives* by Hisashi Kashiwai, *Tokyo Express* by Seicho Matsumoto, *The Full Moon Coffee Shop* by Mai Mochizuki and *A Perfect Day to Be Alone* by Nanae Aoyama.